BEHOLD FAITH
AND OTHER STORIES

Tom Noyes

Dufour Editions

First published in the United States of America, 2003
by Dufour Editions Inc., Chester Springs, Pennsylvania 19425

ISBN 0-8023-1338-8

Library of Congress Cataloging-in-Publication Data

Noyes, Tom, 1969-
    Behold faith, and other stories / Tom Noyes.
       p. cm.
    ISBN 0-8023-1338-8
    I. Title.

PS3614.O83 B45 2002
813'.6--dc21   2002026430

Printed and bound in the United States of America

BEHOLD FAITH
AND OTHER STORIES

Author Biography

Tom Noyes' stories have appeared in numerous literary jour-
nals. He holds degrees in Creative Writing from Houghton
College, Wichita State University, and Ohio University. Originally from Pennsylvania and Upstate New York, he currently
teaches Creative Writing at Indiana State University in Terre
Haute, where he lives with his wife and daughter. This is his
first book.

for A. J.

Acknowledgments

Some of the stories in this collection first appeared in the following publications:

"Vehicles" in *Tamaqua*; "Burying Agnes" and "Parables" in *High Plains Literary Review*; "Meat" in *Third Coast*; "One Removed" and "Behold Faith" in *Ascent*; "Truck's Testament" in *Image*; "All You Want and More" in *Whetstone*; "The Hardest Season" in *Worcester Review*; "Considering Work" in *Permafrost*; "Crowd Pleasing" in *Wisconsin Review*; "Stumps" in *Blueline*; "Sleeping Through Mountains" in *American Literary Review*; "In-Between Places" in *Pleiades*; and "Georgia, Would You Mind?" in *Mochila Review*.

Contents

Vehicles

Once, half sober and on my knees with a brick in my hand, I told my son Buck that God has a place set aside for hustling, lead-off hitting center fielders who protect the plate deep in the count and look to go from first to third on singles to right. I told him this halfway through his senior season in high school. He was in the middle of a miracle.

❧

In thirty games I had fifty-five hits. My father saw every one. He'd rise early in the morning to keep up with his brick-laying jobs so he could watch my games in the afternoons. He yelled my name before each at bat, just before I stepped in the box. "Come on, Buck," he'd say. "Little knock now, little knock." I listened for him. He became part of the rhythm that kept me that season.

In prior years, curve balls had been as great a mystery to me as the Biblical commentaries that lined the walls of my father's study, but during that spring, every pitch looked as simple as a full moon. I'd never seen the ball like that before, like a small planet, its center a white hole and the swirling red rotation of the stitches. I saw some pitches so completely and vividly it would've been a miracle if I hadn't hit them hard. Still, after every flash of perfect unison, my eyes with my hands and my hips and my wrists, I stood on first or second or third and wondered how I'd ever be able to be that perfect again.

It wasn't concentration. In fact, I doubt it had much to do with anything I did. It was something truer and easier than effort. After my tenth game, I told my father how it was, how quiet and focused.

"And spiritual," he said. "There is something of that in a hitting streak." He smiled. "Willie Mays said so."

It did not matter that year who was pitching. Even though I faced the best pitcher in the league only during practices–he and I both played for Chenango Forks–I know that what I saw of him was his best.

Timmy O'Malley was a junior my senior year. He was a six-four tow-head with three pitches, and a scout had come to watch him in a summer league game when he was fourteen. His slider was sharp and hard and broke right at the front of the plate where most guys are already in full swing. During games, I had a good view from center field, and when he had his breaking stuff working, I could see hitters' knees buckle and their heads jerk. Some tried stepping up in the box to catch it before the magic, but if Timmy noticed a guy cheating like that, he wasn't afraid to send one in high and tight. Buddy Butler, our catcher, jammed two kitchen sponges between his hand and his mitt when O'Malley pitched, and he genuflected before every inning.

In inter-squad games, Coach Wiedner regularly had O'Malley throw two or three innings between starts, and O'Malley had become used to mowing down our lineup just like he did our opponents'.

One practice I came up after hitting a triple–I had pulled one of O'Malley's outside fast balls down the right field line– and he sailed one behind my head, just missing my neck. I stayed on the ground concentrating on trying to breathe while Buddy threw off his mask, mitt, and kitchen sponges to go after Tim. Coach said it was the first time he'd ever seen the catcher charge the pitcher. "Now that's intensity, men."

After that practice, there wasn't a game in which the moment didn't pass at least once through my mind, that part of a second when my eyes lost the ball behind me and my breath stopped, and I'd have to call time and take a long stroll out of the box to clear myself. I learned early that season that my hitting was beyond me, and only if I stayed out of it and kept my mind quiet would good things happen.

Near the end of the season, Coach Wiedner filmed my swing during practice with his camcorder, and after showers the whole team watched. He played me in slow motion, and then he rewound and played me again.

"Watch how he addresses the ball, guys. See how still his head is? Watch his step, watch his hands, watch his follow through." He chewed on his moustache and marveled. "Now that's pretty," he said more quietly and reverently each time he rewound. "Now that's real nice."

☙

I told my son his swing that season was not of this world. "God has blessed you, Buck," I said. "You're his vehicle right now. You're the one picking up the bat and putting on the helmet and stretching it out in the on-deck circle, but what you're doing up there isn't just you. Sometimes, I don't know, maybe it's your mom up there with you too. Just relax and enjoy the ride."

I was at one time, before Buck was born and when he was very young, a minister. My wife told me I was a good one. She was killed in an automobile accident during Buck's freshman year in high school, three weeks before his first j.v. game. "Everything," I told Buck the night of her death, although I don't know now if I wholly believed it, "has purpose."

The one thing I didn't like about being a preacher was that I couldn't stop and think behind the pulpit for too long without it coming across like I wasn't prepared and didn't know what came next. In seminary I had a professor who told me frequent pauses would say to my congregation that I wasn't sure about my message, and if they thought I wasn't sure, soon I'd be talking only to myself, my wife in the front pew, and to God. "And God and your wife will be listening only because they have to."

I took his advice and trained myself against such lapses, but I never felt good about using notes or memorizing what I'd written or read earlier in the week. Although I preached like this, and people told me I was a good preacher, my words often rung in my own ears as contrived and uninspired, and I was often tempted to share with them truth as it came to me, as it was conceived, when it was all truth.

When I talked to Buck in the truck on the way home after ball games or on weekends when he helped me lay bricks, I could take my time and say things right. "You've been chosen, at least for a while. Just remember: quick hands, don't guess, keep your head down, keep your weight back, and thank Jesus, son, thank Jesus."

❧

Before she died, my mother told me my father never preached sermons about tithing—he thought that was a matter of an individual's conscience—and he never pretended to heal anyone or have visions in which God told him secrets.

During the years my father was a pastor, he sealed the church driveway, twice painted the church inside and out, mowed the yard, laid down carpet, vacuumed the carpets, varnished the pews, cooked Salisbury Steak four years in a row for the annual Mother/Daughter Spring Banquet, built a tool shed, preached two sermons every Sunday, one every Wednesday, and took two pay cuts. He visited the hospitals in Binghamton two nights a week, and he made regular visits to pray with and administer communion to shut-ins who couldn't get to church. He did everything except stop drinking. I don't know if he tried to do that.

He liked to go down to Barney's Bar and Grill and empty a few with the regulars after a trying deacon's meeting or a day of visitation. He called it evangelizing, but some didn't, and finally something happened, something like a last straw, although neither he nor my mother ever told me more, that marked the end to his ministry. Soon after, he began contracting bricklaying jobs.

Even though I was very young, I remember the night the church accepted his resignation. He came home late, smelling stronger than usual, I noticed, when he bent over me in the dark to kiss my forehead, and he and Mom cried at the kitchen table together, out loud and shamelessly. I heard him pray then. His sentences were slow in forming but were not slurred. "Help us, your servants, Lord."

After Mom died, a few nights a week he'd call me from Barney's, and I'd ride my bike down, and we'd throw it in the back of the truck with the wheelbarrow and the bricks and the trowels, and I'd drive him home. I liked walking in the bar my senior year. The men would pound me on the back and call me Slugger or Killer and toast me with their brown bottles. My dad would say something loudly when he saw me. "Buck hit the fence in left field three times last week against Oneida," he'd put the last swallow to his lips, it was a chain link, "and the way it rattled," and then he'd bring the bottle down hard on the bar and grin widely and give a personal goodbye to those who'd turn and look, like his leaving meant the end of something.

As he rode next to me in the dark, he sometimes talked about some guy who'd been at the bar that night and how he was empty and what he needed. "To reach the lost, you have to go to them," he said once, and he rolled down the window and leaned into the rushing air to breathe deeply and clear himself. "I pray still that the Lord will use me," he yelled to me over the wind, "that he is using me."

One summer day as we worked he said, "Sometimes it's not up to you." We were rebuilding the fireplace of one of his ex-deacons. My father and his customer both thought they were doing the other a favor. My father worked fast but was never sloppy, even in the afternoons after lunch at Barney's. He laid every row as straight and as quickly as the first. "I haven't chosen much, Buck," he said.

That was before the spring of my sweet swing.

❧

I am aware of some who know me, some well, who believe they know why my wife died and why my church was taken from me. They think that there are reasons. Some genuinely tried to help my son and me, and I appreciate their sincerity and kindness—how could I not?—but I don't understand those who believe they can know how or where or why God moves.

My wife, like most of the church members, didn't drink, but neither did she view me as an unusually depraved sinner because I did. She saw me as a man who needed all of God's mercy and grace to transcend life, like she saw everyone, like she saw herself.

I didn't announce to people in the church that I drank—I certainly didn't ask permission—but it's just as true that I never went to any lengths to hide the fact. When they hired me, they didn't ask me about my views on drinking—I wouldn't have lied—but instead wanted to know my thoughts on eternal security and my expectations of salary. My answers matched theirs, and I was hired.

Mrs. Woodrow, a pleasant, elderly woman to whom I took communion on the first of every month, died peacefully in her sleep the night my head deacon, Art Wilson, came into Barney's to find me. It was late, but the family of the deceased wanted me there with them, to pray. Art had been at the hospital with the family—he was always a good and responsible deacon—and he'd told them he would get me.

My wife answered the phone and Art apologized for calling so late. Then he asked for me. She had no choice but to tell him. She could've told him I was in the bathroom and then called down to Barney's and gotten me, but that, I know, would have been deceitful. I'm glad she didn't lie.

"Pastor," Art tapped me on the shoulder and looked at me straight when I turned around. "Mrs. Woodrow died tonight." I met his eyes and nodded and put my bottle down, lightly. "We should get over there," I said, and I put my hands on the bar and pushed myself up.

"I'll take care of it," he said. He spoke loudly over the other voices and the juke box, like one who didn't frequent bars and didn't know how to talk in them. "I'll tell them you're not feeling well." People around us were listening now, and behind the bar Barney stepped closer, polishing invisible spots off the glass he held in his hand.

"I'm fine, Art. They want me there. I'm their pastor. I'll come with you." I rose.

"Don't," he said red-faced, and he scanned the room quickly before pivoting to leave, then turned back toward me, toward the bar. "You should have been honest with us," he said. "You should have been."

"I don't know what to say," I said. "I don't think I've been dishonest."

He left then, and behind me Barney said quietly, "You don't have to say anything, Preach."

❧

One week after I graduated, a scout called. My father and Coach Wiedner had both assured me one would.

The scout had been at several of our games, initially to watch O'Malley pitch, and he offered me a contract over the phone. He said chances were I wasn't going to get drafted–I came out of nowhere my senior year–and this might be my chance to get noticed. He scouted for the Utica Blue Sox of the New York-Penn league, and even though they weren't affiliated with a big league club, they played teams that were. "Think it over, son. Talk to your mom and dad about it. You can always go to college later if you don't think it's working out, and a few of our guys take classes in the off season."

"I'm not going to college," I said.

"Well there you go," he said like he'd proved something. "What are you doing?"

"Laying bricks with my father."

"I'll meet you at the Utica Greyhound station the day after tomorrow, son. Get ready to play some ball."

❧

Buck came down to Barney's to find me immediately after the call from the Blue Sox. In minutes the news was all over the place and I stood on a chair and announced the next round was on me. "Praise be," I said.

"Amen," everyone in the place said, and they laughed, and they cheered.

❧

I started in center field my first night in Utica. The guy I was replacing had just become a father and decided to retire. When I walked into the locker room and introduced myself, he smiled, shook my hand and said, "It's all yours."

I was to replace him completely. I wasn't only taking over his position, I was getting his uniform, his locker combination, and his road-trip roommate, a shortstop from the Dominican Republic who didn't know any English except a few mouthfuls of obscenities his teammates had taught him.

Two hours before the game that night, I waited by my locker as old center field moved his stuff out and told me how to play each of the Oneonta Yankee hitters. "Drake is the one you have to worry about. The infielders will play him to pull on the ground, but he hits the other way, a ton the other way, in the air. Shade toward right plenty, especially because we have McAllistar throwing tonight, and he gets it up there in a hurry. Most of the hitters are going to be behind him a little anyway."

"How about their pitchers," I said. "What do they throw?"

He smiled. "Just relax and don't guess. Take a couple and get comfortable. The first time you're up, they'll probably throw one inside on you. Don't flinch. Know it's coming." He stuffed the last roll of tape in his duffel and zipped it before standing and making room for me on the bench. "I got a baby girl, you know. My wife just delivered Tuesday."

"I heard," I said. "Congratulations."

"I never before last night thought of what it's going to be like not playing," he said, and he smiled again. "Last night we're losing 5-1 when I come up in the bottom of the eighth. There's no one on base, so it isn't much of an at bat, really, but I know it's probably my last one, and I start thinking how I'm never going to see another pitcher stare past me for the sign, except maybe in some sorry bar softball league. Before I get up this last time, in the on-deck circle, I send one up, a prayer I mean, that I'll get a good piece of it, get the sweet part of the bat on it. You know what I mean. That I'll get to feel it in my hands. Not a dinger or anything—you know Ted Williams hit a dinger his last at bat?—but I want to hit it square."

"Sure," I said, and then there was silence between us, and I felt I should ask. "So how did it go?"

He slung his bag over his shoulder. "Grounded out to shortstop," he said. "Hit it off the handle." He paused. "I guess that's the difference between me and Ted Williams."

"He must've prayed better," I said, and I felt like it was all right to say.

"Something," he said on his way out. "Good luck."

He was right on two counts that night. The first time the monster Drake got up I played him over toward right and didn't have to move to make the catch.

The first time I got up, first pitch, I didn't budge and the ball just missed the brim of my batting helmet. The second pitch was right down the middle, and I slapped it hard between left and center for a triple, and I thought, "this is a good beginning."

❧

Buck called me after each game to tell me how it had gone. In his first twenty games as a pro he hit .380 and didn't have an error.

"Any other teams come talk to you yet?" I asked once.

"Not yet," he said. "It's only been a month."

"It's just a matter of time, Buck," I said. Just keep doing what you're doing, and keep being thankful. Don't forget that."

"I don't," he said. "I won't."

❧

We went to Schenectady in September for our last series of the season. There was no score when I came up for the second time, but we'd threatened in the first inning. With one down I'd stroked a double down the line and gone to third on a ground out to the right side, but our clean-up hitter looked at strike three, and that was as close as either team had come.

Swinging two bats in the on-deck circle before leading off the fourth, I watched the pitcher warm up and look at me once or twice between pitches. "There's no way he's going to give me anything tight after what I did with that last inside fast ball," I said in the direction of Martinez who was swinging and watching next to me. "First pitch is going to be away. I'm going to left for a single and get something started."

I don't know if Martinez was listening or not, but before I started toward the plate he made a fist and shook it. "Little rap gets us going."

Again I didn't see it. First pitch. A curve ball that didn't curve or a slider that didn't slide. Some of the guys told me later that when it hit my face, I dropped instantly without stepping or hesitating, and before I began coughing and gagging on dust and my tongue, they thought I was dead.

"Get some ice."

I focused briefly on a hazy, hovering umpire, watched him lose his mask.

"Keep still, son."
I felt myself fading.
"Get him out of the dirt before he chokes."
"We should not move him yet."

※

It didn't turn out to be a serious injury. He spent two nights in the hospital for observation and that was it, but when spring training came around, he told me the ball wasn't large and focused anymore, it was too small and fast and it was indiscernible. He swung through air and met nothing but air, and his feet were busy and his head quick to pull, and long walks out of the box could not empty his mind.

"We're going to let you go," his manager told him a week before opening day. I was planning to be at the game. Buck and I both thought it might help. "There's no shame in it now. Know that," the manager said. "The club will keep in touch. Take it slow. You're a ball player, Buck. Be a shame if you can't get it turned around."

He didn't, although each night after we laid bricks we went to the batting cage, and I gave him quarters, and he drove the rubber coated balls consistently hard into the canvas at the back of the lot. People stopped to watch him sometimes. Fathers pointed him out to their little leaguers, made them watch his hands and the turning of his hips. They'd say quietly, "That's how you do it, just like that," and the boys' capped heads would nod.

He couldn't, however, stand in against live pitching. When I called Timmy O'Malley and asked him, he said yes, and the three of us met down at the high school field. He started Buck off slowly, throwing three-quarter speed, big, easy-hanging balloons that even I could've stroked. I stood in center field, hopefully deep, my wrong hand stiffly jammed in Buck's lefty mitt. "Little knock now, Buck, little knock," I said, and I thought, "No matter what he does, this is both ending and beginning."

Buck's swings were so weak they hardly stirred the air. He managed to foul a few into the back stop and dribble some back to Timmy before he said maybe this wasn't the day.

Even after Buck and I were off the field, Timmy stayed on the mound a while, working at the dirt with his cleats. Eventually he made his way over to us at the truck. He took off his cap and wiped his forehead with his sleeve and said to call whenever we wanted, even tomorrow if we wanted. Buck said thanks and held out his bat like it was his hand, and Timmy gripped and shook it like it had fingers.

When I pulled the truck into our driveway, I thought about letting Buck out and going to Barney's, but I didn't. I turned off the engine and clapped him on the knee. We sat there until he opened his door, then I got out and followed him inside.

❧

Sometimes I feel like I want to get in some swings, so after work my father and I go to the cages. The first few times I tried tricking myself into imagining the machine as a real pitcher, and I fooled around with my stance, dropped my hands, straightened my knees, but now when I go I just get in the cage and I don't think. I usually don't even change out of my work boots. The mechanical arm slings me the ball and I step into it and hit it.

My father and I work well together. I carry the bricks and mix the cement, and when bricks need to be cut specially for a project, I do that. When I'm caught up with things, I take a break to drink coffee out of our thermos and I stand behind him and watch.

Sometimes I think he's going to turn and say, "This is not our work," but he doesn't. He sets and scrapes, and when a row is finished he goes on to the next one.

In-Between Places

Quinn's wipers scrape, ice on ice. Defrost can't keep up. His own breath is part of the problem. The hole he's looking through shrinks. The edges fog, then freeze. He cracks open his window, but that doesn't help. He drags his forearm across the glass. Better at first, but when the smear ices over, worse.

Snow, then sleet, then snow again. Quinn's headlights don't burn through what's coming down, they illuminate it. A bleary stretch of outer space dense with shooting stars. Quinn could make wishes. The tail lights of a semi hover fifty feet ahead like planets. Quinn's looking to stay in the tracks while hanging back far enough to avoid the spray.

Quinn could pull over onto the shoulder for a break, rest his eyes for a few minutes. He's wearing a warm jacket, has a wool blanket in the trunk, hat and gloves lying on the seat next to him. There's an unopened bag of M&M's in his cupholder. He could lock his doors, ease his seat back. What he should do is take the next exit, find a room, eat some eggs. He's got $23 cash and a MasterCard. A lot of times they put diners across the road from or next door to motels. This isn't a storm he's going to drive out of. This isn't weather he can weather.

He's not due in Albany at a certain time, or even at all. The last thing Rachel said to him over the phone was "See you when I see you." She wouldn't be shocked if that was never. She has no expectations. "Not even low ones," she said. "Burn me once, shame on you; burn me twice, you can go screw yourself." Rachel and Quinn share a past, maybe a future. Rachel's pregnant, twenty-seven weeks. That's how long it's been since she visited her parents in Cleveland, ran into Quinn, her ex-boyfriend, at the grocery store. They reminisced, got along. A few days later she returned to Albany, to her job behind the customer service desk at a bank. She opens accounts, closes accounts, and irons out discrepancies. Worked her way up from teller. She's good at smiling in a crisis.

She let Quinn in on the baby a month ago, after the sonogram. The doctor couldn't tell sex–the baby's legs were scissored, like a runner's stretch–but confirmed a straight spine, a sound heart, four whole limbs, and two brain lobes. Rachel mailed Quinn a copy of the image. She'd drawn arrows on it in red pen. She'd labeled HEAD and HEART. She'd labeled PLACENTA. Quinn checked out *What to Expect When You're Expecting* from the library, found out that the placenta's the afterbirth. There are two deliveries. First the baby, then the placenta. You love and nurture the first, you pitch the second. You think you're done, but then you're not.

Quinn carries the sonogram in his wallet. He's not sure if he's looking down on the baby or if it's a side-view. Either way, it's hard not to see the two jellybean-shaped brain lobes as large eyes, the head as a raccoon's, a possum's.

The travel advisory stretches along Interstate 90 from Cleveland all the way to Syracuse. This year's Blizzard of the Century.

In Erie, Pennsylvania, the DJ cancels high school basketball games, prayer meetings, bingo, a quilt exhibit, and a real-estate class. "In summary, whatever you were going to do tonight, forget it," he says at the end of the list. "Your plans have changed." When the meteorologist comes on for the hourly update, the DJ delivers the obligatory line about the weather being her fault. The meteorologist laughs. "I'm only the messenger," she says. "Don't kill the messenger." The DJ says, "No, of course not. There will be no killing. It's just weather." The meteorologist says, "Just weather?" like she's offended because weather, after all, is her job. It's what she gets up for in the morning, to see if the world's carrying on in the way she foresaw. They laugh.

Quinn doesn't know what, if anything, is behind him. Occasionally he glances in the rearview out of habit, but there's nothing to see. He has no rear defrost, no rear wiper.

Ahead of him, the semi groans. Its brakelights flash. Before coming to a complete stop, it skids softly to the right, ends up with a few of its eighteen tires on the shoulder. Quinn stops twenty feet behind. This is the closest he's been. Baby blue plates. New Jersey. Stickers from New York, Pennsylvania, Ohio, Michigan, Indiana, Illinois, Ontario, and Quebec. Chunks of slush slide off the mud flaps.

Quinn turns off his engine and switches on his hazards. The wind's quieted, and what the meteorologist called the "wintry mix" has almost stopped. Quinn cranks his window down the whole way and rubs his eyes. He unhooks his seat belt and rolls his head in a slow circle. His neck bones crack in his ears. Ice flakes blow onto his cheeks.

Quinn is scanning radio stations when the semi driver comes to his window. The man puts one hand on Quinn's roof as he leans in. He smokes a cigarette. "Looks like we're sitting tight for a while," he says. He's not wearing a coat, only a flannel shirt with the sleeves rolled up over his biceps. He has a ski hat on, though, the kind with the pom-pom on top.

"Can I get a smoke?" Quinn says.

"Sure." The driver pulls the pack from his shirt pocket and shakes one loose. Quinn takes it and pushes in the lighter on the dash.

"Storm's lulled for now, looks like," the driver says. The lighter pops.

Quinn lights up, takes a drag, blows the smoke into the car, away from the semi driver. "Any idea what's going on?" Quinn says.

"Jack-knifed rig. Heard it on the CB. There's a bridge about a half-mile up. They get slick."

"Thanks for the cigarette."

"Watson," the driver says. He reaches his hand in Quinn's window and they shake. "Like Sherlock Holmes. I get it all the time from the guys at the garage. They're always like, 'Elementary, my dear Watson.' We have a good time. Everybody has their thing."

Quinn smiles and nods. He clears his throat.

"This other driver, Henry, he gets a tic sometimes in his right eyebrow. Like a muscle twinge. Everyone who talks to him while it's happening is like, 'Henry, your eyebrow's twitching,' like it's a new development. Over and over again. It's the repetition."

Quinn ashes his cigarette out the window. "Poor Henry, huh?"

"No, it's not like that," Watson says. "He joins in. Sometimes he'll beat you to it. You'll be talking with him and out of the blue he'll be all, 'Hold on, man. My eyebrow. Lookit. Isn't that spooky?'"

"I'm Quinn. I'm sure your crew would have fun with me. My name, I mean."

"Oh, sure," Watson says. "Quinn. I can't think of anything right off, but it wouldn't take us long."

"So what we have to do is wait this out," Quinn says.

Watson nods, drops his cigarette, grounds it into the snow with his foot. "Dinnertime," he says, "and I'm not eating."

"You want in?" Quinn says. "I'm going to roll up this window."

"Sure," Watson says. "Company."

Watson circles the car to the passenger door, and Quinn starts the engine to let the heat run. He's worried. His fuel gauge is broken, so he has to keep an eye on the odometer between fill-ups. Usually he's on top of it—he writes the mileage on a pad he keeps in his glove compartment—but he's not sure about this tank. He forgot to write anything. He had some things on his mind. Today's Wednesday, and he filled up last Monday or Tuesday, so that's eight to ten days of around-town miles—maybe a hundred and fifty back and forth to work—plus the seventy or eighty highway miles he's knocked off since leaving Cleveland two hours ago. He gets about twenty-four miles a gallon. When he tries math in his head, the numbers pile up in columns, like on a chalkboard, but that doesn't help him get anywhere. He'll either run out of gas or he won't.

Watson's made himself at home. He's wearing Quinn's gloves, eating Quinn's M&M's. He says, "Your heater doesn't work for shit."

"You're kidding me," Quinn says.

"What are we sitting in, anyway?" Watson says. "Some kind of Plymouth? A Buick?"

They're listening to oldies. Frankie Valli, Stevie Wonder, America, a string of commercials, then The Beach Boys. "This will warm you up," the DJ says. "Think sand. Think palm trees."

"You want to sit in my cab? Like a toaster-oven in there. That's why I don't have a jacket. Don't need one."

"How long do you think this is going to take?" Quinn says.

"We're waiting for the wrecker," Watson says. "In my cab we could monitor the situation on the CB."

"Looks like it's starting again out there," Quinn says. "Right the hell over our heads."

"Well, I'm making a move to a warmer climate," Watson says. He crumples the M&M's wrapper in his fist and drops it on the floor between his feet. "Thanks for supper. Coming?"

"In a minute," Quinn says.

Watson nods. The pom-pom on his hat bobs. He needs both arms to force the door open. As he pushes, the back of his neck wrinkles like a pack of hot dogs. The door hinges crackle, then squeak. "Deep freeze," he says. "If I were you, I wouldn't lock."

When Watson shuts the door behind him, he disappears. Quinn's windshield and windows are white curtains.

After a few more songs, Quinn turns off the radio, cuts the engine and pockets his keys. His options are limited. He can stay or go. He said he'd go. If he doesn't show up soon, Watson might come back to check on him, and that would be awkward. Quinn grabs his hat off the passenger seat. Watson had been sitting on it, so it's warm. Quinn pulls it on, stretching it down over his face like a ski mask without mouth or eye-holes. You lose fifty to seventy-five percent of your body heat out of your head, your face. Too many cavities. Your ears, your mouth, your nostrils. Like drafty windows. Quinn's got a chill between his ears. His brain lobes. Two buried ice cubes. He can see through the tight knit of the hat, but just barely. The world's patchy. When he opens his door, he has to use his shoulder.

The wind's picked up again. It isn't blowing in any one direction, it's swirling. This kind of wind, you can lick your finger and stick it up in the air if you want, but you won't learn anything. At a ball park this kind of wind will wrap a flag around its own pole. It will knock down one hitter's bomb at the warning track and launch the next lazy looper into the upper deck. As a boy, Quinn thought for too long that a grand slam was a home run hit extra deep, one really crushed. He played little league for two years before he had it right, before he realized that it depended on how your teammates set the table for you.

Puffs of snow rise from the road and the roof of Watson's truck in small tornadoes. The terrain Quinn negotiates is treacherous. The hat is itchy, especially on his nose. He's sacrificing that for warmth. It's itchy on his cheeks, too, just below his eye sockets.

Quinn slides along the highway like he's wearing skis. His toes don't leave the ground, only his heels, like cross-country. He swings his arms like he has poles. Get the blood moving. That event in the Olympics where you ski with a rifle strapped to your back and stop occasionally to shoot. Where you have to be a world-class skier and a world-class shooter. Where the more tired you get, the harder it is to steady your gun. It has a complex scoring system. No American has ever won it. The biathlon. No American's even come close. The champ is always from Denmark, Norway, or Austria. Fritz and his icy blond beard. Johann and his cinder-block thighs. They know how to change gears, how to turn it on, shut it down, then turn it on again, how to steady their hands with their hearts pounding hot in their heads, icicles dripping from their moustaches.

The wind gusts just as Quinn reaches the cab. It blows through the hat, up the tunnels of his nose. Ice caves. Stalactites, stalagmites. Quinn folds the front of the hat up onto his forehead, off his face, and knocks on the door.

Watson's voice is lilting, sing-song. "Who is it?" he says. He's fooling around.

Watson's on his way to Kingston, Ontario, but not tonight. Neither he nor Quinn is going anywhere. Route 90 is now officially closed from Cleveland to Syracuse. No one's come up behind Quinn. He's last in line. Directly in front of Watson's semi there's a white Lincoln, and in front of the Lincoln there's another semi. Beyond that, who knows?

Watson's been on the CB. When the bridge is cleared, everyone will be forced off the next exit for the night. It's slow going for the wrecker. Watson talked to the driver of the jack-knifed truck. "He called himself a moron," Watson tells Quinn. "He's taking it hard."

Tomorrow Watson will cross the border at Niagara Falls. "Some winters there's an ice bridge across the gorge," he says. "You can't walk it, but it's solid. Gulls land on it. It's something to see at night with those colored lights they have. Like a 3-D rainbow."

"The mist," Quinn says.

Watson nods. "It freezes. But not every winter. Conditions have to be perfect-o." When he says this he brings his fingertips to his lips and kisses them, like he's just eaten a good pasta.

"This is news to me," Quinn says. He's heard that Niagara Falls is ruined. A polluted tourist trap. U.S. and Canada both.

Strip bars, Made-in-Taiwan trinket shops, gull shit, and barrels of chemical waste. "I've never been, but I've heard it smells."

"You should make a point to see for yourself," Watson says. "Ice bridge or no. It's more than just water falling over rocks. When you go, do this: think of yourself as an explorer–Lewis or Clark or whoever–and imagine you've just come out of the woods and the first thing you see is The Falls. Imagine you've found it like that. Like luck. That's the mind-set to go in with. Like you're the first."

"Or like an Indian," Quinn says. "Long before any explorer."

"Sure," Watson says. "Wear moccasins."

"I don't know," Quinn says. His hat's on his lap, his hands buried in it like a muff. "All those newlyweds prancing around, nibbling on each other."

Watson smiles. "Go when it's raining," he says. "Go on Christmas. You'd own the place."

"I'll take my kid maybe. My kid and me at Niagara Falls under an umbrella on Christmas morning."

"There you go," Watson says. "Pretty picture. You and your papoose." He drums on the steering wheel with his fingers. "How about Mom, though? Your squaw, I mean. What's she up to?"

"Whose squaw?" Quinn says. "She's waiting in the car. She's at home basting the turkey and doing some last-minute gift wrapping. She's on the phone with her parents. She's on the phone with her boyfriend. She's in a barrel, working her way downriver."

"That's a shame," Watson says. "The mother of your child. You know nobody's ever survived the American Falls in a barrel? Lots have gone over the Canadian side and lived, but not the American side. Too many rocks. One kid, though, fell out of a boat and went over. In the Fifties. Not a scratch. *The Maid of the Mist* picked him up. A boat full of tourists in black rain coats."

"Rachel, my kid's mom," Quinn says, "she'd survive. She'd side-stroke to shore and her make-up would still be in place. Her pulse would be normal. She'd make a mint doing interviews, sign a made-for-TV movie deal, star as herself."

"You guys have a boy or girl?"

"Don't know yet," Quinn says. "Still under construction."

"Like the t-shirt," Watson says. "Congratulations." He extends his hand and Quinn shakes it. "I've got a couple. Live with their moms. Ten and six. Chicago and Toronto. I was hoping to see Toronto on this trip, but I don't know now. This mess could put a glitch in things. Look behind your seat. I even bought a present."

Quinn reaches around and grabs a plastic bag. There's a model kit inside. A tractor trailer. "Not bad," Quinn says. "Christmas?"

Watson nods. "A few weeks early, but I wanted to watch the kid open it. No glue. It's snap-together. No paint either. No mess."

"He'll love it," Quinn says.

"She," Watson says. "Yeah, I hope so."

Conversation tapers and Quinn drifts. His head falls back against the seat and his eyes close. Restless sleep. You know you're sleeping, you're that close to being awake. He's not dreaming exactly, but his mind is working largely and loosely. How it will go with Rachel when he shows up. What she'll say.

"You're here. This is something I wasn't counting on. You're welcome to the couch. It pulls out. If you're hungry, we could get a pizza. It's tempting to feel optimistic, but one thing you can't expect from me is a hero's welcome. I mean, I hope you're not expecting that. You can't show up in my living room looking for me to beam with gratitude and open my robe like my ship has come in because that ship has sailed, friend. Bon voyage! You hear what I'm saying? Iceberg straight ahead! I mean, let's be adults. Look at me. Let's you and me face facts. Let's deal. For once."

Then it's labor and delivery, and Quinn's pacing the waiting room like some sap from a black-and-white movie. Loosened tie, sport jacket, wing-tips. Where did they come from? When nurses pass, they smile, touch his shoulder, and Quinn can't help turning to watch them sway away in their white skirts.

Next thing Quinn knows, the scene's shifted to Rachel's bank. Her water breaks, and they clear the table in the center of the lobby, the one with the chained pens and deposit slips. Rachel's on her back, and Quinn's stationed at the business end of things. He's helping her work through it. "Almost there. Push. You're doing great. I see its head." One of the tellers works the door, asks customers to please use the ATM. "We've got a situation here," she says. "Deposits, withdrawals, and balance inquiries can be done at the machine. For all other business, you can call our 1-800 number, or you can come back tomorrow. As you can see, we presently have our hands full! Over there on the table! I know we advertise full-service banking, but this is ridiculous! I've handled some major withdrawals in my day, but you've got to be kidding me!"

Quinn's head falls forward off his shoulder. His chin hits his chest and his head bounces back. There's a twinge in his neck. "Ouch," he says. Something's out of whack. A kink. He straightens slowly, grimaces, and wipes his mouth with the back of his hand.

"Don't fight it on my account," Watson says. "I'd join you, but I'm full of No-Doz."

"Just wrenched my neck," Quinn says.

"A cup of coffee would be good right now," Watson says. "A little cream, no sugar for me, thanks."

"What are we hauling, anyway?" Quinn says. He massages the spot where his neck meets his shoulder, just above his collarbone. That's where something's pinched or hyperextended, where something's slipped or pulled. "What do we got back here? Anything that would aid survival should our situation take a turn for the worse?"

"Auto parts," Watson says. "Brake pads and rotors, shocks and mufflers."

"That's not going to help at all," Quinn says. "Not a bit.

You got any catalytic converters, any gaskets?"

"What?" Watson says.

"Nothing," Quinn says. He turns to face Watson, slowly, like he's balancing a platter on his head. He hurt himself waking up. "Me making a joke."

In front of them, the tail lights of the Lincoln go out.

"What do you think?" Watson says.

"Me? Nothing," Quinn says. "Hardly anything."

"You want to take a walk, see the mess firsthand?"

"Sure," Quinn says. "I'm done sitting."

They get out of the truck, and Quinn crosses in front of the cab to walk next to Watson. He reaches in the pockets of his jacket for his gloves, but they're not there, so he balls his fists and burrows them as deep as they'll go. He can't completely straighten his neck. He has to tilt his head to the right a bit as he walks, like he has attitude. You don't want a piece of him.

When they come up on the Lincoln, the driver's-side window opens. A woman pulls her scarf down off her mouth so she can talk. "Scouting mission?" she says.

"Right," Watson says.

"We all get off the next exit when this clears?"

"That's what we're hearing," Quinn says.

"Thing is, I have to pee," the woman says. "Sorry to be uncouth, but that's all I can think about right now. I'm floating."

"No one's behind the truck," Quinn says. "Just my car. We won't be back for a while."

"I might have to take you up on that," the woman says. "I'm in a predicament."

"Be my guest," Quinn says.

Most of the vehicles Quinn and Watson pass are running. Three in a row are listening to the same radio station. Someone somewhere is slashing prices. Ahead of them, through the clouds of exhaust, Quinn and Watson see flashing red lights.

"On the scene," Watson says. "Pennsylvania's finest."

The sky is clear in patches. A few stars. Quinn's neck goes back okay, it just doesn't want to go left. His foot slides and he almost trips. The road crunches under him.

"Steady as she goes," Watson says.

"She's peeing back there," Quinn says. "In the middle of Interstate 90."

The trooper's wearing an orange poncho and a wide-brimmed hat covered in clear plastic. His car's on the other side of the bridge, on the other side of the jack-knifed truck. "Not much to report," he says. "Waiting."

Two men appear from behind the truck and stroll over. Everyone nods at everyone else. One of the men has bushy red sideburns that crawl out from under his cap and down his jawline, almost the whole way to his chin. "We keep looking at it," he says, "but it won't budge."

The other man turns his wrist to look at his watch. His nose is sharp like a beak. His chin, too. Pointed at the tip like an arrowhead. "I'm the one who parked it," he says.

"Happens to the best of us," Watson says. "Although I can't say it's ever happened to me personally."

"Me neither," Sideburns says. "Thirteen years of driving truck."

"Not me," Trooper says.

"Nope," Quinn says.

Everyone laughs. The driver of the jack-knifed truck laughs loudest. He doubles over and stomps on the road with his cowboy boot, splattering slush on his pant leg. He hooks his thumbs in the belt loops on his hips, closes his eyes, throws his head back and howls. The other men stop laughing. He could be faking. Like sarcasm. When he stops laughing, he does it suddenly, like someone's cut off his oxygen, and he lights a cigarette.

"Can I bum one?" Quinn says. "I already hit up Watson here, so it's somebody else's turn. Besides, it's the least you can do, considering."

Jack-knife loses his smile and looks at Quinn. He doesn't reach for his pocket. Instead, he points to Quinn with his chin and looks one at a time to the other three men. "Get a load of this character," he says. He takes the pack out of his pocket and tosses it to Quinn. "Don't make a habit of it," he says.

Quinn catches the pack. One cigarette. "I don't need your last one," Quinn says.

"Go ahead," Jack-knife says. "What's the difference? You didn't pay for any of them, did you?" He looks at the other men and smirks. "Smoke it," he says. "Do me a favor."

Yellow flashing lights appear beyond the trooper's car. The men turn and face them. The trooper claps his gloved hands together. This makes a hollow sound, like underground. "We're in business," he says.

All this could turn out good for Quinn.

If there's an early lull with Rachel, even in the first minute, even in the hall outside her apartment door as she's deciding whether or not to invite him in, this is stuff he can use. If conversation needs a jump start or, later, a shift. The wintry mix, Watson and his Christmas present, the jack-knifed truck, bumming the cigarettes, the peeing woman. People ask and answer the question all the time. How was the trip? Things don't happen only in places, they happen in-between, too. Maybe that's an idea that will shape up to be something Quinn and Rachel can use. Maybe they'll turn it into something they can agree is somehow relevant, considering their circumstances. "Imagine if everything was smooth sailing? How boring," Quinn could say. And Rachel could answer, "Thinking along these lines, we've never been boring. We are by no stretch of the imagination boring. In fact," she could say, "maybe we could use a little boring." And then maybe she'd smile and reach out to touch Quinn's arm, or he'd reach out to touch hers.

So this glitch could trigger something. It's happened before. It's not without precedent. In high school, on their first date, driving home from the movies, Quinn crossed a double yellow to pass the slowpoke in front of him, and lights flashed behind him.

"Out of the car," the cop said. County sheriff. Fat guy with a buzz cut. "Hands on the hood." He patted down Quinn hard, grabbed a handful of hair and pulled Quinn's ear back to his mouth. "Girlfriend?" he hissed. His breath, surprisingly, smelled like cinnamon.

"First date," Quinn said.

"If it was my daughter in there, last date," the cop said. "I'd snap your neck right here and walk away with a clear conscience."

"What's going on?" Rachel yelled out her window.

"Back in the car before I do something you'll regret," the cop said to Quinn.

The cop wrote Quinn five tickets. Handed them in through the window one at a time. Passing in a no-passing zone, reckless driving, failure to stay right, speeding, and driving with impaired vision. The last one was for the air freshener hanging from Quinn's rear-view. "You and me have a court date," the cop said to Quinn, then he looked at Rachel. "Miss, I'm driving you home."

"I'm fine," Rachel said. "No thanks."

"A guy like this will drag you down."

"Thanks anyway," Rachel said.

When Quinn got home, he stapled the five tickets together and hid them in a drawer. His parents didn't find out about them until six months later when their insurance rates went up.

"A guy like this will drag you down" became a shared joke between Quinn and Rachel, and the fact that they kept it between them enabled Quinn a couple weeks later to pull Rachel to him, and it allowed Rachel to open her mouth to Quinn's, and it let them kiss each other longer and more deeply than they would have otherwise.

A month later in court, the cop barely remembered Quinn. The judge rolled his eyes at the impaired vision ticket. He also threw out failure to stay right and reckless driving. Speeding and passing in a no-passing stuck.

Trooper and Watson are discussing motels and restaurants off the next exit. Wesleyville. Six or seven miles. The best bet's to hang a right and then double back toward Erie on

Route 20. Two or three miles to Howard Johnson's. Who knows what shape the road will be in? The plows get to it when they get to it.

The driver of the wrecker is short and wiry. He works fast. Quinn's impressed. People in trouble call this guy, and he comes to the rescue. Not a bad gig. You see the effects of your work right away. The stalled car blocks the intersection, you show up and do your thing, the traffic clears. Quinn used to like to cut the grass. Long when you start, short when you're done, and there's a nice smell. His job as a shipping clerk isn't like this. For every box he moves out, another sneaks in. The warehouse is always full. He doesn't make a dent.

When everything's hooked up, the wrecker driver walks over to the other men. "Let's go," he says.

"What do you need?" Jack-knife says.

"I need whoever parked her to get back in her and hold her steady as I yank her."

"I can do that," Jack-knife says.

"You're not going to turn her at all, you're just going to keep her steady."

"That's what I'll do."

As the two men walk away, Quinn turns to Trooper. "Gas station?" he says.

"Right across the road from Ho-Jo's," Trooper says.

"Think they have aspirin?" Quinn says. Quinn's discovered that forcing his head left sends a bolt of numbness all the way down to the first two fingers on his left hand. Not numbness as much as tingling. Prickly. Like they're asleep.

"Carla's working tonight. She'll help you out. When you go in, tell her Officer Mountain Dew and Charleston Chew says 'hey.' That's what I get every night when I stop in. It rhymes, you know, so she calls me that. Officer Mountain Dew and Charleston Chew. She's a cutie."

"And me," Watson says. "I don't know her, but maybe you could put a good word in."

"I'll tell Carla the whole gang says hello," Quinn says.

"Don't tell her anything from me," Sideburns says. "Can't stand her."

"Really?" Trooper says. "Carla?"

"Actually, we've never met," Sideburns says and smiles, "but my gut tells me she's not everything she's cracked up to be."

Wrecker honks his horn and waves his arm out his window. Jack-knife does the same. The wrecker creeps forward, and the tractor trailer slowly straightens.

Ten or fifteen more feet and they would've been fine. This is what they think about afterwards. How close.

The chain creaks, then screams, and the wrecker's front tires come off the road, like a wheelie. When the chain snaps, it sounds like a gunshot, and the wrecker slides across the bridge into the guardrail. One of its tires climbs up and over and then stops. Its headlights shine over the frozen creek, over a white field, into a patch of dark woods. The tractor trailer, now un-jack-knifed and pointing in the right direction, sits there dumbly. It's still attached to the now limp chain, like a fish that swallowed the bait and snapped the line.

"Dumb-ass hit the brakes," Watson says.

"Who?" Trooper says. "What happened?"

"First he jack-knifed his rig across a bridge. And then when he was getting towed, he hit his brakes."

"We're going to need a wrecker for the wrecker, aren't we?" Quinn says.

"Oh, yeah," Watson says. "We're just getting started here."

"Why the hell did he hit the brakes?" Sideburns says.

"Because he has nowhere to be," Watson says. "And none of us does either!" he yells in the direction of the tractor trailer. "Isn't that right, Dumb-ass!"

"Easy," Trooper says.

"Sure, officer," Watson says. "Fine."

Wrecker climbs out of his truck and stomps over to the tractor trailer. He motions with both hands for Jack-knife to come down. He's not saying anything, he's just motioning.

He points at Jack-knife, turns his finger, and points at himself.

"He's not asking Dumb-ass to dance," Watson says.

"Hell," Trooper says. He starts over towards the tractor trailer, and the others follow.

Jack-knife steps down from his cab to square off with Wrecker before the other men get there. There's an exchange of shoves, a clumsy take-down, and then Jack-knife and Wrecker are rolling around in the slush.

"We're not exactly dealing with Ali and Foreman here, are we?" Watson says.

Trooper runs the last few yards. The other men walk. Wrecker starts out on top, but Jack-knife's got forty pounds on him, and it doesn't take long for things to reverse. This is disappointing.

Trooper pulls Jack-knife up by his collar, and Watson and Sideburns arrive in time to intercept Wrecker. He's spitting blood. Jack-knife's left eye is red and puffy.

Quinn stands in the space between the two groups. "All right, gentlemen," he says. "Keep it clean. No funny stuff after the bell."

"You and me," Jack-knife says to Quinn. He's breathing heavy. He doesn't sound good. He sounds like a pack a day. "I would like that."

"Shut up," Trooper says.

"We were going too far right," Jack-knife says. He looks at all the men but Wrecker. "I barely tapped them."

"We weren't going too far right," Wrecker says. "You didn't just barely tap them."

"I say we were," Jack-knife says. "I say I did."

"All right," Trooper says. "Shut up."

It's just after nine when he radios for another wrecker.

Watson wants to stay on the scene, but Quinn decides to head back to his car, wait it out there, maybe shut his eyes for a while. Before he goes, Watson shakes his hand. "I thought of what the guys at my garage would do with you. There's a song, right? 'Quinn the Mighty Eskimo' or something? They'd latch right onto that. Talk about your igloo and so forth. Your pelts. Shiver when you walk by." Watson smiles, hands Quinn two cigarettes. "For the road," he says. "When D-Day comes, though, spring for cigars. Smoke one for me."

No one else acknowledges Quinn's leaving. Jack-knife, Wrecker, and Trooper are leaning against their respective vehicles. Sideburns is pacing the guardrail on the bridge, kicking slush into the creek.

It's snowing again. Most of the vehicles Quinn passes want news. The reactions range widely. An elderly man in a station wagon curses. Two teenagers in a jeep high five and giggle. A woman in a minivan hisses through her front teeth and punches her husband in the arm. A guy in a pickup takes off his Indians cap and bounces his forehead on his steering wheel.

Two of the vehicles Quinn passes are empty. He figures the tractor trailer belongs to Sideburns, but whose Subaru? He doesn't remember it from before, but it had to have been there. There are tracks all around it. Sneakers. Big ones. Like a basketball team.

The last stop is the woman in the Lincoln. "If it's not good news, I don't want to hear it," she says. "Seriously."

"Well," Quinn says.

"I have to pee again," the woman says. "Unbelievable."

"Not much you can do about it," Quinn says. When he shrugs, his fingers buzz.

"Need to make a phone call?" she says. "I have a phone."

"No, I'm good."

"Macaroon?" she says. "I have macaroons."

Quinn eats the cookies in his car. She had cookies but no aspirin. He cracks his window and smokes one of Watson's cigarettes. He can't find his gloves. They're not under the seat. They're not in the glove compartment.

Starting the engine for some heat would be nice, but that's not an option. There are risks, and then there are risks. Quinn can't afford to burn gas that isn't working to get him somewhere.

Here's an idea: He could turn things around. He is last in line. He could head back where he came from. There's an exit back there somewhere. Even if he doesn't want to risk it with his car–the tracks have probably drifted over; it would be dicey–he could walk it. Maybe catch up with the basketball team. But then he'd have to abandon his car. And what if it's one of those exits that leads to no services? One that just leads to more roads?

He'll stay put.

Quinn's to the point where he doesn't have to reach for his wallet if he wants to look at the ultrasound image. It's like a slide in his head. Easy access. He just has to hold it up to the light. Excellent resolution. The thing about the placenta is the blood. Rich and nutritious. If you want, you can save it, recycle it. There are people who will hold it for you. Placenta banks. If your kid needs blood down the line, you can hook her up with the best. There are people with this kind of foresight.

The woman from the Lincoln shuffles past Quinn's window. "Mind your manners, now," she says loudly. "Repeat performance." He couldn't watch even if he wanted to. The rear windshield is three-layered. There's icy glaze on the inside, and on the outside there's another ice layer, and, on top of that, snow.

Each time Quinn told the story to the people in front of him, he aimed to keep it short. He tried not to add dramatic wrinkles or pass judgments. Just the facts in a neutral tone of voice. Like court testimony. Like he was under oath. They had to wonder about his head-tilt, but nobody said anything. No one admitted to having aspirin, either.

If the gas station has any, he'll have to stock up. If not there, then at the motel. Chances are Rachel won't have any. There are things you don't keep around when you're pregnant. No coffee. Forget about beer and cigarettes, of course. There are tubes that connect the baby directly to you.

Rachel used to give great neck and back rubs. Little karate chops.

When Quinn tells Rachel the story, he'll take his time. He'll tell it with his facial expressions as well as with his voice. He'll do impressions of all the characters. He'll occasionally offer his humble opinion. He'll make it last as long as he can.

Burying Agnes

Cal knows what Jan's up to. Her words are aimed to latch onto him, burrow their heads under his skin like ticks. She's taking a break from coffee and the Sunday paper's *Parade Magazine* insert to describe Cal to himself. He hears, "Warped, deranged." He hears, "Morbid." This morning, "Macabre," through the screen door as he heads out to the backyard, Agnes at his heels. "Twisted," Jan calls after him. "Taboo." Cal's out to dig a hole, and Jan's out to stop him.

Cal marches on, twirls his shovel against his shoulder. That last one surprised him, but not enough to break his stride. He says without turning, "Denial ain't just a river in Egypt."

Agnes stops to squat at her regular brown-grassed patch by the concrete bird bath. She's got a bad set of rear wheels, bumps along like she's riding on her rims. Vet says arthritis. This on top of her going deaf, her bad circulation and the deterioration of her teeth. When she sleeps, she wheezes. Sometimes Cal thinks he can see her breath rise in faint green clouds like swamp gas. Agnes is fifteen. That's one hundred and five in dog years. The vet says this winter, Christmas if not sooner. Cal's looking to dig the hole before the ground freezes.

"Grotesque," Jan says, raising her voice. Cal's getting away. "Grisly, gruesome, ghastly."

When he reaches the live oak at the edge of the yard, Cal pats Agnes's large, lumpy head, then sinks the shovel into the ground, stomps on it with his foot. Halfway down, he hits a root. Cal wrenches the blade free, forces it deeper at a new angle, takes a step back, chokes up on the handle and pushes, pries earth from earth. He throws the shovelful a few yards to the left, in front of Jan's rose bush. "There's one," he says. Agnes sticks her snout in the dirt, scrapes with her front paws, snaps weakly at a gray bug. "Watch out now, Miss. This is going to take a while." Cal puts his back into the second shovelful. "You could've been a schnauzer, you know. You could've been a poodle."

"Who do you think you're talking to?" Ernie asks from the yard adjacent to Cal and Jan's. "Your mutt's deaf as a cinder block." Ernie and Madeline have been Cal and Jan's neighbors for eight years. The day they moved in, Agnes chased their cat, Leon, into the crawl space under their front porch. These days there's Leon II, still half-kitten. On sunny afternoons, Agnes lies in the yard and watches Leon II cross and recross the property line as he stalks blowing leaves and grasshoppers and mugs the occasional mole. Leon II sometimes rubs his face against Agnes's face. They touch noses. Jan says, "Eskimo kisses" in a baby-jabber voice and snaps pictures. Agnes's ear twitches at Jan's tone, and Leon II bats it casually, like yarn.

"Agnes knows what I'm saying," Cal says. He pitches the shovel in the ground like it's a flag, like his yard's a planet, like he's just claimed it for his people. "Me and her, we have a rapport."

"Good for you two," Ernie says. He's shirtless in a floppy hat and cut-offs. It's Labor Day weekend, and he's as brown as a nut. He spends his days manicuring his lawn, emptying beer cans, and smoking cigars by his pool. His copper belly's swelled and hard. When he converses, he pats it with the soft pads of his hands like a bongo.

Ernie's been retired for almost a full year. Cal has five more down at the plant, but he's in no hurry. He likes getting up and going someplace, Monday through Friday, seven to four. He's a supervisor. He has a desk on the floor. He keeps track of the younger men and their actions and wins their loyalty by listening attentively to their gripes, asking after their wives and kids, and cutting-up at meetings to undermine tension. He's been to retirement parties where the guests-of-honor talk about finally having time to pick up a tennis racquet or golf club, work with wood, live out of an RV, concentrate on their tomatoes, trace their genealogies, write their memoirs, and he's raised his beer and toasted this new found freedom with everyone else, but he wants no part of it. Retire. To tire again, if you think about it. Jan thinks about words and is good with them. She does the crossword and beats the hell out of Cal at Scrabble. Her boss takes drafts of reports and letters to her, and she marks them up heavily in red. Commas and spelling, sure, but she goes deeper. She cuts and re-organizes. She takes awkward, ugly-duckling sentences and transforms them into graceful swan-songs. She considers the bottom line, makes sure everything adds up. If it's bad news for the reader, she balances resolve with regret, buries the gist. If it's good news, she's up front and out with it. Maybe Jan thinks she's the cerebral and clear-minded one, that Cal doesn't have this capacity or inclination, but he does. He's apt to think through what's worthwhile. Re-tire. Tired once, tired twice.

"Talk sense to him, Ernie," Jan yells from somewhere inside the house. Sounds like maybe upstairs in the bathroom. She has the windows open. In the afternoon she'll shut them, crank on the air, put on a sweater. "He's being spooky. I'm in here wigged-out."

Ernie waves.

"She won't face facts," Cal says.

"Hole's for Flash over there?" Ernie asks. Agnes is sitting up, ears perked, staring back at the house, wondering where the voice came from. She's sure she heard something.

"Right," Cal says.

"I got one for you," Ernie says. He takes off his hat and rubs the top of his head. "OK. Here you go: If it takes two men three hours to dig a six-foot hole, how many hours does it take one man to dig half a hole?"

"No such thing as half a hole," Cal says.

"You heard it before," Ernie says. He puts his hat back on and shakes his finger at Cal. "You're wily."

"Not me," Cal says. "Just knew it."

After dinner that evening, Cal's on his hands and knees in the living room, hovering over Agnes. She's got one sticky eye on him. The other one's buried in the carpet.

Agnes's stomach is gurgling. Jan switched dog food brands to see if something good would happen—she's looking for the canine Fountain of Youth in a can—and Agnes's digestive system is rebelling. "Take cover," Cal says. "She's about to blow."

Cal's armed with a tape measure. He stretches it tail to snout. "Fifty-one inches," Cal says. "Fifty one." He repeats himself in part so he'll remember, in part to torment Jan. She ignores him. She's in the recliner reading **Reader's Digest,** laughing at "Life in these United States." Cal tries to think of something else to say. Tonight, he's out to get her goat. "Aggie likes getting measured for burial," he says, patting the dog's motionless rear end. "She's like King Tut. Maybe we'll make a mummy of her. Buy a couple extra rolls of toilet paper next week, will you?"

"That's not a humorous comment," Jan says. She gets up from the couch, walks toward the kitchen. "It's a weird one. Humor makes people laugh, at least grin. Weird makes them avert their eyes, exit the room."

"I know jokes," Cal says.

"You know maybe two, not counting knock-knocks," Jan says. Cal hears her open the refrigerator, get a glass from the cupboard. "And they both open with the same line."

"Two guys walk into a bar," Cal says. "Lots of possibilities. One of the guys, for instance, could be the pope. The
other gay or ethnic. One could have a parrot, the other a tattoo. The pope could have the tattoo, the ethnic gay guy the
parrot. Let's make the tattoo a hula dancer, the gay guy
Asian. Let's call the bird Mookie."

Cal watches Jan walk back into the room. Ice cubes clink
in her glass of Diet Coke. That two-liter's been in there for a
week and a half. It has to be flat. Jan settles back onto the
couch, takes a sip. Nothing worse than no fizz when you're
expecting fizz. The opposite of refreshing. Might as well drink
maple syrup.

"Spare me," Jan says. "Life is short."

"Don't have to tell me and Aggie," Cal says.

Cal's back at the hole early the next morning. He's
already put in a couple hours by the time Ernie makes an
appearance. "Work's illegal on Labor Day," Ernie says.
"Drop the shovel and step away from the hole or I call 911."

Cal's waist-deep in lawn. The hole is a rectangle–five feet
long and three feet wide. He plans to dig to chest-level and
then call it good. This morning he's unearthed a cap gun, a
doll's arm, a half-dozen nails, and an eyeglasses lens. "I think
I've hit the mother-lode," he says, looking through the lens at
Ernie. He tries to take his hand away, leave it up there in his
eye socket, squeeze it between his eyebrow and the top of his
cheek. If it stays, he'll deliver his next line in a British accent.
When he removes his hand, though, the lens drops.

Ernie's on his patio uncovering his grill. "Hey, we're having a cook-out today. Our boys are coming with wives and
kids. Swimming, burgers, hot dogs, potato salad, watermelon,
beer, etcetera. Madeline told me I had to invite you and Jan.
You're that special."

"That's kind of you, but I don't know," Cal says. "Sounds
like a family thing, like we'd be intruding. For what it's worth,
I like my dogs with a little black on them. Spicy mustard and

chopped onions. Lots of eggs in the potato salad, a dash of celery seed. What time and what should we bring?"

"All day," Ernie says. "Nothing."

Cal leaves his shovel in the hole and walks to the house. Agnes is at the screen door waiting for him. She's been watching him dig. When he opens the door, she slides past him, makes for the bird bath. "Stick around," Cal says.

Jan's eating a bagel at the kitchen table. Her hair's wet and she's in her bathrobe. She's staring at the wall in front of her. "Can't wake up," she says. "I feel blah."

Cal's at the sink, washing his hands with dish soap. "Hope it's not catchy," he says. He scrubs his hands under the faucet, rinses, reaches for the dish towel hanging on the oven door. "Cook-out today at Ernie and Madeline's. We made the guest list."

"Yeah?" Jan says. She pops the last bite of bagel into her mouth, sticks the cream cheese in the fridge and looks at Cal. He's holding the glass lens over his eye.

"I'd appreciate it rather astoundingly if you would please make note of my oracle," he says.

"Your oracle or your ocular?" Jan says.

"Either," Cal says. "Both." He slowly takes his hand away from his face. The lens sticks. "What's important is that it gives me x-ray vision. You, believe it or not, aren't wearing panties." He turns slowly to look out the door. "Aggie, amazingly enough, has no brain in her skull."

"Hey, we're going to this shindig next door, right?" Jan says. She claps her hands. "I'll make a cake. I need a purpose. The whole clan's coming?"

"Right," Cal says. "Ernie says we don't need to bring anything."

"That's what he's supposed to say," Jan says. She picks up the phone and dials. "Have to ask Madeline if anybody's allergic to chocolate. If yes, I'm off to the store for angel food."

Cal walks into the living room, looks at the couch. He's met Ernie and Madeline's sons a few times, but he doesn't

remember their names. Has he met their wives and kids?
He's not sure. He's bored. He looks at the clock above the
television. 10:30. He'd like to find something broken so he
could fix it. He switches on the TV. ESPN has auto racing.
That's not a sport. Anything you can do sitting down is not a
sport. Bowling is, but only when it's your turn. Fishing's not.
Maybe fly fishing, but not drifting around in a rowboat. Cal
switches off the TV and walks back into the kitchen.

Jan says, "Good, good," into the phone. She says, "Bye,"
and hangs up. "Great news," she says to Cal. She taps his
cheek with her finger as she passes him. "Chocolate's a go.
The chocolate allergy gene is not a component of Ernie or
Madeline's DNA. I'm getting dressed."

"Give me something to do," Cal says.

"Jumping jacks and squat thrusts," Jan says without turning. "Four sets of fifty. Ready, begin."

Cal heads outside, stands on the porch. Agnes is next
door, sniffing around the bottom of the grill as Ernie scrubs
the racks with a wire brush. "I have a helper," Ernie says.

"She's good at what she does," Cal says. He sits on the
porch step. In a few minutes, he hears pans banging in the
kitchen. Car's washed. Lawn's mowed. He could scoop poop.
The shovel's in the hole. He gets up and wanders over. Instead
of going for the shovel, though, he picks up the cap gun. He
knocks out the dirt caked around the trigger and in the barrel.

Agnes watches him from next door, head tilted, ears
perked.

The last time Cal held a gun, he got away with it. This was
thirty-five years ago in another city. He walked into an empty
bar on a week night, told the bartender to empty the cash register, and left with a brown paper bag full of money. He can't
remember exactly how much. One-fifty, one-seventy? He ran
a few blocks, walked a few more, dropped the gun in a river,
ate eggs and toast at a diner. The next morning he bought a
bus ticket to the city he lives in now. When he arrived, he got
a room, bought a paper, scanned the want ads, found a barber, landed a job, met Jan.

Things can happen like this. One thing can lead to another, and the old thing can be swallowed up by the new thing. No trace.

Cal spins the gun on his finger. What I wouldn't give for a holster, he thinks. What I wouldn't give for some spurs.

Agnes limps toward him, tail wagging. With her eyesight, who knows, she might be holding out hopes that the blur in Cal's hand is a rawhide chew that she can spend the afternoon gumming up. When she gets to him, Cal holds out the gun, and she sniffs and then turns away like she does when offered celery sticks or radishes. Cal lowers his fist gently onto the top of her head. "Punching dawgies," he says.

Both of the minivans that pull into Ernie and Madeline's driveway have multiple bumper stickers. When driving, in addition to getting where they're going, members of Ernie and Madeline's brood are out to get their say. One of the bumper stickers says, "My kid beat up your honor student." Another says, "Bump! Set! Spike!" Another says, "If you can't run with the big dogs, stay on the porch." Another says, "My yin and yang are no longer on speaking terms."

In the pool, the six grandchildren peg each other from point-blank range with beach balls. They're all blond. They wrestle off each other's bathing suits. Occasionally, a pair of trunks or a bikini top flies onto the deck. Madeline and Jan supervise. They throw the clothing back into the pool when it comes out, and they count for the how-long-can-you-hold-your-breath-underwater contest. They judge the swim-to-the-end-of-the-pool-and-back-again race. When Jan disqualifies the apparent winner because he didn't touch the wall on his flip-turn, he lodges his protest by spitting water in his sister's ear.

Both of Ernie and Madeline's sons are wearing ball caps, one backwards one forwards, and their wives are wearing sun-visors. The two couples team up against each other for mixed-doubles lawn darts. The son who wears his hat backwards throws the darts overhand. When he's up, everyone stands back. There are loud arguments about the score and the rules. There's taunting and pointing.

Ernie's back is to everything. He focuses on the grill. Cal sits nearby in a lawn chair recliner, nursing a beer. Agnes is sitting next to him, panting, taking it all in. Leon II naps under the porch. He's already had his tail pulled, been tossed like a bean-bag from one blond to another. Cal's the one who saved him. He said, "Whoa, now. Put the cat down," and one of the blonds cried. Because of this, Cal's sort of the bad guy. Jan pursed her lips at him. The kid's mom didn't look Cal in the eye during his brief explanation. She hugged the kid, gave him a Coke. No one wanted the cat thrown, but did he have to make the kid cry? That's the question Cal's assuming is on everyone's mind. His answer: It's too bad about the crying kid, but what's worse: a mopey kid or a cat with a shattered spine? Still, Cal feels pressure to make up for it.

When Ernie tells Cal that the meat's almost done, Cal gets out of his chair and goes over to the picnic table, uncovers the serving dishes. He manages to solicit hot dog and hamburger orders from the swimmers and dart throwers. He puts the appropriate type of bun and the appropriate number of buns on each plate—Ernie and Madeline's sons put in orders for two of each—and by the time Ernie's melting yellow slices of American on the patties, the table's filling up. A couple of the kids have changed their minds and make bun exchanges, but, overall, things go smoothly. Jan volunteers to pour iced tea and lemonade, fetch beers, but Cal tells her to stay put. He's hustling. He pretends to spill drinks on the kids, making them giggle. "Not at the table, fellas," he says to the kids' fathers as he snatches their ball caps and throws them like frisbees into the middle of the yard. "Don't push it," one of them says with a forced smile, and Cal gestures to the guy with a tilt of his head, says to the guy's wife, "You go for the tough hombres, do you?"

When Cal settles into his spot on the bench beside Jan, she looks at him until he looks back. When she has his eyes, she squeezes his knee under the table. Cal forges ahead. He picks up his fork, says to the kid next to him, "You know you can use a fork to call birds?" "No way," the kid says. "Yes way," Cal says. "Watch." Cal holds the fork up to his mouth, licks his lips. "I haven't done it for a while," Cal says, "but in a lot of ways, it's like riding a bicycle. Just no banana seat." Jan looks straight up into the sky. She flexes her neck muscles. She knows what comes next. Cal inhales deeply and screams through the fork, "Calling all birds!" A couple of the blonds fall backwards off their benches. The youngest looks like she's going to cry. Their lives will be rough ones, Cal thinks. So easily shocked.

Agnes hunches at the foot of the table, alert for falling scraps.

After eating, Ernie and his sons go inside the house to watch a ball game. "You coming, Cal?" Ernie says. "Orioles, Yankees. Mussina, Clemens."

"I don't watch American League," Cal says, dragging his chair out of the shade and into the yard. "I'm against the DH. I have scruples."

The women put on their bathing suits, take to the pool. The daughters-in-law in bikinis, Madeline and Jan in one-pieces. Madeline's suit has a short skirt at the bottom and comes up high on her chest, almost to her neck. If she stayed dry, Cal thinks, she could easily go to the grocery store in it and no one would bat an eye. Maybe even a job interview. "Bathing beauties," Cal says as they pass by. Agnes lies beside his chair.

"Don't be fresh," Jan says. She has her sunglasses pushed on top of her head, holding her hair back. She has tan lines on her shoulders and thighs. White meat, dark meat. Just like Thanksgiving. Cal winks at her.

It's been decreed that the women get the pool for one hour, and then the kids can have it again. To pass the time, the kids play three-on-three wiffle-ball. Cal's the center-field homerun marker. He's reclining on the property line. His left half's home, his right half's company. If the ball comes to him, he's allowed to catch it, but he can't get out of the chair, and he at no point gets to hit. He's taken to calling all of the kids "Blondie" in his play-by-play. "Blondie toes the rubber, winds up, here's the pitch. Blondie swings and misses. Way out in front on that one. Blondie knew Blondie was sitting on the fast ball and took something off, fooled Blondie badly." There are two fielders, one on either side of Cal. The right-fielder says to Cal, "Why don't you shut up?" The left-fielder says to the right-fielder, "Why don't you?" Cal says, "Looks like there's some discord in the outfield between Blondie and Blondie. This could prove horribly detrimental to Team Blondie's chances this afternoon."

In the middle of the third inning, runners on first and second, one out, Cal dozes off. His hand slips off Agnes's neck, tips over his beer. Aggie rises, stretches, licks the top of the can, the grass, and lumbers over the property line to her porch, lies down.

Cal wakes when he hears the scream. One of the bikinied daughters-in-law from the deck of the pool. She saw it happen.

Cal turns to see where she's looking. The blonds are gathered around the hole. Five of them. Cal rolls out of his chair and goes over. They part for him. Some are crying. At the bottom of the hole is the sixth blond, motionless, sprawled awkwardly. There's blood seeping out of his hair, and there's blood on the shovel by his head, and there's blood in the dirt. The wiffle ball rests against his thigh. "He was going back to make the catch," one of the blonds says.

Cal eases himself into the hole and picks up the boy. Everyone from the pool and the house is running across the lawn to the hole. The boy's father squats at the edge of the hole, stretches out his arms. "Give him here," he says to Cal. Cal hands the boy over gently, then hoists himself up. The boy's father lays the boy on the grass, puts his ear to the boy's mouth. "He's breathing," he says. He takes off his t-shirt, wraps it around his hand, and presses it against the gash on the boy's head.

The boy kicks his leg, rolls to the side, moans. "Hang on, Stevie," the boy's father says. "You're all right. Take her easy." When he says, "Call an ambulance," his wife runs inside.

By the time the ambulance arrives, the boy's sitting up, crying. Cal's moved back away from the boy. He's behind everyone. "What happened to you, Tiger?" one of the paramedics says, placing a hand on the boy's shoulder. When he kneels to inspect the head wound, he moves the boy's father's hand away. He reaches into his kit, grabs some gauze, tape and scissors. He holds the gauze in place, goes three times around the boy's head with the tape, snips. When the tape comes off later, some of the hair will, too. "This will keep pressure on it until we can get you some stitches," the paramedic says.

"I fell in the hole," the boy says. "I got knocked out."

"We'll need to get him on the stretcher and take him in," the paramedic says. "Get him fixed up. They'll probably want to keep him for observation tonight. Probably a concussion. Either mom or dad is welcome to ride along in the ambulance."

"Mom will go ahead and the rest of us will follow," Ernie says. "This family sticks together." He places each of his hands on a blond head. "Looks like Stevie's going to pull through, so you all are still going to have to split your inheritance six ways." He gives each a squeeze on the back of the neck. "Let's take a field trip," he says.

Within a few minutes everyone is piling into minivans, Jan included. The women don't change out of their bathing suits, they simply wrap their towels around their waists. When Jan climbs in one of the vans, Cal's on her tail. Before sitting down next to her, though, he sees that the driver, the hurt boy's father, is glaring at him, and he notices that the man has replaced his blood-stained t-shirt with one of Ernie's golf shirts. On the left breast of the shirt, where a pocket might be, two drivers are crossed in an "X." "Maybe stay here, Cal," Jan says quietly. "I'll call."

Cal backs out of the van and stands to the side of the driveway, watches them pull away. He rounds the house, crosses through the backyard, stands over the hole. In his periphery, Leon II streaks out from under Ernie and Madeline's house to attack a wind-blown paper plate.

Cal's left hand is in his pocket. He's running one finger around the chipped edge of the lens.

If Cal had x-ray vision, he'd know. He's a man who sees things through, but not a man who sees through things.

Eight more inches of digging? He'd hit a water line.

Madeline's skirted bathing suit? It could cover a patch of moles on her inner thigh which Ernie used to rub with his thumb when they made love. The soft pack of Camels buried in the glove compartment of the minivan Cal tried to board? Eleven cigarettes and a couple amatuerly-rolled joints which son and daughter-in-law will pass back and forth on their patio later tonight after the kids are in bed. The blond who hit his head? He's fine, but his younger sister has a hole in her heart, about the size of a breath mint. The paramedic on the scene? A bit of a mean streak when he drinks and an intense desire—it came on him suddenly, like smells hit you, like colds do—for the hurt blond's mom. Jan? Sitting in the back seat of the van, heading west, she slides her glasses down off her head, onto her nose, wonders if she should've stayed back at home with Cal. She's wishing she had.

That bartender Cal stuck up thirty-five years ago? If Cal could've peered into the guy, he might've turned the gun on himself, or at least laid it on the bar and walked out into the night with his hands shoved deeply into the pockets of his jacket, ashamed at how much his victim had been through already in his life.

Aggie? No surprise, her lungs slowly fill with fluid. She'll drown from the inside. Cal and Jan will miss her, more than they expected. So deeply, in fact, that it's doubtful they'll replace her. If they come to a place where they want to, they won't name the new dog Agnes II. That's for sure. It won't eat out of Aggie's bowls or wear her collar. These things, along with the gun, the doll's arm, the nails, the lens, and the wiffle ball, will hover in the earth around Aggie, orbiting her like planets.

Meat

When Mr. Q splits the swinging doors of the meat room, the radio's up way loud—"Been a long, lonely, lonely, lonely, lonely, lonely time"—and Stevie, my part-time kid who comes in afternoons and weekends, is dancing a fryer across one of the work tables. The chicken flaps its clammy wings, Rockettes-kicks its drumsticks, unleashes a series of inspired shivers, spins, and struts, collapses into a James Brown split. The bird's got moves and they're all about funky. The bird's got it going on. Mr. Q's thinking, Shenanigans. He's thinking, Monkey business. He tilts his head, cradles his chin with his thumb and forefinger, thrusts out a hip, shuts one eye. Stevie's back is to the doors and the radio's blaring just above his head, so he's oblivious, no clue. The bird's getting a groove on. It's shaking what it's got. Laying it down. Working it out.

Lance, my only full-time cutter on staff—Mr. Q says I'll have another before Labor Day, but that doesn't help me today with ground chuck flying out of the store at 89 cents a pound—is clocked out, stretching lunch, two and a half hours now. He met his girlfriend, RayAnn, for an argument. Their agreement is that they'll never walk away, hang up, or go to bed angry. They've closed restaurants, missed dentist appointments, watched three consecutive sunrises in the same parking lot. Lance warned me this morning. He can feel one coming on. I said, "Not today." He said, "I hope not." I said, "Don't hope not. Make sure not. I can't spare you. Stay off the touchy subjects. Tip-toe around the time-bombs. Be agreeable. Be a pleasure. Hold one of her hands in both of yours and give her a soulful gaze. When she sneezes, say 'Bless you.' Ask if she's lost weight." He said, "Tucker, love is anything but cause and effect." I said, "Lunch is one hour." He shrugged. "I've been fired before for her. And twice arrested."

Cindy, my only wrapper today, is in the ladies' room. She's slow even in there. Twenty minutes and counting. When she comes back, she'll look like she did when she went, like she's just this side of awake. She goes through the whole day with puffy face, slits for eyes, and pillow head. She's perpetually stretching and yawning. No matter how many sticks of gum she's chewed or cigarettes she's smoked, at three in the afternoon she still has morning breath. My other wrapper, Frieda, is at home. Her story is she's sick. She called early this morning to make her case, and I said, "Frieda, the ground chuck," and she said, "Nausea, headache, dizziness, fever rash, must get off phone, need rest."

In a pinch, Stevie can work the wrapping machine, but his packages are an embarrassment to the meat department. They droop and sag. He uses the wrong size styrofoam boats and too much wrap and doesn't pull tightly enough. The plastic bunches and gaps. Air gets in and turns the meat brown. Within minutes the case is a soggy mess. If a customer's desperate, puts a package in her cart, it leaves a trail of blood spots all the way up to checkout. Cashiers and bag boys scowl if one comes through their lane. They're forced into double-bag mode. They have to wipe their sticky fingers on their jeans.

Stevie's funny, though. Jokes. The kid's a natural performer. He wants to go pro.

People can't get enough of the 89-cent ground chuck. It's going to be like this all week. You see the love of beef in their eyes as they tenderly finger the packages, the unbelievably reasonable price stickers, the "Ground Fresh Today" labels. They consider ground beef's efficiency, convenience, and flexibility as they load up. They think family bar-b-ques, picnics, casseroles, Sunday meatloafs. They think Hamburger Helper, Sloppy Joe mix, tacos. They think how sick they are of chicken. Their mouths water, their stomachs groan. They think they'll make room in their freezers. They think definitely tonight for dinner, and maybe a small patty with two eggs and an English muffin in the morning. Protein. Brainfood. All tomorrow they'll be on their toes. Nothing will get past them. Some customers are walking away with twenty or twenty-five pounds worth. I'm barely keeping up. My next move has to be to get out there to the sale signs with a magic marker and set a per-customer limit.

Mr. Q's down from the office to ask me how the ground chuck's moving, to tell me the cases are looking a little light.

Stevie's hilarious. He says he wants to go on the road when he gets out of school, do stand-up until he gets a movie contract or his own sitcom. Sometimes with the dancing chicken bit, he sticks a rubber glove down into the cavity, so the chicken's dancing plus it has this five-fingered head flapping around, and sometimes the kid does this voice, this clucky chicken voice, and the chicken sings as it dances. Whatever comes on WPYX 106.5—The Best of the 60s, 70s, and 80s. The kid changes the words on the spot. "Born to Be Stir-Fried." "Ice-box Hero." "Take It to the Giblet." "Pinball Gizzard." Whenever he sings "gravy" instead of "baby," Cindy has to run out of the room, go pee. It's the fastest I've seen her move. But now's not the time for comedy with Lance turning lunch into a day off, Frieda playing deathbed, Cindy perhaps napping on the toilet, and Mr. Q on site with questions and concerns.

Stevie with his chicken still doesn't know Mr. Q's behind him. The situation is getting uncomfortable. I make

eye contact with Mr. Q and get the feeling that I'm not to
say anything, but I'm not sure if I'm supposed to go about
my business or watch the chicken. It's hard not to watch.
It's really got its mojo working.

Suddenly, a second chicken enters, stage left. Slam-danc-
ing commences, white meat to white meat. The newcomer
loses a wing but continues to stand in, shows real pluck. Mr.
Q keeps moving his folded arms higher up on his chest.
Another few seconds he'll run out of chest.

Frieda's not sick. I'm no schmuck. She's alive and well
across town at the new Grand Union filling out an applica-
tion. Word is they pay a buck fifty more an hour than here
at Q's. They have a seafood department, a sprinkler system
in produce, a video section, and a sit-down
restaurant/espresso bar behind the deli. Lots of free-sample
tables. A profit-sharing plan. An annual employee family
picnic complete with softball game and free pony rides for
the kids. Frieda's good. She'll get the job if she wants it.
Magician-quick hands. Every package beautiful. She can
wrap a crown roast perfectly first try without puncturing the
plastic with a rib, and when she's caught up with the wrapping, she'll take the pricing gun, load up a cart with cases of
hot dogs and bacon, and fill holes in the smoked meat case.
She earns her check and then some.

When the song ends, one chicken bows, the other curt-
sies, and they both flop down in exhaustion. Mr. Q takes two
steps and reaches over Stevie to turn the radio down, past
the mark he scratched on the dial a few months ago with a
paper clip. The sign he made, "VOLUME DOESN'T GO
PAST MARK ON DIAL. ANY QUESTIONS, SEE MR. Q,"
is still taped to the shelf beside the radio. Someone, either
Lance or Stevie–I know I didn't do it, and Frieda and Cindy
write too neatly-scrawled, "IS CHEAP" with an arrow pointing to "MR. Q," but Mr. Q misses it. When Stevie turns, Mr.
Q stares him down convincingly. He's been waiting for this.
Stevie looks like he's swallowed a rock. He drops the chickens into a tub and shuffles to the saw. Women in housecoats

are heaping ground chuck in their carts like it's just been
announced that beef will prevent cancer and make husbands
more personable and easier to live with, and the kid's thinking he should quarter chickens.

Stevie's talented. When he breathes it's funny. Bottom
line, though, is that he's got no instincts for the meat business.
When Mr. Q's done glaring, he turns to me. "Tucker," he
says and points to the ceiling. "Can I have a word?"

We're going upstairs. His office. I take off my apron, toss
it on my block and follow. He steps on a piece of beef fat on
his way out, slides half a foot, but keeps his balance and continues on through the swinging doors like nothing's happened. Out of the corner of my eye, I see Stevie flipping Mr.
Q the bird. Not one of his chickens, his finger. "Watch it,
funny man," I say to him on my way out. "Get the hell off the
saw and on the grinder. Chuck's in the cooler. Cut up a case
and start grinding. Don't stop grinding."

"Aye Aye, Captain," he says. Scotty from **Star Trek.**
Dead-on. The kid's going places. Someday I'll be watching
him in my living room.

On the stairs, Mr. Q is four steps ahead of me, then five.
He's widening the lead. Before he hits the top, though, I close it
to three by skipping a couple. I'm on his tail. Time is money. I
understand this. For the last six months, the meat department's
had the widest profit margin of all the departments. At monthly
manager's meetings, when this is announced, Betty from bakery folds her hands and frowns at her lap. Every morning at
8:40, when she ducks out for her first cigarette, I swing by,
swipe an apple fritter and a Boston cream. I eat them brazenly
as I walk through the aisles back to the meat room. I'm liable
to stop off in dairy and crack open a pint of chocolate milk.
Who's to stop me? Meat makes more than bakery and dairy
put together. If Mr. Q passes me, he winks and smiles, tells me
his golf score from the afternoon before, brings me news and
gossip from the front of the store, lets me know—I don't ask—
what Darla the head cashier is wearing, brags on where he's
taking his wife and kid skiing over Christmas.

Mr. Q's kid, Wally, has a smart mouth and goes to private school. When things got crazy over the holidays last year, Mr. Q made him work the store. He wanted the kid to understand a day's work. Wally spent his first day in the meat room. Within the first half hour, he was using one of Lance's knives to open boxes. I had to send Lance to lunch at 9:00 in the morning so he could cool off. Wally said, "What's the big deal, Tucker?" He said, "What's with that guy?" He said, "Technically, this knife belongs to my father, not to that Neanderthal." I said, "Technically, that Neanderthal could kick your ass." Stevie laughed from across the room at this line. I can be funny, but only normal-guy funny. Not like Stevie. He takes it to another level. He's an artist. His comedy culminates in something more than the sum of its parts. It's funny for its own sake.

Wally transferred to produce the next day. That afternoon, a friend of his came in the store, and Wally got excited, threw a nectarine. The nectarine hit an old man in the temple and knocked him off his feet. When the old man got back up, he received a month's worth of free groceries. Wally was sent home by his father. On his way out of the store, he kicked over a salsa display. It was a scene. We all have problems. I don't have kids, but I was one. My father didn't own anything, but we tangled. There are at least two sides to most things.

What's amazing about Stevie's talent is how good he is on the spot, how quick. And his delivery. Bod-a-bing, bod-a-boom. When Frieda came in the meat room and told us that Wally had just dumped the salsa display, Stevie rushed to the door in a frenzy with one hand on his hat like it was going to fly off his head—little touches like this make the difference—and screamed, "Hot or mild, Frieda? Was it hot or mild?" No punch line. Just the way he did it. Flying to the door like that and the screaming. Timing. Improvisation. He's got a flair. Nails it every time.

In the hallway leading to Mr. Q's office is Carrie Schultz's desk. She's Mr. Q's assistant. She's not at the desk. Word is that she and Mr. Q have something on the side, that that's the only possible way she could've held onto the job this long. She calls in sick at least once a week. Calculators and typewriters mystify her. She wears short skirts and clingy blouses and heavy eye make-up. Her hair is long, blonde, parted down the middle and feathered back, like *Charlie's Angels.* She doesn't smile. She's always coming out of or going into the ladies' room. Cindy sees her there a lot, comes back and reports that she thinks she's heard her crying in the stall or might've seen her swallowing a handful of pills at the sink. I don't know. I talked to Carrie once in the break room. I put down the sports page to answer her questions about pork roasts. She said her father was coming to visit that weekend and that her mother, while she was alive, used to make him a pork roast with sauerkraut and mashed potatoes twice a month. Carrie wanted to do this for him during his visit as a surprise. I told her I'd cut and tie one for her special, and I suggested roasting it with raisins and apples. She seemed to appreciate the time and effort I put into the conversation. She's beautiful, and I wonder if maybe that's part of the reason why stories about her float around the store. The latest is that she's pregnant, Mr. Q, and he wants her to get rid of it. I don't know what to believe.

Maybe a younger brother or sister, no matter how illegitimate, would steady Wally. It's strange sometimes what will do the trick. Maybe he'd take the sibling under his wing, teach the kid the ropes. "Convince Dad that you want to go to public school," he'd advise, his arm slung around a pair of narrow shoulders. "Here's another thing: resist the urge to throw fruit."

Mr. Q raps his knuckles once on the wall as he walks into his office. He sits behind his desk and motions me into a chair across from him. He says, "Ground meat case is half empty. Everything going smoothly? Problems with your crew? Enough beef in the cooler?"

"It's moving quickly," I say. "Maybe too quickly. I think setting a limit would be a good idea. Ten pounds a customer, maybe. This would serve to regulate the consumption." Sometimes I surprise myself. Mr. Q's impressed when I use phrases like this. He thinks to himself, "In front of me is Tucker, an uneducated steak slinger, a common chicken packer, burger grinder, nonetheless, an employee who understands and has a knack for the business." In the last manager's meeting, I delivered a short lecture on the success of my stuffed pork chops. I take a normal rib or loin chop, which usually sells for about $2.69 a pound, slit it down the middle, dump in a spoonful of Stove Top stuffing, and jack the price to $3.99 a pound. I said, "I'm happy to report that this new product has been an unequivocal success. A very slight increase in overhead and labor has yielded a sizable increase in profit." When I finished, Mr. Q nodded, clapped his hands together once and rubbed, and looked at the other managers with arched eyebrows as if to say, "And the rest of you?" Bakery Betty's face fell softly into her hands, and she kneaded her temples.

"I trust your judgment, Tucker," Mr. Q says. "Go ahead and set a limit. Let the cashiers know, though." He leans back in his chair and folds his hands behind his head. How he sees it, there's no crisis he can't handle. "Anything else?"

"I did want to discuss something with you when I had the chance," I say. "I was wondering about getting another forty or fifty cents an hour for Frieda. She's coming up on three years. My best worker, really. Fast. Conscientious."

Mr. Q leans forward and rests his elbows on the desk. "Frieda. Now she's the one with the ponytail? Nose-ring? Smoker? The one Carrie says she's always seeing in the can?"

"No, that's Cindy. Frieda's older? Shorter? Fast walker?"

"Right, right." He closes his eyes and scratches inside his ear. "Tell her fifty cents. It'll be on her next check."

I stand up. "I appreciate it. Frieda will too."

"All right then, Tucker. Let's get some ground chuck in the case. And tell the wise-ass kid I'm watching him. Tell him he's on his last leg, that there's plenty of bag boys up front who'd love the chance to move back into the meat room, that he's expendable, that funny doesn't mean shit in the real world, that funny grows on trees."

MEAT   63

"Right."

On my way back downstairs, I pass Carrie going up. She's carrying a purse. Just getting back from the bathroom, or lunch, or maybe a doctor's appointment. She smiles and I nod. Who knows what she's headed for? It's hard to read someone when you pass them on stairs. It's the angle. You're on the same level for just a brief moment.

I can't know any more than this: She gets to the top of the stairs and drops her purse on her desk. Mr. Q looks up when he hears her. Whether he gets up, goes to her, gathers her in his arms, assures her that he's there, or tells her to get on the horn and cancel his afternoon appointments so he's clear to go to the driving range and work out his slice, I don't know.

As for me, I know where things go from here. I proceed downstairs, set a limit to how much ground chuck shoppers in West Sand Lake, New York, can buy, and then I get on the grinder, try to fill the cases and maybe stay an hour or two past 5:00 to back-up one hundred pounds or so for tonight and tomorrow morning, and then I go home, open a can and eat, anything but a burger, watch TV until I can't take any-more, think how Leno and Letterman are losing it, that in a few years the time might be right for Stevie, maybe even the dancing chickens, and meat eaters of West Sand Lake will see it and laugh.

Before I do anything, though, I'm calling Frieda with the good news about her raise. Maybe she'll stay, and we'll all pull together, come back from lunch on time, take fewer on-the-clock bathroom breaks, keep the comedy to a minimum, and we'll get through ground chuck week, and next week we'll be able to breathe a little easier, put something like bottom round roast on sale, turn the radio up a notch, laugh a little.

When I walk into the meat room, Stevie's on his tip-toes, arms and head over the top of and inside the grinder. I get a sick feeling deep down. "What," I say. His head pops up.

"Problem, Tucker," Stevie says. "I left my knife in the tub of chuck, and then I dumped it into the grinder with the meat. Now, grinder's broke." He stepped on the foot pedal to demonstrate. Clackity-clack, clackity-clack. Like a set of keys flying around in a dryer. "Sorry."

Having said this, he studies the floor, pulls on the bill of his Q's Supermarket hat. I know what he's thinking: There's nothing inherently funny in this, but that's, ultimately, the comedian's challenge, to point to the everyday mishap that life is, expose it as tragedy, but at the same time get people to laugh at it. Nothing's come to me yet, but something will. I have confidence in my instincts. At the exact right moment, a joke will be uttered.

I give him almost a full minute. Nothing. He looks up once, opens his mouth to speak, but then clams back up. He meanders slowly to the walk-in cooler and shuts the door behind him. He needs some alone time. I head for the phone.

First I call the grinder company. The voice who answers says, best scenario, they can have someone come out middle of the week. "The flu's ripping through here," the guy says. "Half my staff's down." I say, "We've got ground chuck on sale this week. 89 cents a pound." "Ouch," the guy says. "Hurt me."

I hang up and call Frieda. She picks up on the first ring. "Tucker, somehow I knew it was you. Grand Union just called. I start a week from today. You can't beat them, so don't even try. You were good to me, but I was good to you, too, so we're even. The way I see it, I owe you nothing, not even a week's notice. Nothing against you—I know you're just a cog, a spoke, a monkey, so to speak—but I know ground chuck's on sale this week, I know you need me, and that's why I'm not coming in. Shamefully enough, I'm out to hurt you. 'You' I mean collectively. I'm out to hurt Q's. Do me a favor and tell Cindy she's a lame-o, tell Lance he's half a man, and Stevie that there's a difference, albeit slight, between laughing with someone and laughing at someone. Aloha means goodbye."

"The grinder's broke," I say.

"Bonus," she says.

I hang up the phone and turn. Lance strolls in. His eyes

are red. His lips are trembling. "We're through," he says. "Me and RayAnn. She left half-cocked. If she'd had her different purse, she would've shot me with her handgun. Her last words to me were nonsensical but aimed to injure." He walks over to his table, ties on his apron.

"The kid broke the grinder," I answer, "and that was Frieda on the phone. She's gone. Message to you is you're half a man. All is lost."

Cindy walks in just in time to here my pronouncement. She loses her legs, slumps against the wall. "Lame-o," I say.

The door to the cooler opens and Stevie walks out. When he sees Lance, he smirks, ducks back in, and re-emerges with a beef heart. He smiles widely. His face is all mouth. He walks over to Lance, pulsing the bloody mess with both hands. "Romeo, Romeo, don't tell me, Romeo. More trouble in paradise?" He lets the heart splat on the table. Drum roll please. "And you thought your heart was heavy." Rim-shot.

At that moment, we all know he's lost it, that his future's dim, that he's doomed. We weren't expecting this. He's trying to read our faces, but he can't make it out. He doesn't get it.

One Removed

Cam's speech is almost back to normal, his pronunciation nearly perfect. I can still hear the occasional slur or stutter, and he talks more slowly—during pauses he swallows purposefully, like he's downing pills—but these imperfections somehow make him seem insightful and introspective. Believable. His words weigh in and settle one at a time. His sentences line up like this, measured, single-file, like they must be going somewhere.

I don't know for sure the specifics of the night my husband was attacked—he says he doesn't remember much, that he doesn't want to—but I've imagined it. I've worked it out, the whole thing, blow by blow.

It's winter, a week before Christmas, and Cam is leaving his lover, Dot, for the night. He walks out of her apartment building and turns north onto Stratford. He leans his shoulders into the wind, tucking his chin under the top button of his jacket. His hair's wet from Dot's shower and freezes quickly. The snow has picked up. He hears a plow come up from behind him and moves across the sidewalk to avoid the spray.

When he comes to Elm Street, he turns west and lifts his head. This is when he sees his car, still parked under the streetlight where he'd left it so it would be safe. Both doors are flung open, bent on their hinges, and, along with the hood and roof, deeply dented. The tires are flat, and all the glass is broken, including the sun roof. When Cam comes closer and looks in, he sees that the seats are shredded, the stereo smashed, and he sees small shifting snowdrifts shining on the dashboard, on the passenger seat.

He's already taken a couple blows to the back and shoulders, is already face down in the sidewalk slush when he realizes what is happening. There are three of them, Heath and two of his friends, Ray and Patrick. They've been waiting for Cam behind the hedges across the street. Heath is the one with the baseball bat.

After the initial flurry, the attackers are winded, and eventually the blows stop coming in bunches. The attackers slow down, take their time, take turns, fall into a rhythm. After a while, Ray and Patrick, the two using their hands, have sore, split knuckles–they instinctively bring their fists to their mouths, dab at the blood with their lips–and they think it's finished. The physical exertion and the cold air pumping their hearts has sobered them, and it's snowing, and it's late, and there's work tomorrow, and the guy they were out to get is lying motionless on the sidewalk in front of them.

But Heath isn't finished. He drops the bat, takes a couple deep breaths, and aims a kick at Cam's head. He does this again.

When Heath stops kicking Cam, it's not because he has to, because he hears a siren or sees a pair of approaching headlights, or because a voice yells out a window that the cops have been called. It's not because Ray and Patrick grab him and tell him it's enough. When he stops, it's because he's finished, and he doesn't run away, he walks.

Two days after the attack, I knew their names, and I knew all three of them had been drunk, and I knew that they'd used an ax and a knife on the car and a bat on Cam, and I knew that Cam had been sleeping with Dot. I first learned all this not from Cam, but from police reports. All three attackers confessed and pled guilty and are just beginning their prison terms. Ray and Patrick got two years each–they'll be up for parole in six months–and Heath, because he used a bat and kicked a man in the head when he was down, will serve a minimum of five years.

I imagine Heath was acting according to jealousy and pain and the part of him that believed women could be owned, and the other two, Ray and Patrick, went along because their friend had been wronged, and helping him was an act of justice. They would've expected the same loyalty.

One of the things I wonder about is how Dot felt when she learned that Cam was in the hospital, that her ex-husband had put him there. Once, in my senior year in high school, I broke up with a boy to date his friend. They stopped being friends because of me, at least that's the way it seemed then, and although a part of me felt low, another part of me liked the drama and passion the three of us acted out. I fantasized about them hurting each other over me more than I did about loving or even sleeping with either of them.

The bad feeling between them didn't result in anything more than empty threats and stare-downs in the hallways between classes until one night early that summer. A week or two after graduation, my boyfriend, Dan, and I walked into a party where Andy, my ex-boyfriend, was. It was Andy's last night at home. He'd be leaving for army boot camp the next day, and he'd already gotten the haircut. It was the first time I'd seen it–I couldn't believe how different he looked, how much older, more serious–and a part of me wanted badly to go up to him and run my hand up the back of his neck and above his ears.

When Andy saw Dan and me, he broke out of the circle he was in and made his way towards us. Our presence, combined with the emotion of all the good-byes he was giving and receiving and all the bourbon and Cokes he was drinking, was too much for him. His exit was angry and inspired–a shoulder-to-shoulder brush, a silent stand-off, a slammed door–and when Dan and I left the party a couple hours later, we discovered on the driver's side of the cherry-red Camaro he'd just received for a graduation present a deep scratch in the paint stretching from headlight to tail light.

When I got home that night, I dialed Andy's number. When his mother answered, I hung up. If he would've answered, I would've told him I was sorry and wished him good luck for the future, and I would've asked him where we could meet.

When Heath, breathless and slurring his words, called Dot from a bar after he and Patrick and Ray left Cam on the sidewalk along Elm Street–I don't know for a fact that he called her, but I believe he did–I wonder if, along with the feelings of fear and guilt and disgust that she had for him, she also felt a desire to have him in the room with her, to have him touch her.

After three days in intensive care, when he was stable enough to move, Cam was transferred from the hospital in Pittsfield to Boston. He spent six weeks there. I stayed in Boston, too. I took a leave of absence from my high school teaching job and got a room at a motel a few blocks away from the hospital.

Cam had reconstructive surgery on the left side of his face. Now it's held together by a three-inch steel screw, running from just below his eye into his jaw. The screw is undetectable–Cam says he doesn't even feel it–but even now, three months after the operation, I still have trouble looking at him when we eat without visualizing the movement of the screw as he chews, worried that his next bite might snap or shift or somehow lock-up his face, that he'll scream out in pain. When he eats apples, I have to leave the room.

In addition to his shattered jaw, there was enough brain and nerve damage to result in impaired motor skills and some emotional trauma. One of the doctors compared his condition to that of a stroke victim. Extent of recovery is wait and see. He still goes regularly to physical therapy and speech therapy sessions, and he still sees a counselor, although not as frequently as he did at first. There were days early on when he didn't want to get out of bed, and there were days when he went back and forth between wanting to be alone to being nervous when I wasn't in the same room as him. Sometimes I'd get home from the grocery store or the bank to find him sobbing, worried that I'd left for good.

Overall, though, improvement has been steady. He can finish a crossword puzzle now–I hold the pen and he tells me what to write–and if we bring home a movie for the VCR, he can follow the plot if every once in a while I hit the pause button and remind him of who's who and what they're up to. He still can't drive, though, or handle a steak knife, or work buttons or zippers, or open a jar, or use a bottle opener. Occasionally he has trembling spells in his hands. They twitch and shiver, turn into small, nervous animals–you want to hold them, pet them–and he has to concentrate on slowly opening and closing his fists to change them back into hands. It's mesmerizing, and a little frightening, like a magic trick.

What's most frustrating for him is that he still can't get around the house without his walker. On bad days and in public he still has to use the wheelchair. Making love is possible, but in discovering this, we've also realized that it's awkward and painstaking, almost not worth the effort for either of us.

The night Cam was beaten, he called home from the store to tell me he'd be late. I was in the kitchen. The phone rang and the tea kettle whistled at the same time. I answered the phone first, told Cam to hold on, went to the stove, took the kettle off the burner, and then picked the phone back up. "It's late for tea," he said, and I said, "Herbal," and he said, "Oh."

I asked him how business had been, and he said great, that's why he was going to have to stay. He wanted to go over some numbers, do some restocking, get everything he could out of the back room and onto the floor for the final rush that would come that weekend, the last weekend before Christmas. The more he talked, the more specific his lie became. "Skiing equipment is moving like crazy, so that section's a mess. I have to get that squared away. And I need to figure out what to put on sale. I have fifteen left-handed catcher's mitts in stock. You believe that? I don't know what I was thinking there. And I'd like to find a way to move more rods and reels, maybe put a display up front. Anyway, I'll be a while. You'll be all right?"

I didn't believe him, and I tried to hide my disbelief by saying as little as possible. Lying is difficult, but being lied to can be harder, I think. I've learned this during my time with Cam. The liar hides behind the lie, but so can the listener, and when this happens, a kind of guilt-based bond is formed. For these two people, lying becomes like a sacrament, a point of commiseration. It becomes a way for them to share in loss and to ease into lives without one another because to stop loving on one's own is too abrupt a truth.

When I hung up the phone, I undressed and got into bed. The next day was the last before winter recess, and I had some student papers to finish grading. I put down my pen once when I thought I heard a car turn in the driveway, and then a few minutes later when I thought I heard someone on the porch, but both times it was nothing. The call from the hospital came hours later, after I'd turned off the light by my bed, after I'd fallen asleep.

I don't know what Dot looks like. She didn't attend any of the court proceedings. I know this because after the sentencing last week, on the way home in the car, I asked Cam if she'd been there. He shook his head without looking at me and then leaned forward and fumbled with the radio, but he couldn't get his fingers to work together well enough to turn the knob. When he sat back, I could tell he was frustrated, and I was sorry I'd brought up Dot's name. At the next red light, I reached over and switched the radio on, and we didn't say anything. When the light turned green, the car lurched forward and stalled, and it took a few moments for the engine to catch again when I turned the key, and Cam broke the silence between us by saying we needed to get the car to the shop for a tune-up. It was probably something simple. Maybe the fuel filter.

When I picture Dot and Cam together, it's usually just before they've made love for the first time, or just after. The image of two bodies in bed is less disturbing to me, and somehow less important, than the moment Cam decided to be unfaithful to me, the first button he undid, or maybe even before that, the first time he touched her hand, the first time she laughed at something he said. I also think about the moment immediately after the fact. How long did they linger in the bed, or on the couch, or on the floor? Who got up first? What did they say?

In my mind, Dot has long, dark hair and dark eyes. She's a few years younger than me, not yet thirty-five, and she wears jeans and boots and turtlenecks and ski sweaters and dangling earrings that shiver when she laughs and when she brushes them with her hand as she tucks wisps of hair behind her ear. She is like every woman who lives in Pittsfield who might stop by the sporting goods store on a Saturday afternoon looking for a new jacket, and she isn't looking to meet a man, but it's always a possibility because, if she isn't beautiful, she's close, and she's alone, and when she's smiled at, she smiles back.

She's got a jacket on, a blue one, down, more than she can afford, and she's looking at herself in the jacket in the mirror outside the fitting rooms when Cam walks up behind her—in the mirror she watches him notice her, slow, turn—and he reaches towards her hip, catches the price tag attached to the side pocket, reads it, and puts his hand over his heart and closes his eyes like he can't believe what he's just seen, like it pains him. He tells her he didn't realize the clerks had been marking the prices so low, he doesn't know how he's supposed to make any money selling high-quality, top-of-the-line merchandise at such bargain basement prices. He can't tell her not to buy the coat–it's her right as a consumer–but he wants her to know that taking it home at this price is contributing to the demise of an honest, community-conscious business man. They both smile in the mirror.

A few weeks later–maybe just days later, maybe later that day–the two of them are in the apartment on Stratford Avenue. It's the middle of the afternoon, and Cam's told the assistant manager at the store that he's in charge, and he's to tell anyone who asks that Cam had to make a run to Albany to meet with one of the suppliers. Dot and Cam are in the bedroom, quiet, and Dot is at the closet, pulling on a faded terry-cloth robe, and Cam is sitting on the edge of the bed, the sheets pulled across his lap, and he's reaching down to the floor for his pants, or the two of them are in the living room, and Dot is at the stereo putting on a CD, laughing at something that Cam just said, and Cam is stretched across the couch, smiling, one arm dangling down to the floor and the other bent under his head like a pillow.

The phone rings. They don't look at each other during the three rings, during the time it takes for Dot to get to it across the room. When Dot picks up, she hears Heath say, "You've got someone there right now, don't you? Don't you?" and she says, "I'm sorry, I think you've dialed the wrong number," and she hangs up.

One night in his hospital room in Boston, just a couple days after the operation on his jaw, Cam told me he'd been thinking about things. He paused to take a careful sip of water from the paper cup beside his bed. Most of the swelling from the beating had gone down, but there were still faint traces of purple around his cheeks and eyes and across the bridge of his nose. He kept one hand on his jaw when he spoke to make sure his mouth wouldn't move too much–he looked and sounded like a bad ventriloquist–and he tried to be concise. "To forget, to forgive, you have to know what it is you're forgetting and forgiving. I know I need to tell you. I just don't want what I've done to ruin what we're starting to rebuild. Lot's wife, you know. Can't go forward if we're looking back."

He proceeded to tell me that it had been a fling, said it was just a few times, a few moments of weakness. They'd met sometime around Thanksgiving, flirted, she'd given him her phone number, and things had gone from there. Always at her apartment, never our house. He wanted me to know that he'd never do that, bring another woman to our home.

Maybe what bothered me that night in the hospital, bothers me now, even more than the fact that I was deceived and betrayed, is the nagging feeling that I don't know the whole story, the realization that there is a degree of finality for everyone involved except me. There's prison for Ray, Patrick, and Heath, the end of an affair for Dot, a beaten but now healing body for Cam, but for me there is nothing. I am one removed from everything, and Cam is the one who removes me. Maybe more than everything else, this is what I cannot forgive him for, the way he links me to the pain and tragedy and at the same time distances me from it, doesn't allow me to fully embrace it as my own. I feel bullied into love by a man who I sometimes have to help to the toilet in the middle of the night, who occasionally bursts into fits of laughter or tears without knowing why, who used to lie and now tells the truth because he has no other choice. If there was not a screw in Cam's face, if he could walk, if he could cut his own meat, if he could make love like a normal man, if he could still lie, I don't know if I'd be where I am.

So I didn't say what I wanted to that night in the hospital. I didn't ask what Dot looked like, what they talked about, if they talked about me, if she even knew he was married, if he loved her. I didn't ask him where we'd be at that moment if the beating hadn't happened, if he wasn't in a hospital bed. Instead, I asked two questions I already knew the answers to. I said, "How could you?" and then "What do you want from me?"

Reading is slow going for Cam, but lately he's been able to work through some books on positivity and the power of the mind in healing the body. His doctors say that he's been making great strides in rehab lately, and he attributes it all to his new frame of mind. Over dinner the other night, he quoted from one of the books. "Looking back sells the future short," he said. He put down his fork–to control it, he has to hold it in the middle of his fist and stab at his food like a child–and looked me in the eyes before delivering the line. He wanted me to realize its full weight and wisdom. A few moments before, out of nowhere, I'd asked him how he and Dot had left things the last time they saw each other, the night of the attack.

"I'd be so happy if I knew you were moving on, Robin. It would help me. When you bring up what happened out of the blue like this, it makes me wonder if you've forgiven me."

"I understand."

There have been moments when I've felt a kind of pity for Heath, even identified with him. I understand that his beating of Cam was, in essence, intended to punish Dot. Cam was just a body to be broken, a stand-in. You can't be betrayed by a stranger, but Heath had to do something. He couldn't just stand by and let Dot hurt him. I doubt he's that kind of man. I imagine he's a passionate man, a man of action, probably quiet.

When Heath first knew for sure that Cam was the one–perhaps he'd followed Dot to the store on several occasions and that's how he knew–he'd probably tried to keep himself under control, stay calm, see how things developed. But the day of the attack he must've seen something he couldn't put out of his mind. Perhaps that morning he'd seen Dot and Cam kissing in the store parking lot, in broad daylight, and after watching Dot climb in her car and drive away and Cam walk back inside the store, he'd gone into the store and bought the baseball bat, a thirty-five inch Louisville Slugger, and on the way to the cash register he passed Cam, and Cam smiled and asked if he'd found everything OK.

Later, at the bar that night, after following Cam from the store to Dot's, Heath simply tells Ray and Patrick what he knows to be happening at that very moment in Dot's bedroom, and he tells them how it makes him feel and what he intends to do about it. Ray and Patrick are sitting next to Heath at the bar, one on either side of him, and they're noticing how tightly he's holding his bourbon, how he hasn't taken his coat off, and the more they hear, the worse they feel for him, and when he pushes himself away from the bar and gets up, takes his wool hat out of one coat pocket, his gloves out of the other, they get up too, and one of them, Ray, claps Heath on the shoulder, and Patrick nods and presses his lips together, and they walk out in single-file, silently, into the cold, and Heath can't stop thinking about Dot's body being touched, about someone other than him touching Dot's body, and his stomach lurches, and he spits on the sidewalk and wipes his mouth with the back of his glove, and Ray and Patrick think about how horrible it is to feel like Heath's feeling—they know—and the three of them walk to Heath's pickup, and out of the cab they grab the bat and a knife and an ax.

I think Cam wants to avoid talking about the attack and the affair because he thinks that by not talking he and I will be able to forget. Maybe all the physical therapy he's been through in the last few months has him thinking of memory as a muscle, and he thinks that if we don't exercise it, it will atrophy, wither. Despite his silence, though, I know he hasn't forgotten. Occasionally I wake up in the middle of the night to his whimpering and moaning. It's frightening, but something makes me listen for a while before waking him. I know what's happening in the dream, but something prevents me from stopping it right away, from stepping in. A part of me wants to leave him alone. Finally, though, I always reach over to the other side of the bed and touch his shoulder. "Cam," I whisper. "Cam, wake up. You're here with me."

For the past few days, Cam's been talking about selling the store. He says he thinks he can get a fair price for it, and he's thinking maybe he'd like to move to Arizona or New Mexico, some place warm where he can get more fresh air, maybe buy another sporting goods store or get into real estate. He says we should get into something together. He says since I'm not teaching right now, maybe this is the time to make a move. A window of opportunity. The past few months have been tough on him—Massachusetts winters aren't compatible with wheelchairs or sore joints—and he thinks that a change of scenery might do us good, serve as a concrete expression for the new start we're making in our marriage. He says no pressure, it's up to me too, but he wants me to think about it.

Yesterday morning I asked Cam if part of the reason he wanted to move was because it was hard for him to be in the same city as Dot. Not from a temptation standpoint necessarily, but more because knowing she was right across town made everything seem too close, too immediate. After all, it was entirely possible that we would eventually bump into her at the mall, or on the sidewalk, or at a restaurant, and maybe she'd be by herself or with a girlfriend, or maybe she'd be with a man. Either way, it would be awkward for everyone.

We were in the car, on the way to the hospital for a rehab session. Cam had the newspaper open on his lap, and after I was done talking, he clumsily gathered it into a ball and threw it at the windshield. He looked at me and then out the window and then back at me. "You're not doing your part," he said.

When we came to the intersection of West and Onota, the car died at the red light. I tried repeatedly to get it started, and Cam told me not to crank it so long, that I'd damage the starter, and then he told me to give it some gas, and when that didn't work, he said to wait a minute, that I'd probably flooded it, but after a minute it still wouldn't turn over. It was rush hour, and we were in the left-hand turning lane. Cars honked and weaved around us, music and news spilling out open windows. It was the first truly warm day of spring.

Without saying anything, I switched on the hazards, got out, and walked across the intersection to a 7-Eleven where there was a pay phone. I took the Triple-A card out of my wallet, picked up the receiver and dialed. I told the man who answered where we were, and he said twenty minutes. I hung up and turned back to the intersection, watched the light change, the flow of traffic swell in another direction. I thought about going into the store for a cup of coffee. Cam's arm dangled down the side of the car. We looked at each other.

Perhaps no one driving through the intersection stopped and helped because they didn't know that the man in the passenger's seat was unable to get out and walk, that he'd taken a beating, that he'd lost a lover. They couldn't have known that his wife was watching from a pay phone across the street.

Truck's Testament

We were running the no-huddle last Saturday against
Rensselaer when I had my vision.

Down by one, with the last minute and a half tick-
ing away, I received, out of Schwartz's right hand, four consecutive, perfectly thrown, wrong-way rotating spirals. Each
of the passes spun towards me, inexplicably, clockwise. There
was no wind. Not one was tipped.

When I pause now and look back over my seventeen
years, I realize how I've been preparing for this my whole
life, how I've been set apart. In hindsight, my premature gray
seems especially meaningful, like a symbol, or at least a hint.

Twenty-five hundred years ago, Ezekiel saw flying wheels,
watched skeletons rattle to life in front of his eyes, and
decided that his people were in trouble. I don't claim that my
vision measures up to Ezekiel's–I don't know exactly what to
make of it–but I know I was part of a miracle. The minimum
requirements were met. Nature's laws were defied, however
subtly. God's presence was evident, if only to me.

Of course, in the moment, there's no time for reflection
because we're driving, and miracle or no, we're against the
clock. First, two square-outs for first downs that stop time and

move the chains, and then a hook-and-go for thirty-five yards. (What knocks the cornerback's ankles together and sends him sprawling? On the game film he has a bead on me, but then suddenly collapses, like something or someone unseen has sledgehammered his knees. Not a blocker within ten yards.) Finally, after our last time-out, I find the seam between the linebackers and the secondary and catch a 22-yard post route that gets me in the end zone. I cradle the ball into my chest like a newborn and drag a safety the last seven yards.

The kid hanging off my jersey is scrawny, legs like linguini. No business being on the field. When I cross the goal line, I shake him off like dust. He rights himself, kneels, removes his helmet, and cries. I bend to him and put my hand on the back of his hot neck. There is nothing he could've done. He's been used. He's one of the thousand Philistines that Samson introduced to the business end of a donkey's jaw bone. I feel for him until he reaches up and gives my ponytail a yank, pops off a one-liner about Grecian Formula. It's at this point that I grab his ear and twist. His body, of course, follows. Before the ref breaks things up, the kid's done a couple somersaults. When I let go, I tell him to get his ass out of my end zone.

Even in the middle of a miracle, I still have too much eye-for-an-eye in me. I can't resist last licks. This is one of my many deficiencies. My heart, I know, has to change.

The clock shows zeros. The ref picks up the ball, gives me a stare, and my teammates storm the field and bury me. At the bottom of the pile—this is the second part of the miracle, the most substantial part, also the hardest to put into words—I hear God's voice, not just with my ears but with my whole being. He says, "Truck, I claim you" in a voice that vibrates in me like low thunder, like a seashell held up to my ear. The voice is somehow loud and quiet at the same time, and it's slow, like its batteries are running out, and what it tells me, what I know it means, is that the weight I feel is more than just guys in pads. What's squeezing the breath out of me is God's deep love for and disappointment with humankind.

The weight of the world. I weep.

At the bottom of the pile, I weep for us all. The pipe-cleaner skinny safety with the twisted ear becomes a symbol for me, and I let out a long and loud wail for how far we've fallen. The guys pile off sheepishly. Someone wonders aloud if they've crushed my ribs. They stand around me, slack-jawed, hips cocked, not sure what to say or do. They give me room. They know what I can be like.

I can't see clearly beyond my face mask. Everything's shimmering, colors and blurs.

Three days AV (after vision) and I'm still in a kind of limbo, wondering what comes next. Lots of questions, not many answers.

We go full pads practice on Tuesdays. First play from scrimmage is a 20 Blast. No cuts, no jukes. Right up the gut. Bread-and-butter. I can come out of the backfield and catch the ball if I need to like I did Saturday against Rensselaer, but I'm at my best pounding it. This is the play: me, the 2 back, through the 0 hole, between the center and the right guard. Nothing fancy: square your shoulders, drive your legs. No jab steps, no misdirection, and, in this case, no blocks to follow because, despite Saturday's touchdown, I'm still in Coach's doghouse, and all this week I'm running behind the scrub line, a pathetic row of five sluggish cows. More than anything they get in my way. The whole herd of them might as well stick their thumbs up their asses, graze their way over to the other side of the school, and watch the girls' soccer game. We can't see the game from our practice field, but we hear the crowd erupt just as we're lining up for the 20 Blast. The cheers could be for Kristen. She plays left wing, runs like a gazelle, and has a great foot. I don't have to be watching her to see her: the pink tip of her tongue peeking out the corner of her mouth as she dribbles up the sideline, shin guards pumping, thighs and calves smoothly swelling like a dancer's. I take the ball and look for an opening. Nothing. Have to make my own.

As I shed a linebacker and break into the open field, I can still hear the cheers from the soccer game. I imagine they're for me. I smell end zone. Zuccari, our all-league safety and a pretty good hitter, is the last guy to beat, and he tries to tackle me high, and I give him a straight arm under the chin that I know he feels in his mouthpiece like a jawful of bees. When I get to the sideline, I switch the ball to my outside arm—I'm a fundamentally sound player all the way around, even Coach, presently one of my many detractors, would attest to this—and although no one has a chance of catching me now, I run hard the rest of the way, maybe even pick up speed.

As I concentrate on my form—long, even strides, pumping my arms—I imagine how I must look to everyone behind me: a 215-pound seventeen year-old fullback streaking down the sideline with his long gray ponytail bobbing behind him in the wind, and I think about how my father once told me that years ago, before I was born, before even he was born, there was a All-American halfback nicknamed the Galloping Ghost, and I think, That's me, I'm the Galloping Ghost, scaring the hell out of everyone with my power and speed and head of old man hair.

My next thought, though, is of God looking down on me, reading the prideful mind of His newest prophet—maybe He's wondering if I'm going to work out after all—and when I cross the goal line, I'm humbled and ashamed. With my back to everyone, I drop the ball, take a knee, remove my helmet, spit out my mouthpiece, and bow my head. To acknowledge His presence, I grab two handfuls of turf and toss them underhand into the breeze. It's the only thing I can think to do that seems significant. I keep this position for another second or two: on my knees, my palms upturned towards heaven in silent repentance.

Just before I get to my feet, I remove the rubber band and let my hair fall down my back, halfway to my ass—I've been growing it out of fear of baldness and death since seventh grade, the year I started going gray around the temples, because I didn't know how long I'd have it, how long I had—

and I feel freer somehow, like I'm on the verge of something, like the big picture is coming into focus, like soon I'll know something for sure.

I pick up the ball, put my helmet back on, and sprint the fifty yards back to the line of scrimmage—I wish someone had a stopwatch on me—and everyone's looking at me and then at Coach, back and forth slowly like badminton, but I just take my place in the huddle and wait for the next call. Coach turns his back to the field so no one can see his face. He could be crying, he could be smiling. He could be swearing under his breath. He could be reciting Hail Mary's. I don't know what he's doing. I'm a prophet—I'm almost positive of this—but I'm not that kind of prophet.

Running with the scrubs in practice this week is only part of my punishment. What really hurts is my one-game suspension. I'm slated to sit the bench this coming Saturday, our second game of the season. Coach says he doesn't care if we're winning by thirty in the fourth quarter; I'm not getting any snaps. He knows we'll cruise. The reason I didn't serve the suspension last Saturday, the afternoon of my vision—I'm sure God had a hand in this somehow—was that Coach knew he needed me against Rensselaer. Hudson's a different story. They haven't won a league game in two years. They're small, but they're slow. We could put our cross-country team out there without shoulder pads and still whip ass up and down the field.

My trouble can be traced back to last Friday night, the night before our season opener, the night before I received the sign from God that has given my life new direction. On this night, I temporarily lost my mind and rammed Chad Schwartz's head through a microwave. The fact that he was not seriously injured because he was wearing his helmet at the time—he always attends pre-game parties in his headgear; it gets him pumped—has not, in the least, eased anyone's disappointment in me. Schwartz is our quarterback. He has an arm like a slingshot, flicks passes up and down the field like he's killing Goliath—so far no sign from him, by the way, sug-

gesting he's aware that he was throwing magic balls last Saturday—and the two of us are friendly, but he's a wise guy,
always has a line, and last Friday night at Jen Vandervliet's
party, he got tanked and started in on my hair. He gets
between Kristen and me, slides his arm around my shoulders,
presses his face mask to my ear and says, "What's up, Silver-
ado?" and then looks around for laughs. I admit that my hair
is a topic I can't be lighthearted about, a defect that, try as I
might, I'm unable to laugh off.

Schwartz is not the first. If God is really looking to use me,
I know I have a long way to go. I have to learn perspective,
patience, how to see the connections between things rather
than just the things themselves. My vision needs to change.
Bottom line: I'm too much of this world. What I need is to
find a way to dissolve into spirit. Let them try to tackle that. A
shivering, shaking cloud of karma.

On top of missing a game or two and being demoted to
scrub-level in practice, I'm expected to pay for the
microwave, so cash is another problem. I have none, and
when I mentioned this predicament to my father last night, he
covered his ears with his hands and walked away. A lot of this
from him in the last three days. The microwave was state-of-
the-art: rotating tray, automatic defrost, a button just for popcorn. It doubled as a convection oven.

On top of all this, Kristen, star left wing and, up until a few
days ago, my main reason for existence, has given up on me.
She says she has too much self-respect to continue as is. She
says I'm out of control. She says she's bailing. She says last
straw. All this to my face the last time we talked, at the party
Friday night, just minutes after Schwartz and the microwave.
Since then, nothing. No contact. I'm trying to think positively,
along the lines of like maybe we're on a break, and that's the
best thing for us right now, some cooling off time.

I sympathize with Kristen's position. She's frustrated with
me, and she has a right. But what we have has nothing to do
with last straws. When we finally talk again, I'll tell her this,
that what we share is above all the normal give-and-take,

back-and-forth, start-and-stop, boyfriend-girlfriend stuff. I'll tell her that it's beyond even us.

She'll get mad, as in angry, but also as in a little crazy. Her eyes will get so big that her lids will disappear. There will be so much she wants to say. She'll lead with something like "What good is our love if it's beyond us? What does that even mean?" In answer, I'll reach out my hand and try to touch hers, but she'll fall back two steps and deliver a look that tells me one more false move and I'll be on the receiving end of one of the most precise and powerful left feet in the state. I'll put my arms up to show temporary surrender, and I'll tell her that I don't completely understand either, but some things can't be explained. I'll tell her that she's thinking too much, trying to figure out what's between us like we're calculus, and she shouldn't do that. Getting to the bottom of some things ruin them. "We're like a poem," I'll say, and her eyes will roll. "Seriously," I'll say. "You screw around with a poem too much, try to paraphrase or dissect it like they do in English, try to cut the theme out of it like a spleen, like the poem's a lab frog, and you end up destroying it."

Maybe then I'll recite the poem. The one by me about her. If I haven't had the chance to memorize it, I'll pull it out of my pocket and read it. I haven't as of yet written this poem, but I'm thinking in that direction. I have ideas. I've noted, for instance, that "Kristen" half rhymes with "listen" and "missin," and I'm considering the metaphorical potential of the figure-eight swirling of her tongue when we're deep into a kiss. I've bought a dictionary/thesaurus.

I don't know what happens after I tell her the poem. I'm thinking a lot depends on the poem. I'm feeling some pressure with all that's happened this past week–understandably, I think–and it's affecting my creative process.

At some point, of course–maybe when she's still in shock from the poem–I'll have to tell her about what's happened, my new role in the world. I'll tell her that I think, overall, the whole God's messenger thing might be good for my character, help me mature, make some improvements.

Eventually, of course–after I get more of a handle on this thing myself–there will be a lot to explain, not just to Kristen but to everyone. The world. Once the visions start rolling, people are going to want to know the hows and whys. I'm not exactly sure yet how God will use me, but I have some ideas. Rather than telling the future or reading minds–I doubt that God has need of a Let-me-guess-your-weight, I-know-what-cards-you're-holding type of sideshow freak–I have a strong conviction that my focus will be on pointing people towards truths already evident in the world and themselves. As I can't see myself behind a pulpit, I'm thinking poetry. I've been reading some. Metaphor and rhythm. Get people to listen with their whole selves. This is quite an assumption on my part, I know.

Since my vision last Saturday, though, the world's been different. I've been seeing it differently, anyway. It's not that things aren't as they were before, but that they are so intensely and totally what they've always been. I feel like everything's opened up to me. Colors are sharper, voices throatier. Here's something: I can hear heartbeats. This afternoon at lunch, a cafeteria full of them. In the halls, I know without looking when someone's behind me just from the thumping.

This is difficult to communicate, but that's half the prophet's job, the communicating. This is where I think metaphors can help. Bridge the gap. Make the message more accessible. They'll help people begin to see, suggest to people how to make the connections they need to start making between this world and the next, between their bodies and their souls.

Something like this: We're in a tough spot down here, backed up against our own goal line. We've got a long way to go, and a lot of us are banged up, sucking wind. Sometimes, though, you have to play hurt. You have to want it. God's drawn up a play to get us out of trouble, but not every head's in the huddle.

I've read more these last few days than I have in my whole life. Along with the poetry, I've been into the Bible. There's a lot in there to think about, but I can't believe God's had his full say, that that's all there is. I'm thinking He needs somebody, a go-between, a liaison, to fill in the gaps. I'm thinking this is maybe where I come in. One thing, though: I don't know why me. I do know, though, that all the prophets who've come before me have had the same question. It's a characteristic of the position. Moses thought wrong number, that God really wanted his brother. It took a burning bush, twelve plagues, and a parted sea to convince him otherwise.

One thing I've got going for me is willingness. I've got faith. I've got the capacity to admit I'm flabbergasted while continuing to move forward.

So I'm trying to think things through, explore possibilities, do a little research, but, at this point, I don't have much to go on, and I know nothing's up to me. It's true about Him moving in mysterious ways, and I've only had the one vision. I don't know what Jonah was thinking, but he wasn't thinking whale. Daniel wasn't thinking lion's den. A certain degree of unexpectedness is to be expected, I realize.

At the moment, I'm between revelations.

Coach stops the scrimmage to do walk-throughs with the first team offense, so both Schwartz and I are sidelined, flanked by scrubs. Coach is sending a message. He won't tolerate delinquents. After a few reps, though—the second team quarterback is short-hopping balls into receivers' ankles— Coach calls for Schwartz. I stay put like cement.

It was a bad scene last Friday night. Cops, Jen Vandervliet crying over what her parents were going to do to her, Schwartz dazed on the kitchen floor, his face mask pulled down and twisted sideways, and Kristen fighting tears as she delivered to me her final speech. She slipped my football jacket off her shoulders, let it drop right where she was standing, and had Bernie Hanson drive her home. I'm hoping she didn't do anything with Bernie just because she was pissed at me. I want to ask her what went on in his Honda, but I know now is not the right time to show my jealous side.

I've tried to call Kristen a few times this week. Her mother answers every time, says Kristen's unavailable. If I ask, "Does that mean she isn't home, or that she's home and doesn't want to talk to me?" her mother says, "Think about it, Truck. What's the difference?"

One of the cops who showed up at Vandervliet's to sort things out says to me in the patrol car as we're backing out of Vandervliet's driveway, "Aren't you Truck Dombrowski? Don't you play fullback for Mount Union?" and I say, "And some inside linebacker. Coach has me going both ways this year," and the cop's partner, the other cop, the one who's riding shotgun, turns around and says, "You messed up, Truck. Don't you guys open tomorrow against Rensselaer? What are you thinking putting your quarterback's head through a kitchen appliance?" and I say, "I guess I wasn't thinking," and he says, "I believe you've identified the problem," and his partner, the driver, looks at me in the rearview and nods slowly with pinched lips like I'm in the middle of a life lesson.

In some ways, Friday night prepared me. I was broken up by what I did, and, because of this, I was ready to accept what God had to show me the next afternoon. Another way to look at it, though, is that my whole life since seventh grade—the year of my growth spurt, the year I started playing football, the year my hair went gray, the year I stopped visiting the barber, the year I began to realize how different I was—has been designed to condition me. A program to whip me into shape for what was to come. For what's still to come.

My father didn't like it when I started growing my hair out, but he never pushed me. It's been just him and me for as long as I can remember, and because of this, I think, he's always been careful to not come down on me too hard. Maybe he's even been a little easy on me. Right now, though, I think he's feeling like he went wrong with me somewhere, and I'm worried that when I tell him how God's called me, he'll be even more convinced that he's failed with me. I'm not yet sure how to handle this. I'm trusting that when the time's right, something will come to me.

When my hair started turning, the first thing my father did was take me to the doctor to make sure the gray wasn't a symptom of something more serious, and when I got a clean bill of health—I wasn't convinced; I still felt doomed—he took me to the Dunkin Donuts across the street. Over hot chocolate, he told me that everyone has at least one thing. He took off his right shoe and sock and showed me that his big toe was webbed together with its neighbor. "All around you," he said. "Just in here right now, the girl behind the counter has a black wart on her neck that looks like a beetle, and the guy sitting over there by the front window has asymmetrical ears. The left one's shaped like a circus peanut." He lifted his mug and sipped. "Your mother," he said more quietly, "was born without tonsils."

Of course, when God's involved—when isn't He?—it may be thinking too small to try to point to one thing, like one year, one life change, one freak attribute. It's probably true that the whole thing, my whole life, is part of a plan, one that was set into motion long ago, before I even was, before my mother and father even were.

It's possible that I'm part of *the* plan.

It's amazing how things have worked together to put me where I am right now. It's somewhat of a miracle in itself, for instance, that Schwartz wasn't injured, not even a scratch. Had he been hurt, there's no way I would've played the next day, Rensselaer or not, and I wouldn't have had my vision. At the sheriff's office, Coach used the word "lucky." He accompanied my father to pick me up. Outside in the parking lot, I made no denials and offered no excuses. My father stood by silent—anger and disappointment clam him up; he's not a yeller—so Coach asked the questions. Had I been drinking? Yes. Had I fought with Schwartz? Yes. Did I understand that drinking and fighting violated team rules? Yes. If I were him, would I let me stay on the team? I don't know.

Coach exhaled loudly, rubbed the back of his neck with both hands, and motioned to my father. The two of them turned away and huddled. When they were done talking, they faced me. Coach spoke again. "I asked Schwartz what he thought I should do with you."

"Is Chad all right?"

"Don't interrupt me, Truck. Don't interrupt me again." Coach slapped his forehead and spun around in place. My audacity amazed him. My father stood by in a slight crouch, his feet shoulder-width apart and his arms tensed and bent at the elbows like he was ready for action, like if I tried to make a run for it, he'd plant me. "Schwartz is fine," Coach said. "Lucky for you. He tells me he was wearing his helmet? Why the hell, I don't know."

"Friday night ritual," I said. "It gets him up."

"Did you just interrupt me again!" His rage came somewhere from deep inside him, somewhere that not even football had ever reached. I looked at my father for help. He looked back. He had his game face on. He bit his bottom lip.

Coach took another deep breath. "Schwartz said part of the whole thing was his fault, that he provoked you, and he admitted that he'd also been drinking." He folded his arms across his chest and looked up into the sky as if there were answers up there to this dilemma of his. He swallowed, and his huge Adam's apple bulged. "Schwartz is reporting to my office at 7 a.m. I want you there, too. As I watch you both run suicide sprints, I'll decide what to do about the rest of your season. You've put everyone in a lose-lose situation here, Truck." That was the last thing he said. He shook his head, clapped my father on the back and started towards his car.

After Coach left, I followed my father to our car. We got in. We put on our seatbelts. My father put the key into the ignition, but he didn't start the engine. He rolled down his window and reached for the pack of cigarettes on the dashboard. I knew he'd been trying to quit, and I felt guilty. He pushed in the cigarette lighter, and we waited for it to pop. When it did, he lit one. After he smoked it, he smoked another. When I said, "Sorry," he took a third cigarette out of the pack and wiggled it slowly between his fingers. He said softly, "What do you think your life will come down to,

Truck? How do you think it will all turn out for you?" He lit
the cigarette, started the engine, and shifted into drive. When
I began to speak, he interrupted. "Let's not do this now. Let's
just think a while."

That was the last we spoke. I don't think he's mad at me
anymore, I think he's at a loss. He's back up to half a pack a
day. I think he thinks that there's something he needs to tell
me, something that will help me, something that I can take to
heart, and he's waiting for it to hit him. I'm not the only one
waiting on a revelation. "Truck," he wants to be able to say,
"here's the thing."

Saturday morning, Coach had Schwartz and me out on
the field in full pads for an hour of sprints. When Schwartz
puked, he let us quit. Afterwards, he walked into the showers
and said, "My office." When we didn't move right away, he
screamed, "Now!" and his face purpled, and that Adam's
apple of his pulsed and strained like it wanted out of his
throat. We grabbed our towels and marched. We dripped all
over his carpet. Schwartz's hair was still frothy with shampoo.

Coach said he didn't want to wait to talk to us because he
was scared time might change his mind. As he spoke, he
kneaded the top of his head with both hands and kept his
eyes shut. What he said came down to this: We'd put him in
an impossible situation. He didn't know who all knew about
last night—he could get in some real trouble if word got
around to administration—but he realized he wouldn't be punishing just the two of us if he kicked us off the team and held
us out of the game today, he'd be punishing the whole team,
and that wouldn't be fair. He'd talked to the Vandervliets, my
father, and the Schwartzes, and they'd all agreed that if we
swore we'd learned lessons, if the two of us promised not to
drink or fight for the rest of the season, and if I promised to
pay for the microwave, we could stay on the team and play
today. "After this week, though, no promises. Truck, you
especially are looking at some bench time in the future. You
not only drank, you assaulted a teammate. You make me
sick. Questions?"

Schwartz shook his sudsy head and ducked out. I said, "Thanks, Coach," and extended my hand, but he left it there. "Disappear, Truck," he said. I turned and concentrated on how quietly I could close his office door.

The soccer game has to be late into the second half by now. There's about twenty minutes left in practice. I know this because Coach just blew his whistle and yelled for the no-huddle drill. On Tuesdays and Thursdays, we always work the two-minute offense just before we hit the showers. My absence from the first-team huddle has created opportunity for Buddy Spivak, my back-up. He's tough, but he has no hands. In the hurry-up, when the fullback moves into the slot and runs patterns, he's out of his element.

I have half a mind to sneak over to the soccer game, walk right onto the field and up to Kristen, ask for forgiveness. The refs would call time, look at me uneasily. The players and coaches would be perturbed at first, perhaps even a bit frightened. Maybe when Kristen and I embraced, though, the crowd would erupt and everyone would relax, appreciate the moment.

The fact that every prophet in history has had to sacrifice greatly to fulfill the position isn't lost on me. I'm clear on that. The reality is that maybe I'll lose Kristen. Maybe that's His will. For now, though, I'm staying positive. I've only been without her for a few days, but I can tell the way I feel isn't something that's going to go away over time. I'm worried that God perhaps is overestimating me if He thinks I can do this without her.

All of this waiting on God is new to me. Even though I've always tried to keep an open mind about the big questions in life, I've never considered myself the religious type. Of course, having received what I believe to be a direct sign from God–a sign that I interpret as a preliminary gesture, but still a gesture, like a tap on the mike to make sure it's on– these questions have become more personal. I feel I have a stake in them now. When I came across The Gospel of John this weekend, in the first chapter, where it talks about in the beginning was the Word, and the Word was with God, and the Word was God, the fact that the 'W' in "Word" is capitalized gave me goosebumps up and down my arms.

I've also been reading John Donne over the past few days. In English last Friday, before the microwave, before the vision, before any of this, we were each assigned a poet to report on. Of course, now I know it was no accident that I got Donne. I didn't get around to cracking the book until Sunday night, after my life had changed–I needed a break from the Bible, and my English book was on the floor beside my bed–and I was amazed at how Donne's poetry fit into everything that was happening to me. When I read, "If ever any beauty I did see,/Which I desired, and got, 'twas but a dream of thee," I picked up the phone and tried Kristen– when her mother answered again, I hung up–and when I came across, "Pour new seas in mine eyes, that so I might/Drown my world with my weeping," I got a feeling in my stomach like I'd just swallowed glue.

Donne writes, "Our creatures are our thoughts, creatures that are born giants, that reach from east to west, from earth to heaven: my thoughts reach all, comprehend all." I can't make any such claims yet, but I feel like I'm close. "My God, my God, thou art a figurative, a metaphorical God," Donne writes, and I think I know what he's saying.

When you're a prophet, God's silences weigh in heavy, like a pair of dumb-bells on your heart.

At times, especially at night, I can barely hold myself together. The stress of waiting is getting to me. The last few mornings I've found clumps of hair, more white than gray, around my pillow. From the time I get up in the morning to the time I lie back down at night, I try to prepare myself for what's coming. Any moment now. My head's been pounding off and on, and I can't stand the sight of food. I'm considering a fast, maybe force His hand a bit.

I haven't shaved. My beard's coming in salt and pepper. It's itchy under my chin-strap.

The poems, when they start coming, will be recorded with a medium-point blue Bic, cap chewed severely, on yellow, college-ruled paper. The last couple nights I've spent awake on my back, pen in hand, pad on chest, waiting.

I screwed up this afternoon before practice. I passed Mrs. Monahan, the school shrink, in the hallway after last bell, and I took her presence as a sign because it's Tuesday, and she usually comes in only on Mondays, Wednesdays, and Fridays. She smiled and asked if there was anything I'd like to talk about. I followed her into her office.

Eventually I'm going to have to learn how to discern a true sign from just plain coincidence. There are a lot of both in the world.

When I told Mrs. Monahan what I had to tell–I have to admit it felt good getting it all out–she removed her glasses, let them dangle from the silver chain she had around her neck, and asked me if we could set up a regular time to talk. She pulled out her date book.

I'm sure Monahan will eventually call my father–I suspect she's already talked with Coach; he hasn't looked me in the face all practice–so we're going to have to talk soon, ready or not. Maybe even tonight. Perhaps being straight with him is the way to go. Everything right up front. I'll tell him I finally know what my life comes down to, and then I'll warn him that what I'm about to say will not bring him relief or pride, and then I'll just come out with it: your son's a prophet and a poet. He's to be a light and a voice.

When practice is over, instead of heading for the locker room, I make my way over to the soccer field. I'm thinking about my first prophecy. I have high hopes. When it comes, I know the hardest part will be getting people not to see me, but to see the message. I'm just a vehicle, and I need to work on being just this. I've been practicing in the hallways at school. I try to be transparent, invisible, and it works sometimes. Whenever I pass Kristen's locker, she looks right through me, like there's a window in my chest. Her heart, though, is a drum solo.

As I walk, I bang my helmet against my right thigh pad, and I keep remembering this one thing about last Friday night. This one moment. I think this is why I'm walking to the soccer field. I'm not going to make a scene, and I know Kristen still won't talk to me—chances are, when the ball's across the field from her and she has a chance for a quick glance into the stands, it will be Bernie Hanson she's looking for—but this one thing I keep remembering is making me go.

It was at the party, before Schwartz and the microwave. In this moment, not even a part of me was considering the nature of truth or how fragile the boundary is that separates human life from the celestial and supernatural. In this moment I was not yet poet or prophet. I was only about one thing. My focus was singular.

It's Kristen and me outside on the crowded porch, and there's a cool breeze blowing that smells like brown leaves and mud, and I've got my hair pulled back in a ponytail that she tells me in a soft, thick-lipped beer whisper looks like Christmas tinsel. We've set our beers on the porch railing, and she's leaning back against me, and she has a turtleneck on, and over that my football jacket, and we're holding hands in the pockets, and at one point I slip my fingers up underneath her shirt and rest them on her warm smooth belly, and I think about moving them up, but I have to keep fighting these drunk ideas because Kristen takes things slowly—I respect this—and we're in public. When no one's looking, though, I use my chin to sneak her collar down a couple inches off the back of her neck, and I put my nose and mouth into her skin and tell her how good she smells, like a bag of apples, and I kiss right where her neck meets her shoulder, where it's not really her neck and it's not really her shoulder and it's not really her back, where it's just a place that I kiss, just above the top button of her spine, like a cherry under her skin, and I want that to be just my starting point, but she says, "Truck, not here."

That quarter-sized spot on Kristen's neck and everything about it. That, God-willing, will be my first metaphor.

Georgia, Would You Mind?

Abe feels a twang in his chest, like a plucked banjo string. Fifth or sixth time today. This is what he's just confessed to Vera, that it's been going on for a few weeks, that he has an appointment tomorrow for a stress test. He wants her to know—she has the right, twenty-three years together and counting—but doesn't want her worrying. He wants her thinking, No sweat.

When Vera shakes her head and looks away, reaches for the soapy sponge in the sink, Abe senses that action is necessary. He turns to the counter, to the bunch of bananas at his right elbow, rips one off, sticks the stem in his ear, talks to the black-nubbed bottom. "Hello? Just a sec." He extends it to Vera. "For you."

"Not here," she says without looking up. She scrubs a saucepan, rinses, sets it in the drainer.

Abe coughs into his fist, clears his throat, gets back on the banana. This time the stem's at his mouth, the nub's in his ear. "She's in a meeting." Abe snaps the stem, pulls the peel down in thirds, takes a bite. Bart sets up camp at Abe's feet, perks his ears, watches Abe chew. Abe looks back. "You a fruit fan now?" He crouches on his haunches, holds the banana out to the dog. "Our boy's jonesin' for potassium," Abe says. Bart noses it up, decides he's not interested.

"Who was it?" Vera asks.

"No message," Abe says. "It's a mystery."

Vera moves past Abe to the other side of the kitchen, sponge in hand. "Not another one," she says. Bart takes Vera's place in front of the sink, explores the baseboard with his snout.

"Where's the mousey, Bart?" Abe says. His voice is mushy, his mouth full of banana.

Vera leans over the table, wipes a wide, damp 'Z' across it, turns back to face the sink, squares up and lets the sponge fly. Bends her knees, leads with her elbow, smooth release. Count it. Bart looks up at her, swings his tail slow and low like a pendulum.

"Some things about me that you should know by now," Vera says. "I shoot straight. I'm up front. No secrets. With me, people know where they stand."

"Right," Abe says. "I know I'm standing here. Good for you." His heart bangs heavy in the bottom of his gut. Something bangs. He's no expert. A weird feeling, like everything crucial has fallen, like his kidneys are behind his knees, his liver in his hip pocket. Like he's collapsing into himself, a human sink-hole. "Listen up, Barty Boy," he says. "Lots to learn. We're in the presence of Vera, the great communicator. If you don't know where you're standing, she'll tell you. She has that capacity."

"Who said great?" Vera says. "I'm saying adequate. Functional. All I am and all I'm asking."

"Duly noted," Abe says, moving away from the counter toward the living room. He's heading for the couch. Here's hoping it's simply a matter of taking a load off. "Me, I'm one of the flawed. With me, it's like the bumper sticker says: Be patient. God isn't finished with me yet."

"So you're under construction? A work in progress? What I see now isn't necessarily what I'll end up with?"

"More or less," Abe says. "Yes and no." Abe's hand

dangles off the couch. Bart nudges his head under it, wears it like a hat.

"The suspense is killing me," Vera says.

"I'm sorry about all this," Abe yells into the kitchen.

Vera comes into sight, stands at the edge of the carpet. Sometimes Abe can look old in the face. Not usually, but sometimes. He's mostly clear with periods of clouds. Depends on light and shadow, the time of day. "Sorry doesn't get the laundry folded," she says. "Sorry doesn't plow the field."

Abe drums his fingers on Bart's head, nods. "Sorry doesn't butter the biscuits."

The nurse shaves five patches of Abe's chest before she tapes on the electrodes. The razor's pink, the electrodes white. "We can rebuild him," Abe says. "We have the technology."

"What's that?" The nurse says this without looking up. "I'll give you some lotion to take with you when you leave. These spots might get itchy later." Her hair smells like Band-Aids.

In the opposite corner of the room, the doctor's looking over the *USA Today* sports section. "The Cavs don't have much this year, do they?" Abe says. "They're hard to watch. The whole league. Just dunks and three-pointers. Everything's one-on-one."

The doctor nods, closes the paper.

"Bring back the give-and-go," Abe says. "Bring back the pick-and-roll."

When the nurse is done, she steps back from Abe and surveys her work. She tilts her head slightly. "All hooked up," she says to his chest.

"I don't know about you two, but I'm feeling a little wired today," Abe says as he gets on the treadmill.

The doctor flips a switch. "Start you off slow," he says. "Every now and then we'll pick it up a bit. Let's shoot for twenty minutes."

"Sure," says Abe. After a few seconds he's adjusted his pace to the machine's. "Sometimes I feel like my life's at a standstill, Doc," Abe says. "Like I'm not getting anywhere."

The doctor looks up from his clipboard. "Are you comfortable? Get comfortable. You can hold onto that bar in front of you, or you can let your arms swing at your sides. Either way."

"Choices, choices," Abe says.

"You mind if I turn on some music?" the doctor asks.

"Your office," Abe says.

The doctor turns to his nurse. "Georgia, would you mind?"

"Don't know that one, Doc," Abe says. "Maybe you could hum a few bars?"

The nurse goes over to the cabinet and switches on the portable stereo. Contemporary country.

"Howdy, pardner," Abe says.

"Any dizziness or pain, let me know," the doctor says. "I'm going to turn it up a notch now."

Abe likes tests. He's shirtless, in sneakers and shorts, and he feels like he could go all day.

"Don't get carried away," the doctor says. "Let the treadmill dictate the pace. This isn't a race. I don't want you pressing. Stay within yourself."

"Right," Abe says. "I'm just glad to be here. Just looking to help the team."

"Sure."

"If the jumper's not falling, I'll take it to the rim, draw contact, get to the line."

"Right."

"I won't try to get fancy. I'll just go with what got me here."

"You're a good-looking prospect," the doctor says as he watches the computer screen, scribbles notes. "We here in the organization have high hopes for you."

Abe's on the couch reading when Vera gets home from work. A true-life mountain-climbing tragedy. Six went up, only one came down. Wrote a book. Abe's suspicious.

Bart hears Vera's car pull into the driveway and stations himself at the door. He stares at the knob as his tail sweeps back and forth across the floor. When Vera makes her entrance, he steps in her way, turns in a circle. "Coming through," Vera says. Bart backs up. Vera closes the door, sits in a chair, drops her bag. Bart checks it out. "You smell the kitty?" Vera says. She kicks off her shoes, says to Abe, "Linda got back into town today, stopped by the office with JoJo the feline fuzz ball."

"Mommy's home," Abe says and lays his book on his chest.

Vera scratches Bart's head, bends down to talk into his ear. "You'd like JoJo, Barty. Yes you would. You two would be buddies." She looks up at Abe. "You're alive."

"Strong like bull," Abe says.

"Yeah?"

"Doc says no test is one-hundred percent, but he sees nothing out of the ordinary. He says I'm reaching that age. Maybe stress and caffeine, maybe diet. It might even be skeletal or maybe stomach or esophagus."

Vera stands and hangs up her jacket. "What do you think?"

"He asked if I did cocaine, and I said, 'No, Doc, do you recommend that?'"

"Hey," Vera says. "How's all this settle with you? Are you thinking second opinion? Chiropractor? Gastroenterologist?"

"I'm in wait-and-see mode."

"From now on you're decaf. You're birds, fish, and leafy greens. No more mammals." Vera folds her arms across her chest, sticks out her hip. "This isn't something to fool around with, friend. We're talking chest pain."

"Wait-and-see isn't fooling around. It's legitimate strategy."

"You'd know," Vera says. She stoops to peck Abe on the mouth on her way to the bedroom. Her lips are dry and her breath smells like stale coffee. Her forehead's warm and shiny. She unbuttons her blouse as she walks away. Bart's at her heels.

"Momma's boy," Abe says. The book on his chest is propped up like a tent. He watches the rise and fall of it. He slips two fingers onto his neck, under his jaw. He looks at his watch, counts for fifteen seconds, multiplies by four. He does this again.

When Abe's heart wakes him, Vera's on her stomach, facing away, and Bart's snoring at the foot of the bed. Abe reaches over to his night stand, puts on his glasses and looks at the clock. 3:11. He turns and leans over Vera to get a better look. Her eyes are closed. Her mouth, too, but her lips are out of sync. The bottom one's off to the side a bit, curling up over the top one. This overlap is where Vera exhales every few seconds. Her spout-hole. Abe brushes her cheek gently with his thumb, like he's wiping away an eyelash, and slips out of bed. The mattress creaks. Bart raises his head, thumps his tail once. Abe puts his finger to his lips. "Shh." Bart stays put. Abe closes the door behind him.

Standing in the middle of the dark living room, Abe concentrates on breathing. He's not suffocating, but he can't get quite enough air. He can't find the rhythm. He tries to relax. The question is: What exactly is happening? Dull pain, and he feels his chest contract and expand, like a fist opening and closing, and it feels like the fist is floating around beneath his rib-cage. It feels like something's come untethered, like a balloon, like a small animal has slipped its collar, broken loose. Like a puppy's scurrying around inside him. Like he's filled with helium. Gravity's a law. Something's got to give. It's either going to get worse, or it's going to get back to normal. It won't stay like this. This isn't stasis. He's beginning to feel woozy. His stomach flips, whines. He wonders if it's possible that he's digesting his own heart. His juices are flowing. He walks back down the hall to the toilet. He pulls down his boxers and sits. Waits. That dump was normal. That dump didn't do him in. He stands and looks in the bowl. Nothing out of the ordinary. No organs, no pets. He flushes. His heart is quieting now. It's staying put. Things could've gone the other way, but they didn't. He hears Bart jump off the bed in the next room. After washing his hands, he goes back out into the hall and opens the bedroom door. Bart steps out. "Let's sleep," Abe whispers. The dog jumps back up on the bed, waits to lie down until Abe's glasses are on the nightstand and Abe is under the sheets.

When Vera comes out of the bathroom wrapped in towels, Abe puts on his glasses. Bart's sleeping beside Abe, curled up on Vera's side of the bed.

"Yo, Bartlett," she says, walking to her dresser. "Off the pillows." When the dog doesn't budge, when he only raises his head and looks at her, she removes her head towel and starts to twirl it. Bart growls. "Gonna getcha," Vera says. She snaps the towel at him. Bart snatches it out of her hand, jumps off the bed, gallops down the hall to the living room, back to the bedroom—Abe's seen this before; Bart's ears are back, his eyes rolling in his head—and then down to the living room again. Abe looks out the bedroom door after Bart. The dog sits and waits at the end of the hall, the towel at his feet.

"Barty's a couple beers short of a six-pack," Vera says.

"He's ready for ripping and tearing," Abe says.

"How about you?" Vera says. She pulls off her body towel, twirls it, and snaps Abe's arm. He tries to catch it—he saw it coming the whole way—but he's too slow. Vera smiles and re-twirls. "Are you planning on getting out of bed, or is this the day the world comes to you?"

"Look at you," Abe says, swinging his legs over the side of the bed. "Talking trash and naked."

Saturday mornings they go to breakfast. Omelets, home-

fries, toast. They don't eat again until evening. They don't get
hungry again until seven o'clock or so.

This morning they both start with a cup of regular, but for
the rest of the meal, when their waiter swings back around
offering warm-ups, Abe switches to decaf.

"Did you get up last night?" Vera says. She sits back in
her seat to give the waiter room to pour. "Around three or so?"

"I didn't think you were awake," Abe says. He watches
her stir in cream. "Sorry if I woke you."

"I was half awake. You half woke me."

"What you just said, that's like something you would say,"
Abe says. "'You half woke me.' Once you said to me, 'I'm
close to the point where I'm almost tired of this.' With you,
it's like that a lot. Half, close, almost."

"You say things, too," Vera says. "You're not without
quirks, believe me." She blows softly into her cup and sips,
smacks her lips. "Hot," she says.

"I don't say things," Abe says. "What do I say?"

"You're just weird," Vera says. She taps her temple. "Loco
in the cabasa."

Abe forks a pile of egg onto his toast. "Like how? Give an
example."

"Keeping this whole heart thing from me like it's nothing."
Vera wipes her lips with her napkin. "Now you're going to
say, 'The example you gave is not of something I said, my
dear, but of something I didn't say.'"

Abe puts his finger up, finishes chewing, swallows. "Then
you'll say, 'You know what I'm talking about. Use your nog-
gin for something more than a hat rack.'"

"Then you'll say, 'I do. I use it to keep my ears apart.'"

"Then you'll say, 'I'm not saying it's something you can
help, I'm saying this is how you are. It's a condition.'"

Vera smiles, points her fork at Abe. "Like the backs of our
hands," she says.

"I knew you were going to say that," Abe says.

At the front of the restaurant, a teenage boy drops a coin
on his way to the cash register. An older man bends down to

pick it up and pretends to put it in his pocket before giving it back to the boy. They smile at one another. Vera sees this. The older man could've bitten the coin with his side teeth as if to check its authenticity, or he could've said, "Flip you for it," or he could've stuck the coin in the kid's ear and pulled the kid's arm, like a slot machine. Instead, he went for the pocket. Vera would've liked to see him do more with the opportunity. She would've liked the moment to be interesting enough to mention to Abe.

All Abe sees is Vera looking over his shoulder.

A few years ago, on the way home from a vacation, Abe shook hands with Muhammed Ali in the Savannah, Georgia, airport. The Parkinson's was just beginning to set in. Ali shuffled along stiffly and slowly, but the members of his entourage were careful to stay behind him. Ali led. When people approached to shake his hand, one of Ali's assistants, a small, striking woman in a gray business suit and a black scarf which covered her head and fell onto her shoulders, handed out Muslim pamphlets autographed by Ali. She politely denied requests for pictures. When Abe reached out to shake Ali's hand, the champ faked a surprisingly quick right jab to Abe's jaw. "Careful, sir," the assistant said loudly to Abe. "I think you remind The Champ of Leon Spinks." Ali glared and nodded. Passersby loved it. Abe laughed along, pleased to be part of the schtick.

When they shook, Abe was surprised by Ali's hand, its size and heaviness. The palm was broad and soft like a well-oiled baseball mitt, the knuckles flat and round like bottle caps.

Vera was in the rest room for all of it, missed the whole thing. Even after Abe showed her the pamphlet she was suspicious. Abe had to have a nearby stranger vouch for him. Vera asked the guy to swear to it. The guy raised his right hand. "On a stack of bibles," he said.

Now, years later, in the middle of a Saturday afternoon, Abe's unfolding the pamphlet. The words AS SALAAM

ALAIKUM are printed on the front. Underneath, PEACE BE WITH YOU is written in black pen, and under that, in the same handwriting, is Ali's signature. Abe wonders if Ali's the one who signed it. Probably not. He imagines a pen in Ali's hand. Like a match stick in another man's. Anyway, with the Parkinson's, Ali would be too shaky, and the writing looks like a woman's. Even, billowy letters. Maybe the assistant in the gray business suit was Ali's wife.

Vera and Bart are on a walk. Abe's at Vera's dresser, hunting in her junk drawer for super glue. That's how he came across the Ali pamphlet. He's surprised to also discover an old office i.d. of his from a few years ago. He remembers that Vera liked the picture. There's a head tilt that suggests cool casualness, nonchalance, and the angle squares his jaw a bit. The lips are closed and straight. The right eyelid droops down a bit further than the left eyelid. The hair falls over the forehead in three dark wisps. He hadn't tried to look like this. It just happened. "Who's the stud?" Vera had said when he'd come home with it. "This guy plays the drums, drives a motorcycle. He has an enigmatic past and takes his time. Where's he been all my life?"

On the Savannah trip they'd hit the beach every day. Two weeks on Tybee Island. Vera tanned darker than either of them had imagined she could. Her white bikini top glowed.

Abe shuts the drawer, crouches to open another. Summer stuff. Shorts and tank tops, Vera's red one-piece. He rummages until he finds the white bikini. In one hand he holds the bottom, in the other the top. He brings them to his nose. They don't smell like anything. They smell like clothes, like the drawer.

He hears the kitchen door at the other end of the house open, then close. He hears Vera talking to Bart, then water running. She's filling Bart's water bowl. He hears the door again. She's putting Bart outside on the porch. Abe flops on the bed, still holding the bikini. The bedroom door swings open and Vera comes in. She sees the bikini in Abe's hands. "What have we here?" she says. "Am I interrupting something?"

"Peace be with you," Abe says. "Where do we keep the super glue?"

Vera sits on the edge of the bed, nods to the bikini. "Not your size," she says.

Abe holds it out. "Would you mind?"

Vera pats her waist. "Not exactly in bikini shape at the moment," she says. "Off season."

"Please."

Vera considers for a moment, then reaches out for the bikini. Abe hands it to her. She stands and heads to the bathroom, closes the door behind her.

"Question," she yells from the bathroom. "What's in it for me, indulging you like this?"

Abe gets up and stands in front of the mirror. He takes off his shirt, sucks in his stomach. He tries to flex his pecs.

The door opens and Vera walks over to Abe. "Hey, did you hear me?" she says. Her head's tilted and her eyelashes are fluttering. She's swaying her hips and rolling her pale shoulders. "I won't be ignored," she says in a husky voice.

Abe pulls Vera to him, runs his hands down the length of her back, hooks his thumbs under her straps. "What was the question?" he says.

Vera rolls her eyes, looks down to his chest. She pokes him five times, once in each hairless patch. "You look like dice," she says.

Abe suggests that Vera driving him would be faster than calling an ambulance, so that's how they get to the emergency room. He'd woken in the middle of the night drenched in sweat, heart thumping in his ears, left arm and jaw buzzing. When he sat up, he vomited on the bedspread. Vera had to close Bart out of the room to make sure he didn't get at it. Abe thinks of this in the passenger seat, that they hadn't cleaned it up. That it's still there. That Bart's not able to get in the bedroom and up on the bed where he's most comfortable.

They don't talk much on the way to the hospital. Although Abe knows it's not the case, he feels that the silence between them is a familiar one, a post-argument silence. An aftermath silence. Vera does, at one point, however, rub Abe's knee. She does, at another point, say, "Hon."

Abe's chest feels full, like someone's over-inflating it with a hand-pump, like it's going to pop. Way past the recommended psi. Like if someone tried to dribble it, it would bounce up over their shoulders. Like if someone shot it long, it would carom high off the back of the rim, over the top of the board. Rebounders would jump, land, and then have to jump again.

Abe looks out his window and wonders at the houses with lights on this time of night.

There's no waiting in the emergency room. Vera says, "Heart," and Abe is escorted to a bed. A nurse helps him off with his t-shirt, slips a nitroglycerin between his lips, under his tongue, hooks him up to the monitor over his bed. His heart beats in waves, one after the other. High tide, low tide. They ask, "Where?" and he says, "Chest, jaw, arm." They say, "How'd the nitro make you feel?" and he says, "Big headache." They nod, tell him they're after blood, stick his arm. "For an enzyme test," they say. An EKG machine rolls up. The technician smiles at Abe, says, "I see you're pre-shaved." "Like dice," Abe says. After the EKG, they slip a plastic clamp onto his middle finger. Now under the waves, there's a number.

Vera stays back, lets people do their jobs. Her hand's over her mouth. Instead of watching what they're doing to Abe, she watches the monitor. The line goes up, the line goes down. The number blinks. This can only be good. Right up there on the screen.

After a few minutes, Abe senses that the hospital people are relaxing. He still feels puffed up, like his heart doesn't fit, but his arm and jaw have stopped throbbing and his nausea's gone. A doctor with a clipboard walks up to Abe. He flips pages. "No heart attack for you tonight," he says. "We'd like to admit you, though. Run some tests."

Abe says, "Sure." Vera moves in closer, says, "Sure."

Vera had stayed for a few hours in the chair beside Abe's bed and then headed home early in the morning to feed and run Bart, shower, change clothes, grab Abe's toothbrush and razor, and call work. She dials Abe's office first, gets the machine, and realizes it's Sunday. She punches in Abe's extension, leaves a voice-mail. "Honey, it's Vera. Remember, you don't have to be a world-beater your first day back. Love you. See you tonight."

When she returns to the hospital, there's a different receptionist at the front desk, and the ladies room is open. When Vera left, it had been closed for cleaning. She'd had to wait until she got home.

Vera arrives at Abe's room just when the echocardiogram equipment is being pushed in.

"You look tired," Abe says.

"I'm the wife," Vera says.

The technician, who's set up her cart beside the bed and holds a plug, stares at the already full wall outlet. "Well," she says. She yanks one, and the digital clock on Abe's night stand goes dark. She plugs in. She tells Abe to fold down the top of his gown. She needs him bare-chested. She says, "You two have kids?"

"Nope," Abe says.

"Well, one," Vera says. She helps Abe untie his gown and then settles into a chair at the edge of the bed. "But he's adopted. Bad manners. He's home."

"What we're going to do is just like a sonogram," the technician says. She squeezes clear jelly onto the tip of what resembles a plastic microphone. "Instead of a fetus, though, we're honing in on the heart."

"Command central," Abe says.

"This will be cold," the nurse says as she applies the tip of the microphone onto his chest with one hand and turns the dials on her machine with another. A picture comes into view on the monitor.

"That doesn't look like a heart to me," Vera says.

"That's the liver," the technician says.

"I think I've already seen this one," Abe says. "What's on ESPN?"

The technician moves the microphone up over his left nipple. "There," the technician says. She turns some dials, flips a switch. "I'm going to measure your valve now."

"Should I leave you two alone?" Vera asks.

The technician moves the microphone over and up an inch. On the screen, what looks like a wide-open mouth with a swinging uvula appears.

"I think I know him," Abe says.

"Listen," the technician says. "Silence, please." She turns a knob, and there's a loud, hollow sound, like water sloshing around in a bucket.

"Listen to my heart," Abe says.

"Sounds like scuba," Vera says.

"Shh." The technician puts her finger to her closed lips.

"Does it sound and look like it's supposed to?" Abe whispers.

The technician waits a moment before answering. "From here it does," she says. "But I don't read the measurements and pictures, I just take them."

"Those types are in another department," says Vera.

The technician slides the microphone to a new position. What looks like a mouth of a cave shows up on the screen.

"Who lives in there?" Vera says.

"Wait and see," Abe says.

"Now we need to be quiet again," the technician says.

"Or he won't come out," Abe says.

"He could be a she," Vera says.

"Either way," Abe says. "Just so it's healthy."

"Shh," the technician says.

All You Want and More

Megan, a remarkable typist, an extraordinary bowler, lived most of the time with her family in south Troy, above A Rose Is a Rose flower shop and across the street from Uncle Sam's Diner. The apartment was small, just two bedrooms, a kitchenette, and a cramped living room, so if Megan and I wanted to sneak a smoke or a kiss, we had to climb out the bathroom window and onto the fire-escape. When I think of Megan now, I see the rusty grating beneath our feet and hear the tinny squeaking of the railing as we press against it, and I feel her mouth on my ear, whispering warm, sweet smoke.

Megan didn't always stay at the apartment. Occasionally, Megan's mother, Roxie, would decide it was time to make a change, to remind her husband, Vic, that she'd expected more of life, and she'd move out, dragging along with her Megan and Megan's ten year-old brother, Nicky. On moving day, I'd help the three of them throw things into boxes. I'd do the heavy lifting. I'd be the positive one. I'd pack and smile. I'd spring for burgers. I'd drive the get-away truck.

Moving day worked like this:

At 6 p.m., Roxie gets home from her job as a nurse's aid at Tranquil Hills Retirement Home and knows exactly what she has to do. She's had a chance to think it over on the bus ride home, and she now has five or six hours to get everything packed and loaded before Vic lumbers home from Clancy's Bar. She calls one of her sisters–there's one in Albany, another in Schenectady–and makes arrangements for an extended visit, just until she's able to find a place of her own. It's Megan's responsibility to phone me and ask if I can get my father's truck for a few hours. Her voice on these occasions is more irritated than genuinely sad or upset.

When I hang up, I first listen to my mother hope aloud that, for my sake, Vic doesn't pick tonight to come home early, and then I argue with my father about getting involved too deeply in problems that aren't my own. Eventually, though, he gives up the keys, telling my mother that if their son is ever going to learn anything about life, they are going to have to let him make his own mistakes, and I escape with the Bronco, dazed with love and the puffed-up feeling of being needed. I accelerate through yellows, pass on double solids, and park illegally in the alley next to the flower shop.

Megan and I pile boxes and suitcases in the back of the truck while Roxie has it out with Nicky over whether or not to take the TV. Roxie always wins this argument; the TV never makes it. "We take this TV, and your father, just to get back at me, bounces a check at Sears for some wide-screen jumbo-job bigger than the living room. TV stays. Maybe you'll read a book."

There is always a feeling of high drama, at least for Roxie. She offers a short speech in the crowded cab of the truck as we pull into traffic. With dewy eyes, she looks at Megan and Nicky, touches them, squeezes their shoulders, and says something like "I know it's hard on you kids leaving your home and your father like this, but sometimes doing the right thing is hard. There aren't blueprints for life. You don't always know what's ahead, but if we have faith, the Lord will take care of us." Feeling less inspired, she might stick to nuts and bolts. "Kids, as you know, your father's a drunk, lying sonofabitch. I for one have had enough."

During her parting comments, whatever tone they take, Nicky is in the middle of pulling the knobs off the stereo or stretching his skinny arms up to open the sun-roof even though it's raining. Roxie interrupts herself by delivering a backhand to his ear, and he cries out, "I've been hit! I've been hit! Take cover, men! The jungle's thick with them!" and Roxie sputters and coughs, somewhere between laughing and crying, and she strokes her son's cheek tenderly with the same hand that has just swatted him. Megan takes advantage of the diversion to inch closer to me, hug my arm, and whisper something about McDonald's drive-thru, something Roxie overhears.

"Of course! Dinner! You kids must be starved! What am I thinking?" She then opens her purse and pulls out two or three dollars. "Looks like we'll first have to stop at an ATM. Scott, do you mind? I hope Vic hasn't overdrawn the account again."

"Dinner's on me, Mrs. Binkowski."

"Oh, Scott, you've done so much already. I wouldn't feel right."

"No big thing," I say. "Glad to."

At this she shakes her head slowly and looks heavenward, as if in thanks and disbelief of how she's been blessed, and she touches Megan on the knee. "Hold onto this one, Hon. He's the right stuff." She then turns back to Nicky and begins telling him how she still loves his father, but how she thinks it would be best for everyone if they live apart for a while, give Vic some time to re-evaluate his priorities, and Nicky leans forward and twists the rearview mirror sideways, smashes his nose and tongue against the windshield, flips the bird to oncoming cars, and Megan buries her soft mouth in my ear, twirls her tongue slowly, whispers how she longs to be a dentist's wife, how my generosity will be rewarded in heaven, but first here on earth.

Three weeks later, when Roxie, Nicky, and Megan return to Vic and the apartment–three weeks is the longest Roxie can stand to live in the same house with either of her sisters–I help with that, too. I drive Vic's family back to him, and he's there to meet me at the driver's side window before I can turn the engine off. To get out, I have to go through him. "Thanks so much for bringing my life back to me," he says, crushing my hand in his, peering at me steadily through the thick, yellowed lenses of his prescription safety glasses, not for a moment forgetting who'd been behind the wheel when they'd left him in the first place.

During the ten months Megan and I were together, most of our senior year in high school and part of the following summer, Roxie left Vic four times. My parents kept count. They didn't approve. They were nervous about Megan and me and where it was headed.

A week after graduation, my father cleared his schedule one afternoon–a couple routine check-ups, a fluoride treatment, an impacted wisdom tooth–and took me to play nine at the club.

At the first tee, as he slowly waggled the head of his driver behind an enamel-white Titleist, he told me how sowing wild oats is acceptable and expected and even healthy for a young man as long as he realizes that it eventually is going to end, that sooner rather than later he's going to have to get himself on track and begin building his future. Hell, he wanted me to know that even he himself, my own old man, had kicked up a little dust back in the days before he'd met my mom. How summers home from college he'd done all right for himself. How the chicks had known his name well enough.

Here he interrupted himself, took two quick shallow breaths, swung long and clean, and the ball disappeared, then dropped out of the sky like a wounded dove, floated down softly, silently, two-hundred yards away, an easy eight or nine-iron from the pale watermelon-green of the green. "Perfect," he said.

I teed up, took a practice swing with my three wood–I sliced severely with my driver, a tendency my father said was all in my head–and stepped back to take a last look down the fairway. "I hear you," I said. "But Megan and me, we're for keeps. I think we're going places."

My father grinned and winked. He unfastened the velcro on his golf glove and flexed his fingers. "If you didn't think so, Scott, you wouldn't be the kid your mother and I know you are. Good-hearted and conscientious. A man of integrity. We're proud of you, and we want you to have fun. We do. Megan seems like a good kid. And I hope it's okay for me to say that she's not hard on the eyes in shorts and a tank-top." He raised his eyebrows and poked me in the ribs with his driver before dropping it in his bag. "I just wanted to connect, touch base, be up front with you about where your mom and I are coming from. We love you and, of course, want what's best." He pulled a cigar out of his shirt pocket, bit off the end, turned his back to the wind, spit, snapped open his lighter, fired up, blew a few thick white puffs into the air, and motioned to me impatiently with his hand, like he was a traffic cop. "Go ahead and hit," he said. "We have a threesome coming up behind."

I had to quit after the seventh hole to pick up Megan from her job at the bowling alley. When I told my father where I was headed, he smiled and nodded, told me to make sure to say hi from him, said he was glad we talked.

Vic was, by trade, an independent contractor. He had a tool box. When he needed something for a job that wasn't in his tool box, he borrowed it. Sometimes he returned it. Most of the jobs he could find were handyman-type: he'd build a tool shed, patch a roof, slap on a coat of paint, mow a lawn, unclog a drain, fix a wash machine, or seal a driveway. He pocketed enough for beer and to keep up payments on his pickup. Roxie's paycheck covered things like food and shelter.

Whenever Vic and I happened to be at the apartment together, he'd offer me a beer. He'd come out of the kitchen

with a can in each hand, hold one up and say, "Scotty boy.
This one's got your name on it!" Of course, with Megan
there, I never accepted the invitation. "Megan doesn't want
you encouraging me, right? Your girlfriend won't let you
enjoy a beer with her father. You're awful young to be
whipped already, Scotty," he'd say, popping the top of one of
the cans. "I'll tell the both of you—listen up, Megan—that two
people can't have anything together if they aren't first free-
willed individuals." He'd ease into his chair and raise the beer
to his lips. "Take it from a married man. Going on eighteen
years. A couple needs elbow room." He'd then gauge our
faces for response—I always nodded—and ask us to pass the
remote control.

I showed up at the apartment one evening just before
Christmas, a few months after Megan and I had started seeing
each other, to find Vic there by himself. He told me that one
of Megan's aunts had had an emergency appendectomy, and
Megan had gone with Roxie and Nicky to the hospital in
Albany. They were spending the night at the aunt's house.
"And Clancy's is closed tonight because of his nephew's bar
mitzvah," he said. "The one night I wouldn't have to hear
bitching when I came home past my curfew."

"Sorry," I said.

"You and me both." Vic dropped into his chair and
opened a beer. He looked at me. "What do you say, Scotty?
Have one tonight. You're off your leash. Make the most of it.
It's a Wonderful Life is coming on. You and me and Jimmy
Stewart. We'll sit here, sip a few, and mull it all over."

"Well," I said.

"Atta boy. Grab me another when you're up, will you?"

Vic knew most of the movie by heart. He laughed loudly
at the funny parts and rubbed his lips together when he was
worried. At commercial breaks, we took turns going to the
refrigerator. There were eight commercial breaks.

At the end of the movie, he stood and applauded. I did
too. I put my arm around his shoulders. I told him it was a
great movie and that he was a great man to watch a movie

with because he wasn't afraid to show how he felt. I told him I loved his daughter, that she rubbed her lips together just like he did when she felt sadness coming on, but I had seen this only occasionally because, for the most part, she and I were happy together. I told him that, despite his marriage problems, I had faith that he and Roxie would continue to make a go of it because, if you think about it, that's all two people can do. I told him that when I married his daughter and became a dentist, that's what my old man wanted for me, and I wasn't going to let him down–he and his family would never again have to want for top notch dental care. On the house, I said.

I had more to say, much more, but Vic interrupted. He said he appreciated my sincerity and generosity, that he saw a lot of Jimmy Stewart in me, and he asked for my car keys. He put them in his pocket, picked up the phone and called me a cab.

When the cab arrived, Vic helped me off the couch and gave me back my keys. He asked for my wallet and counted my money to make sure I had enough. Before I walked out the front door, we hugged warmly.

My father woke me the next morning. With bleary eyes and a pounding head, I told him his truck was still at Megan's. "I left the lights on," I said. It hurt to think fast. "Dead battery."

"Why didn't you call Triple-A?"

"Oh," I said.

He looked at me in disbelief and poked my forehead with his finger. "You need to think, Scott. Think." He shook his head. "I'll have your mother drop me off at the office, but you and my truck will be there to pick me up at five-thirty on the dot. Got it?"

After I heard my parents leave, I showered, swallowed some aspirin, and took a cab back to Megan's. When I got there, Vic was gone, and Megan and her mother and brother were not yet back from Albany. I got in my father's truck and drove it home.

Over the next couple weeks, I nervously watched Megan's face and listened intently to her tone of voice. Eventually I relaxed. She didn't know. Vic hadn't squealed.

Six months later I was with Megan at the apartment one night when Vic, drunk but happy, staggered in with good news. When he saw us on the couch, he clapped his hands together and rested them on his cheek. "Well, look at the lovebirds! Megan and Scotty, sitting in a tree, K-I-S-S-I-N-G!" He laughed loudly and took off his glasses and wiped the tears from his eyes. "Meg," he said when he could catch his breath, "go wake up your mother and brother." He said he had great news. He said their ship had come in.

When Megan left the room, Vic sat down next to me, slapped my back, and said he was glad I was here because, in his eyes anyway, I was becoming a member of the family. "I'm not sure if you've won over the old lady yet, Scotty, but you're all right by me. Want you to know that. Maybe someday you and Meg will make it official, huh?" He grinned and punched my shoulder. Then his expression sobered and he stuck a fat finger under my nose. "Piece of advice, though: don't elope. That's what Roxie and I did. She locked herself in the motel bathroom and cried all night. I'll tell you true, Scotty, I wondered that night if I'd made a miserable mistake."

By this time everyone was in the room. Megan stood by the front door with lowered eyes and picked couch fuzz off her shorts. Nicky walked sleepily to the middle of the living room floor and spun around once like a dog before he lay down. Roxie, in a stretched-out, lime-green nightshirt that read "All You Want And More," leaned against the wall and lit a cigarette. "You're in rare form tonight, Vic," she said. "You reek from here."

But tonight Vic wasn't going to be baited into battle. Tonight was his night to shine. He stood and put his finger to his lips. "I just wanted to share some news," he said. "Our luck's changed." Across the room, Megan put on mint chapstick. When we kissed it numbed my lips. "I got a job today. A couple old farts have me rebuilding a cottage down on Crooked Lake. From the ground up. It'll take the better part of six months." He pulled a wrinkled check out of his shirt pocket and waved it. "Best part is, I got a healthy advance that should keep us living the good life for a while."

He had their attention. Nicky sat up, Megan capped her chapstick, and Roxie shifted her cigarette to her left hand and reached out for the check. "Can I have a look, Hon?" she said.

"Sure thing, Babe." He handed her the check and continued. "Now I know that I haven't always been the best provider, but this is the start of something. This is me making a change."

No one spoke. We all looked at Roxie and the check. Everything was quiet except for Vic's stomach bubbling and juicing like it was going to blow. "Pardon moi," he said. "Too much Arby's." He belched quietly and smiled. Nicky laughed loudly and Vic walked over and patted his head.

"You should be happy too, Scotty," Vic said. He folded his arm around my neck. "You get a summer job out of this. I need a good man. You and me Monday morning bright and early. We'll meet here, grab a bag of drive-thru McMuffins, and be on the job by seven-thirty. Five bucks an hour. And benefits. I'll tell you all I know. I'll set you up with my daughter."

A husky laugh came up from deep inside him and turned into a cough. He coughed with his mouth wide open and his tongue curled. His thick neck shook and purpled. Roxie went to him and pounded his back. "Don't leave me now," she said. "The check's made out to you."

Nicky stood up and started clapping and stomping in rhythm like he was in the stands at a high school basketball game. When he had his beat down he began chanting, "Heim-lich! Heim-lich!"

All this provided opportunity for Megan to cross the room, take my hand in hers, plant on me a brief but inspired open-mouth-with-tongue kiss, and tell me quietly–I watched

her still shimmering, ice-minty lips form the words—that, starting Monday, her father staying on the straight and narrow
and, subsequently, her college future depended on me.

Megan had been, hands down, the best typist at Troy
High. She'd easily won the annual Type-Off four straight
years. Roxie displayed her daughter's four blue ribbons on
the refrigerator, under magnets. She saw them each morning
when going for the orange juice, was reminded of the blessing
of her daughter's genius, and it sometimes was enough to
choke her up. Even Vic sometimes lingered for an extra second to reflect on them before grabbing another beer.
    Megan was a natural. Her fingers were limber and quick,
her eyes true. Her concentration was trance-like, unbroken
and passionate. Her form was perfect: steady head, straight
back, perfectly arched wrists. Mrs. Truesdell, her mentor, had
Megan come into her Typing I class for a demonstration in
the first week of each semester, and Megan would hammer
out a blue streak for the wide-eyed freshmen who'd never
before seen such brilliance. For the finale, Mrs. Truesdell
would give Megan a second typewriter, and Megan would fly
through two different workbook exercises simultaneously,
one with her left hand, one with her right. At the end of the
presentation, the students would clap—some even whistled,
whooped—and Megan, red-faced, modest, would stand, carefully open and close her fists, shake out her still-tingling
hands, smile, curtsey, and crack her knuckles.
    Unfortunately, Hudson Valley Community College didn't
offer typing scholarships. In order to get into the Office Assistant program, Megan needed to come up with registration
and tuition. She was eligible for financial aid, but her forms
were lost in one of the moves, and she hadn't been able to
mail out new ones before the deadline. Vic and Roxie were
sympathetic, but they didn't have the money to help. She'd
resigned herself to working at Thunder Bowl, another year of
disinfecting rental shoes, remedying ball jams, and selling

outdated bags of chips and watered-down fountain drinks. Tony, the owner, had promised her full-time and a quarter an hour raise if she stayed on after graduation, and she'd taken him up on it.

Tony was a hairy mass of a man who wore open-necked shirts and Ace bandages on his wrists. His hands were large and strong enough to palm a bowling ball. Without using finger-holes, he rolled violent strikes that made onlookers wince.

He hated me. Whenever I walked in the alley, he was sure to make eye contact with me, and he never looked away first. He talked to Megan about me. He told her he knew my kind. He told her she could do better. He said I had a look about me. When she told him that I was going to be a dentist, he said, "Figures."

It was at Thunder Bowl where I'd first met Megan. We'd moved in different circles at school, but one Friday night I watched her on one of her breaks as she bowled a few frames by herself on one of the end lanes, and I left the group I'd come in with to walk over and ask if she wanted company. I said, "I'm Scott. Need some competition?" She said, "Megan. Suit yourself." So I moved to the scorer's table and flipped the switch on the overhead score sheet. She watched as the shadow of my hand wrote "Megan" on the first line and "Ace" on the next.

"Five bucks a game suit you, Ace?" She reached over my shoulder to stick her wet Juicy Fruit on the corner of the score sheet and then moved to the ball-return, wiggled her lithe fingers over the hand-blower, raised her ten-pounder to her nose, and began her approach: left right left right, ball swinging back, elbow unbending gracefully, ball swinging forward, waist bowing into a quietly beautiful delivery, pro-fessional-like kick and slide, knee almost to the floor, and a complete follow-through and finishing pose. She looked like a trophy. Strike.

She turned and smiled, brushed her hair–almond colored, almond smelling–out of her eyes, and returned to the scorer's table. She reached over me for her Juicy Fruit–her breath, sweet and spicy, smelled like Juicy Fruit–and said, "You're up. Let's get at it. I have twenty minutes left on my break and a hot hand I don't want cooling off."

Within a week we were together. In a short time we'd made long-range plans. Once I had my own practice, she'd be my receptionist. When her father came in the house that June night talking of financial security and positive change, Megan saw everything falling into place. With some help from her father, she might be able to get enough money together by the end of August to enroll at Hudson Valley in the fall. Dreams could start coming true.

The first week of working with Vic was hard. We started early in the morning and quit when the sun went down. Vic wanted to tackle the roof first, so for the first week we climbed ladders, ripped up old shingles, and baked in the sun. Vic was a camel. He could go for hours on one cup of water. Whenever I climbed down the ladder to fill up my jug, he shook his head and whispered to himself. When I jumped in the lake during lunch break on the first day–the cottage had its own dock–Vic told me to cut it out. He said he wanted to convey professionalism. He didn't want his crew goofing off. I was expected to keep my shirt on and wear long pants. I was expected to shape up.

At some point in the middle of the second week, however, the novelty wore off for Vic. We started taking long lunches at the tavern down the road. He bought me the special, linguini and white clam sauce, three days in a row, and told the bartender I was his son so I could get beers. We partnered up and played pool with the regulars. We became regulars. When we'd leave the tavern to go back to work, we'd stop at Shop 'n Save and buy a twelve-pack for the road. We'd drink in the shade by the lake. One afternoon, Vic pulled two air mattresses out of the back of his truck, and we floated around in our underwear and got sunburned. He'd been by his customers' house the day before and asked for and received another check. He told them supplies were running a bit more than expected.

This went on for three weeks. Vic told me he had it all planned out, that we were pacing ourselves. He said that life's a marathon, not a hundred-yard dash. He said it would soon get cooler, and we'd have more energy then. When he spoke, I nodded. I wanted him to know that he could count on me, that I was agreeable and flexible, that I wasn't a know-it-all, that I wasn't a holier-than-thou. I told myself that maybe all the guy needed was somebody in his corner, that although Megan might not understand this line of thinking, she was at the center of it. My getting along with her father was an investment in our future together. I would become Vic's confidant. When he'd go through rough patches, Megan would ask me to talk with him, and I'd be able to smooth things over. It would all pay off.

Whenever I talked to Megan during this stretch–usually on the phone, as I was too exhausted from the combination of beer and sun to see her in the evenings–I told her that things were going great, that her father and I were getting on like pals from way back. She told me she'd gotten a catalog from Hudson Valley, that she had her fall schedule all planned out.

I was passed out in the wheelbarrow the day it ended. When I woke up, Megan was on the dock screaming at her father. He was in the middle of landing a large mouth bass with the new rod and reel he'd picked up the day before.

Before I had fully come out of my daze, Megan was on me. She rapped me on the back of the head with her knuckles. She tipped over the wheelbarrow. She said thanks for nothing. She said she never wanted to see me again. She said forgetting me would be a snap. She stomped to her car and spun her tires loudly in the gravel.

A few minutes later, Vic came up from the lake. He had his fingers hooked under the gills of his fish, and he held it up so I could see. The sunlight danced on its silver scales. I told him it looked like a keeper. Vic went sheepish then, told me that, seeing how things hadn't panned out with his daughter and me, he thought it would be in everyone's best interest if he let me go. "Family comes first, Scotty," he said.

Besides, he'd been fired. The old farts had been by earlier that afternoon, watched us float around the lake on our mattresses for a while, and then called Vic's number from their car phone. Megan had answered, taken the message.

It's been a year now and she still won't take my calls.

I went into Thunder Bowl once to see if she'd hear me out, but Tony saw me coming, met me at the automatic doors, held up a pot roast-sized fist, told me one more step and he'd gladly knock me to Poughkeepsie. The gold chain nestled in his chest hair glistened. The look on his face was one of victory.

This hurts all the more to reflect on now because I just saw in the paper recently that Megan and Tony have become one flesh. My father showed me the announcement, thinking it might serve as a wake-up call, thinking it might snap me back.

Nicky answered the phone when I tried to get through. He said, "Will this be take-out or delivery?" and then I heard a smack and a yelp. Roxie got on and told me that the newlyweds had just returned from their honeymoon in Vegas. She said Megan was starting college in the fall. She said Vic had missed his own daughter's wedding because he'd passed out in the parking lot. He'd gotten drunk with the limo driver. He'd lost the jacket to his tux.

A horn blared in the background. Roxie said she had to go. Tony was double-parked out front with a full truck. She and Nicky were going to stay with the newlyweds for a while until Vic could get things turned around. Tony and Megan had plenty of room at their house in Averill Park. They were thinking of putting in a pool.

Upon hanging up, what I felt, of course, was the deep-down ache of loss and self-loathing.

My theory is that Tony was at first only a shoulder for Megan to cry on, but then love blossomed once more in the smoky world of league nights, automatic ball returns, and stale nachos. I envision this as the moment they knew: Their hands brush together behind the snack bar as they reach for the same soft pretzel.

As for me, my first year of college is over. I barely avoided flunking out of the pre-dental program. When my father found out that I'd been put on academic probation, he took me golfing again. Between holes, he spoke of wasted potential, building a life. He said, "You go around once." He said, "Don't underestimate the power of a positive outlook." He said, "You're young." I said, "Are you trying to say that I shouldn't give up on her?" and he said, "What?" and I said, "Megan," and his face reddened and he helicoptered his new four-iron into the pond off the seventh fairway.

I don't blame my father for his disappointment. I know I've hit bottom. Megan is everywhere. A row of molars and I see typewriter keys. Incisors are bowling pins. During mid-terms, my professor walked in the lab and caught me sneaking a quick huff of laughing gas–I needed something–and referred me to a support group. We meet on Thursday nights, and when it's my turn to talk, I say, "Megan," and all the other group members roll their eyes, fold their arms, and slouch in their seats. I'm simply trying to talk it out. Get to the root of the thing.

After meetings I go to bars. I scope out hands and smiles. I choose a woman with strong, slender fingers–I might admire how they balance a wine glass or the way in which they drum on the bar to the music–and I make my approach. I ask if she's ever picked up a 7-10 split. I inquire about her office skills. I tell her she has great teeth.

One night I went to Clancy's in search of Vic. He told me all he knew. He said all might not be lost with Megan and me. He said he'll talk to her. He agreed with me that Tony's not the one.

Just before last call, Vic broke into song. His voice is a pleasant tenor. People put down their drinks and listened to him, and when he finished, they applauded quietly, murmured soft, slurred words of appreciation. "Danny Boy" was his finale. His voice broke with weeping. When I asked him why, he said he knew too many sad stories. "People and their problems," he said. "Things get to me."

Behold Faith

Lyle's cashier is a fat man with beefy hands. When he hits TOTAL, he does it sharply, like it's a threat, like he's poking another fleshy man in the chest, looking to start something. $2.14. Lyle peels off three ones. He'll get back 86 cents. Would he like a bag? Please. Plastic? Fine. If Lyle stays in the parsonage another week, he'll take the garbage out to the curb on Wednesday night, but before doing that, he'll empty his study wastebasket into the bigger one in the kitchen. He'll then need a new bag to line his study wastebasket, and he'll have this one, the one he's getting now to carry his Mountain Dew and gum drops. The world hums along like this. Lyle's noticed. The universe is a barbershop quartet, one ongoing medley that won't be interrupted, even for applause. When you get a red light, someone else gets a green, and it is good. The traffic flows. If you dig a hole, the next thing you do is fill it up. You inhale then you exhale. Too fast you faint, too slow you suffocate. You stay in step despite yourself. It's in the cells, the DNA. It's in the boomerang blood that flows to your heart, gets pumped out, then flows back again. Wherever you go, you're returning. If you're surprised by anything, it's only because you haven't been paying attention. Lyle pays attention.

Saturday evening and still no sermon ideas, Lyle's bracing for an all-nighter. Buzzed on caffeine and sugar, wide-eyed and aching, he'll spend the next twelve hours leafing through old notes and anecdote books in hopes of patching together another three-point homily on the power of prayer, personal integrity, or ministering to today's youth. Tomorrow morning, cotton-headed and punchy, he'll face his wrist-watch conscious congregation–his own voice will be a hum in his ears, a droning wasp's nest–and when he's finished, benediction delivered, he'll walk down the aisle to the labored strains of the organ, twenty-seven steps to the front door.

It's there in the vestibule each Sunday that Lyle faces a decision. He can stop, turn, loosen his tie, and wait to catch the congregation one by one as they leave, smile, squeeze hands, absorb hugs, bend down to kid with the children, promise prayer and offer reassurance to those who are having hard times, or he can duck outside before anyone's even out of their pew, close the door quietly behind him, hustle across the street to the parsonage driveway where his Chevy Cavalier is parked–he packs his suitcase every Saturday night, places it in the trunk–shed his clerical robe, wad it into a ball and throw it in the back seat, climb behind the wheel, start the engine and drive. No more sermons, weddings, funerals, baptisms, hospital visitations, or marriage counseling sessions. He'll make a fresh start in another line of work. Isn't he good with his hands? Hadn't he, all by himself, put up the youth group's basketball hoop in the parking lot last month? And hadn't he, equipped with only his toolbox and Hayne's manual, installed new brake-pads and rotors, the whole shebang– on the Cavalier last summer? And hadn't it energized him? The smells of grease and hot metal and his own sweat? Hadn't he showered afterwards and put on shorts and driven to this same grocery store to pick up a $10 Porterhouse, three ears of corn, a softball-sized sweet potato, and even a six-pack of beer? Hadn't he realized when he arrived home that he'd forgotten charcoal, and hadn't he had the resolve to return to the store to pick up a bag, even make a point of going through the same checkout line, the same cashier, so he could make a small joke at his own expense and watch the girl's dark eyes appreciate his humility and goodnaturedness?

When this evening's cashier digs out Lyle's change and slams closed the register drawer, it's bells and whistles. Balloons descend, a half-dozen members of the high school marching band high-step single-file into the store from the parking lot, set up by the ice machine, launch into a spirited swing number, and a clown decked out in Hawaiian shirt and puffy pants springs from behind the customer service counter, closes in on Lyle. In his outstretched hands he holds a lei of yellow plastic flowers. For a split second, Lyle's in fight-or-flight mode. He suddenly knows for sure that, if it comes down to it, it is in him to bite the clown's tangerine nose.

The clown, perhaps sensing Lyle's panic, hangs back. He just hulas and points. He's a silent clown with lubed joints, rolling hips. It's up to someone else to explain to Lyle what he's excited about. Enter store manager: wide green tie, severe side part. He gets between Lyle and the clown, slings his arm around Lyle's shoulders. "MegaMart's one-millionth customer!" he yells, raising Lyle's hand. There's applause. The guy in line behind Lyle, number one-million one—a bag of menthol cough drops, a box of Kleenex, a jug of orange juice—drops his chin, sneezes three times, moans.

A cart jam is developing because shoppers are returning to the front of the store from all points to see what's the hubbub. A few small children are frightened, clamped to the necks of their mothers who shoo away the clown when he dances towards them. If you're part of the problem, you can't be part of the solution. Lyle knows this. Across the store in produce, he sees a woman taking advantage of the turned heads. Her purse swells with radishes. Closer to Lyle, just two checkout lines away, a stooped man with a cane, momentarily discombobulated by the ruckus, splatters a jar of spaghetti sauce. He swivels his head to identify witnesses, flees.

The store manager grips Lyle's elbow, steers him left. His advice to Lyle is to smile. Flashbulbs pop. The clown gets in on some shots. Lyle senses that there are rabbit ears being held up behind his head, but he goes with it. "The odds," the manager suddenly says to Lyle. "Think of the odds."

"One in a million," says Lyle. "What now?"

"Paperwork," the manager says, swinging Lyle in another direction, towards a TV camera. "Prizes."

Lyle knows that there are other ways to leave the ministry besides the post-Sunday sermon slip. This evening, waiting in the checkout line, he'd been wondering at his own histrionic tendencies. Why is it not in him to go by the book and simply resign, give a month's notice? He could tell the Board that he's burned out, spent, that he needs to take time to minister to himself, to plumb the depths of his own soul before continuing to plumb others. Plumber, plumb thyself.

He knows the elders wouldn't be surprised. They'd be relieved. They'd shake his hand and wish him well. He knows they talk about him. He knows about the weekly Thursday afternoon conference call they put into his office assistant, Janet, to find out if there's any sign of sermon notes, to get the skinny on unusual behavior patterns, extra-long lunches. One of the senior elders, Harry Towers, stops by the church unannounced two or three times a week, ducks his head and one finger in Lyle's office like he's checking the weather, asks how things are going, reminds Lyle that he's available to talk whenever about anything. Harry says he wants Lyle to know that the burdens of the congregation don't all have to be on the minister, that a church isn't a one-man band. He wants Lyle to share the weight, take a load off, at least make some time now and then to unwind over coffee with a friend. Harry wears suspenders. Lyle's instinct is to pull them back as far as they'll stretch, then release them. He wants to leave marks.

Lyle knows that his sermon this past Easter did not ease congregational concern. From the pulpit, he'd caught a glimpse of Shirley Monroe's bra strap and had completely

lost his bearings. Sitting in the front pew with her husband of
twelve years and their three children, she'd leaned left to
shush her two youngest, give them gum, and the sermon
notes in front of Lyle were suddenly gibberish. Where he'd
been and where he was headed were equal mysteries. A
glance at his watch told him that he was twelve minutes in,
eighteen to go. "So it comes down to this," he'd said to break
his own awkward silence—Shirley Monroe shifted in her seat,
crossed her legs, fingered the baby's breath that peeked over
the brim of her Easter hat, placed a hand on her husband's
arm, fanned her face with her bulletin—"We should live our
lives as He would have us live them. We should live correctly
and well. We should pray. Praying's good. Love, too. We
should love each other."

The sanctuary was warm with bodies and the spring sun.
Shirley Monroe nodded slightly, cocked her head. Her bulletin continued to flap, and the air around her moved. Her
right earring shivered, curled onto her neck. Lyle wished for
a pitcher of iced tea. Lightly sweetened. A couple lemon
rounds and a mint sprig. He'd start with Shirley Monroe and
work his way around the sanctuary. Somehow there'd be
enough for everyone. No glasses, he'd administer it straight
into the mouths of his congregation one by one. Say ahhh.
Like a hairdresser he'd gently guide their heads back with
one hand, and with the other hand he'd pour. He'd hold the
pitcher high like a show-off waiter and bless each swallowing
throat. "May this sustain and refresh you. May it wet your
whistle. May it go down easy and cure what ails you. Cheers
and amen."

Lyle tapped his lapel microphone, concentrated on not
looking in Shirley Monroe's direction, lifted his Bible to his
ear and pointed first to it and then to the congregation. He
tried to make the gesture inviting rather than accusatory. "It's
all in here," he said. "Go in peace."

It wasn't just his sermons. When Lyle visited hospital
rooms or had counselees in his office, he had difficulty focus-
ing. People's problems, and his prayers for them, seemed

repetitive and petty. "Lord, please make everything better. Make everything work out to everyone's satisfaction, and may no one ever feel pain or get sick or die, and may no love go unrequited, and may everyone treat everyone else with respect. Be with the children. Amen."

Lately, the only prayers that Lyle meant and held hopes for were the ones he offered up Saturday nights as he packed. His pacing back and forth between closet, drawers, and bed, where his suitcase lay open, calmed him, emptied him, and he was able to follow through. He asked for strength and direction in the long-haul. He asked reverently, humbly, whether, if possible, he might be afforded a bit of space, a little free rein, some elbow room.

Upstairs in the store manager's office, Lyle signs on the line that gives MegaMart permission to use his likeness in advertising even though he has questions and concerns about this. Against his better judgment, he's already signed away his right to sue in case of injuries received in relation to his prizes. This makes him wonder about the nature of his prizes.

"You've won a shopping spree, Captain," the manager says. He's sitting across the desk from Lyle, feeding him forms. He pops open a can of Dr. Pepper, raises it to Lyle in toast, drains half, burps politely into his fist. The manager's in good spirits. On the way up to the office, he'd let Lyle in on something. Store employees had a pool going, and he was the only one with money down on checkout #4. Two-hundred and forty-seven smackaroos. Lyle's not the only winner tonight.

The clown's taking it hard, smoking a cigarette beside a half-open window in the opposite corner of the office. From what Lyle can gather from the clown's complaints to the manager, some of those smackaroos were his, and, on top of that, he's not at all satisfied with the reaction he received downstairs. He doesn't believe that he was appropriately appreciated. If he'd known it was going to be like this, he would've kept his mouth shut, worked his regular shift in the deli. The way he sees it, people in West Sand Lake wouldn't know a good clown if one hit them over the head with a brick. His wig is stuffed in his back pocket. His round, rubber nose sits on the window sill. He picks it up, squeezes it in his fist, tosses it out the window in an effort towards symbolism, turns to Lyle. "You didn't help things," the clown says. "That look you gave me when I made my entrance set the tone. Especially with the kids. It said, 'This clown's not funny ha ha, he's funny strange.'"

"Sorry," Lyle says as he hands the last form across the desk to the manager. "You startled me. For a clown, your entrance was very confrontational."

"Armed with flowers," the clown says.

"As for me, I didn't get the whole Hawaiian thing," the manager says.

The clown flicks his cigarette out the window and rubs his eyes with the heels of his hands, smearing his face paint. "There's nothing to get," he says. "I was simply trying to create a festive atmosphere. You ever been to a luau?" he asks, turning to Lyle. "Festive."

Lyle nods. He refuses to get into it with a clown. He has to preach tomorrow. He has to get home to prepare notes, pack his suitcase. He reaches under his chair, grabs his bag of gum drops and Mountain Dew. "If you could quickly tell me the nuts and bolts of my responsibilities as prize-winner, I'd appreciate it. I need to be going. I have work."

The manager leans back in his chair, folds his fingers behind his head and smiles. "Not tonight you're not working, Captain. Call in sick." He looks at his watch. "In a half-hour we clear the aisles, and then it's just you and your cart running wild for five full minutes. Whatever stash you cross the finish line with is yours. Free and clear. Not bad, huh?"

"In a half-hour I'll get five minutes," Lyle repeats, "and then I'll be free and clear." Tomorrow morning he'll preach on the transitory nature of life, how we're not built to last. A good farewell sermon topic. A meditation on mortality, and then vamoose. His disappearance will be a good object lesson. Drive the point home. Years from now, around steaming casserole dishes at pot luck dinners, members of the congregation will still be talking about his final benediction: *Go in the name of the Lord God. May He this week shine His face upon you and give you peace. Now you see me, now you don't. Amen.* "And then into thin air. Remember?" they'll ask one another between mouthfuls of beans, baked corn, and shepherd's pie, between gulps of iced tea. "Down the aisle, out the door, gone. Like fog. Like the sun burned him up."

"I'm a minister," Lyle says to the manager. "What I have to do tonight is prepare my sermon for tomorrow."

"No problem, Rev," says the clown. "I'll help you out. Here's one off the top of my head. Feel free to use it." He lights another cigarette, takes a short drag, and then arches his neck and closes his eyes. He swings his head in a slow clockwise circle, stops. "Hallelujah!" he yells out the window, and then he pounds the sill with his fist. "Mercy! Mercy! Mercy!"

At the starting line, beside the salad bar in the produce section, Lyle limbers up. Arm circles, trunk twists, lunges, deep knee bends. The aroma of bleu cheese and cut red onion invigorates him as he listens to advice from the shoppers who line the front wall of the store. "Hit the meat case and load up on filet mignon!" one man calls out. Another assures him that store brands are often as good as, if not better than, name brands. Lyle grips the handle of his cart and revs it like a dirt bike, pops a small wheelie. The Mountain Dew and gum drops slide to the back.

The manager walks up behind Lyle and squeezes his shoulders. "You ready, Captain? We have to get started. Lots of paying customers waiting to get back on the floor. I'll get on the intercom, do the 'On your mark, get set, shop' thing, and you'll be off. Questions?"

Lyle has no questions.

The "go" signal is followed by a static-plagued version of the Lone Ranger theme. Lyle is fast out of the gate, and the crowd is enthusiastic. Lyle feeds off their energy. Coming out of produce and swinging left into aisle 2—his cart is empty; he's forgone all fresh fruits and vegetables—he lifts his eyes to read the sign, get a sense of purpose. DIAPERS, BABY FOOD, JUICE. By the time he hits the end of the aisle, Lyle has two boxes of newborn Pampers, three cans of formula, a couple bottles of grape Hi-C, and a collection of assorted baby food jars: mashed peas and carrots, stewed squash, whipped noodles and beef.

Heading out of aisle 2, Lyle has no strategy. He has no vision. He's winging it. He doesn't weigh the pros and cons of skipping aisle three—COFFEE, TEA, CANDY, COOKIES— he simply skips it. The turn would've been tight, and Lyle's flying, picking them up and putting them down, hauling eggs, delivering the mail. He feels a pleasant tension in the backs of his hamstrings and calves that he hasn't felt since his intra-mural flag football days in seminary. The players formed a circle before each game, held hands, and prayed for protec-tion against injuries. Lyle had shown up late for his final game, missed the prayer. Guys got hurt in each of the first three plays from scrimmage: a gouged eye, a split lip, a twisted ankle. Just before halftime, a fleetfooted missions major by the name of Victor blew out a knee. So be it. His will be done. Lyle had been running behind Victor—he'd been beaten badly on a post route—and was the first one there to help. He was the one who told Charlie, the second guy there, to call an ambulance, and he was the one who'd placed his hand on Victor's back and said, "Help's on the way, Vic. Hang in." But no one remembered these gestures. Instead, they remembered, for weeks, even months after, something that Victor, who was somehow more affable and interesting on crutches than off, would use as his kicker, his climax, when he retold the story of his knee: "Lyle, you know, Lyle, he hears it pop, and he's the first one who gets to me, and the first thing he does, before he does anything else, before he

asks me how I'm doing or where's it hurt or can I feel my
extremities, the first thing he does is pull my flag. Believe
that? Pulls my flag."

Lyle's stacked on top of one another one box each of
honey grahams, chocolate grahams, and cinnamon grahams.
He's collected one jar creamy, one jar chunky, one orange
marmalade, one strawberry, one grape. He has apricot in his
hand but thinks better of it, leaves the jar on the shelf. Cart
space management is becoming an issue. Coming out of the
fourth aisle, Lyle's already at half capacity. The surface area
and density of baking supplies: flour, confectionery sugar,
corn starch, brownie mix, Bisquik. He skips PASTA, RICE,
CHINESE, MEXICAN along with frozen food–this causes a
commotion in the crowd–and heads down aisle 7: GREET-
ING CARDS, OFFICE/SCHOOL SUPPLIES, ENVELOPES,
BATTERIES.

"Two and a half minutes!" the manager's voice booms
over the intercom. Halftime. What is behind is ahead. Smack
between the upslope and the downslope. Lyle's at the card
racks browsing the farewell section when the music starts up
again. Lone Ranger, sure, but originally William Tell. Rossini
was thinking apple, archer father, and target son, not six
shooter, silver horse, and masked man with a past. But see
how it works equally well for both? How especially the strings
reflect, above all–listen to them, they're the whinnies of
horses, the whistlings of arrows–a man on a mission?

The card Lyle chooses has a chimp on the front. The
chimp is wearing a tux. The chimp's cummerbund sags, and
the chimp's mouth is puffed into a pout. His chimp head
droops. His chimp hands are folded on his swelled chimp
belly. I'M NOT GOOD AT GOODBYES, the front of the
card says. On the inside of the card, the same chimp, or
another chimp identical to the first chimp, is eating a neatly
peeled banana with one hand. In the chimp's other hand is
another banana. The chimp is two-fisting bananas. The
chimp's bow tie is loosened, a few buttons of the chimp's
dress shirt are undone, and the chimp's jacket is on the

ground surrounded by bunches of bananas. The inside of the card reads, BUT I'M GREAT AT BANANAS. The clarity of this card is something to be appreciated. See how form matches content? How the card comes with its own customized envelope?

In aisles 8, 9 and 10, Lyle piles on a family pack of toilet paper, a bag each of dog food and cat food, a couple bottles of motor oil, and an aluminum roasting pan. Between aisles, he snatches a fresh turkey from the poultry case. Behind the glass in the meat room, white-smocked workers cheer him on. Lyle hears the thump of their workplace radio. One of the workers has drumstick/thigh combinations fastened in the apron strings on both sides of his hips. When he sees Lyle looking, he draws and fires. Quick hands. Lyle staggers back, arms flailing over his head and then coming to rest on his heart. He dies over breakfast sausage. The meat room erupts. Lyle recovers, bows, moseys.

"One minute!" Lyle flies through the last five aisles. He skips MAKE-UP, HAIR CARE, FEMININE PRODUCTS, SHAVING SUPPLIES. He opts for a bag of salt and vinegar, a loaf of multi-grain, a package of onion bagels, and a gallon of skim milk. He grabs a block of medium cheddar, skips the eggs. Lyle's having difficulty steering the cart. A box of margarine sticks falls off the top. Lyle leaves it. What doesn't kill you, slows you down. Sometimes you have to dump the cargo to save the passengers. Lyle grabs contact lens solution, a box of Band-Aids, a bottle of Tylenol. The finish line's in sight. Straight ahead, everyone is smiling. Even the clown is smiling. Sans nose, but his wig is back on, his make-up repaired. He has his arms around two giggling, squirming children, and a third is climbing his back like a jungle gym.

Jungle Jim the clown with his loud shirt and roomy trousers anticipates, along with the rest of the crowd, closure, and he is surprised, as are the other onlookers, when, fifteen yards from the finish, Lyle detours, swerves towards the bakery counter and disappears behind the stacked ovens. Lyle's cart brushes the backside of a kneading woman. When she turns, Lyle notices flour clinging to her eyebrows and lashes. They're beautiful in their function. Flutter and bat for the sake of the pupils. Lyle spots a service door and heads for it. Getting the cart over the doorstop requires Lyle to run around to the front wheels, bend down and lift. If you're not pushing, you're pulling. Either way you're a force. The objective is to get over the hump. Up is where you need to concentrate your effort, down takes care of itself.

On the other side of the door is the side parking lot. Lyle hangs a Louie, heads for the front of the store. In a way, shoplifting. At least subversive. Not ending up where you're expected is to wreak havoc, even if everything along the way is free.

When Lyle makes the turn around the front of the store, he can see through plate glass the backs of the crowd. They wait for him still. Time's up, but nothing's settled. The philosophy behind extra innings, overtime, Armageddon. For all they know, he's in the back room stockpiling hot dog rolls, bagging warm donuts.

A beige Ford Fairmont with rusted quarter panels pulls into a front row parking space not far from Lyle. Lyle makes a beeline. He taps on the driver's window with one knuckle. A woman turns her head abruptly, eyes him suspiciously. The window comes down two inches. "What?" In the back, two children–the younger one's strapped in a car seat and recovering grumpily from an interrupted nap; the older one's bouncing on his knees with his fingers stuck in his ears–both lock their eyes on Lyle.

"If you open your trunk, I'll put this stuff in it," Lyle says, leaning to the left so the woman can see the cart.

"Where'd you get it?" the woman asks. The bouncing boy is still now, his face pressed against the rear window. He makes a face at Lyle. The face features a smashed tongue and upturned nostrils. The child in the car seat–Lyle can't decide if it's a boy or girl–laughs even though it can't see the face. It's that sure. Behold faith.

"In there," Lyle says, gesturing to the store with a tilt of his head. "I won it. It's free. Thing is, I need you to have it. Thing is, it's yours."

The woman looks at Lyle for a moment before rolling up the window. In her face, in, especially, the dark, creviced line that, like a bookmark, separates her lips, Lyle believes. He's been here before. He'd like to be up in the foliage of a sycamore tree for perspective. Up there he could snap a stick, eat a leaf. He'd like to baptize someone in a river, raise them newly against the current with his back and biceps.

Inside the car, the woman turns around and gives the kids instructions. Lyle can't hear her words, but he notes that they make the oldest child sit back in his seat and fold his hands on his lap, and they make the youngest cry. More than what's said, it's important what's heard. He hopes that tomorrow's speaker realizes this. Barney Sharp could come down from the choir and preach. He has a wise beard, and he strokes his chin in member's meetings. It's a soothing gesture. The congregation could use this kind of affirmation, this kind of hope.

After reaching back and then over to lock the doors, the woman gets out with the keys. She locks the driver's door behind her and, without looking at Lyle, walks around to the trunk and pops it. Lyle wheels the cart over and starts emptying.

"The milk I can't take," the woman says. Her hands are balled up in the sleeves of her sweater. She doesn't help empty the cart. She looks around a lot, like she's got Lyle covered. "Got two gallons at home. It'll just go bad."

"Right," Lyle says. He glances toward the store. All is still quiet. Is it that they haven't caught on, or that he's not worth pursuing? Either way, a clean break. "Milk's mine," Lyle says. "You like Mountain Dew?"

"Sure. And those gum drops?"

"What about them?" Lyle asks, holding up the bag.

"I'll take those now," she says, extending her hand. "I like the green ones."

When the cart's empty, the woman shuts the trunk, gets back in the car. She re-cracks her window, holds her hand up to Lyle. He nods. With one arm he steers the cart across the parking lot to a return rack. With his other he carries the jug of milk. He's hooked two fingers under its convenient handle. Some things are made to carry, to take along with you.

At the return rack, Lyle remembers the chimp card. Too late now. The Fairmont's pulling out of the lot, fan belt screaming. The crowd inside the store has broken up. Lyle sees the manager standing beside the Coke machine, looking out the window, his arms crossed on his chest. Lyle can't tell if the manager sees him or not.

The thing about Barney Sharp is that he spits when he talks, when he sings. He doesn't say it, he sprays it. His moustache is perpetually moist. The ink on his sheet music smears.

Lyle faces the parking lot and scans left to right, right to left. Full house. Coming and going. He knows he's out there somewhere, just not sure where. He jingles the keys in his pocket. Round one's the door. Square one's the ignition. He bites his lip, taps his foot, blinks twice, scans again. Nothing. Total blank. Losers, weepers. He'll remember, though. It will come to him. Give him a second.

The Hardest Season

Nothing breaks up stillness and heat like a clap of thunder and a cloudburst. When it rains in the evenings I walk. The water rolls down the back of my neck, under my shirt collar, and works into a shiver that runs in my spine and across my ribs. I take the new, cool air into my lungs, and I hold it there and taste it.

If I head west from my house and keep at it for a few miles, past where the road turns from pavement to dirt, I eventually come onto a series of turn-offs for hunting and logging trails. I've hiked these trails and know they all cross creeks eventually. The most traveled have sturdy board bridges wide and strong enough to hold a pickup, but if you take the roughest trails, you're left to cross the water one slippery rock or log at a time, and if there's been much rain, you're left to swim.

Sometimes I head east instead, only about three hundred yards from my front porch to the cemetery where my friend Jon is buried. I tell him how the rain's coming down, how darkly the drops stain the dirt and headstones.

Some people in Manchester and Bennington will tell you there are no black bears left in the Green Mountains, but I know otherwise. Three miles into the maples, oaks, and birches behind my house, along the creek that splits my property into two almost perfect halves, I've seen them. Once from the top of a hill, Jon and I watched a bear, waist-deep in the current, bob for trout. When it got one, it waded to the bank, sat on the grass, and bit off the head. And in winter, a January afternoon when the sun on the snow glared brighter than the sky, we saw one that should've been sleeping rip the bark off a maple like it was peeling an orange and then chew deeply into the frozen trunk.

There was another time, a steamy, thick-aired July evening that ended a week of rain. The creek was fast and cold and we were fishing without waders, in just shorts and sneakers. It takes a while to catch your breath in water like that, but eventually it feels good. A few times I held my rod over my head and cooled my chest and shoulders by bending my knees to the rocks and mud of the creek bottom.

Jon was at one of his favorite spots, a shady pool under a black, leaning oak, and I was a hundred feet further upstream, out in the open, trying to get a feel for the fish and what they wanted so I could catch them before they got to Jon. I was standing, changing flies, when I spotted the bear thirty yards away on the nearest bank, a big sow on its haunches eating two-pawed at a raspberry bush. I slowly made my way to Jon, my rod held out in front of me for balance. When he looked at me I pointed.

We stood and watched her. She ripped a section off the bush, picked it clean, and threw it over her shoulder like a bone. "She's a big one," Jon said.

"What do you think?" I asked. "We could move downstream past the bend and be out of her way."

"We could," Jon said, "but this is where the hungry fish are." He held his rod in one hand and let his other hand dangle free in the water, downstream from the rest of him, so it looked like the creek was trying to pull him back to fishing.

"Besides, she looks like a vegetarian."

"She's an omnivore," I said.

"Well, I'm a Methodist." He pulled his line through his hand until he held his fly between his thumb and forefinger. He brought it up to his eyes for inspection, then dropped it on the water and looked back at the bear.

She saw us at that moment and froze, and we froze, and nothing other than the creek moved for what seemed a long time, but then she turned back to her berries, and I sneezed, and Jon's pole jerked almost out of his hands, and line was spinning off his reel, and something was running with his fly.

"I've got one on." Jon raised the tip of his rod, reeled in some line, then let it down again. The bear stretched her neck in our direction and aimed her nose higher into the breeze coming off the water. "Big one," he said.

It took Jon a few minutes to reel in close enough to where I could help with the net. What I saw at the end of the line I couldn't believe. There were two trout, small and shiny steel gray, both hooked neatly through the lip. I lifted the line out of the creek and they dangled angrily, kicking each other with their tails. By holding them still with my hand and looking closely, I could tell which one had struck first.

"Not bad," I said. "Haven't seen this trick before."

Jon smiled and nodded toward the bank. The bear had moved to another bush a few feet downstream. "And we have a witness."

We stayed in the creek even after our shadows had stretched long onto the bank. Until the bear left, I checked on her after every few casts. She took occasional, short breaks from the berries and watched us, tilted her neck and spun her head to follow our quick-dipping flies.

Two weeks later there was another bear. Jon and I were working at the time, closing in on the end of a day.

Besides being friends who fished together, Jon and I were business partners. We owned a wood lot, a tractor, a box-frame wagon, and a plow. In the summer we cut and delivered firewood, and in the winter we moved snow.

We saw many of our customers in both seasons, and they appreciated the work we did. In the heat of July and August, they brought us iced tea as we stacked oak and maple in their garages or on their patios, and in winter, after we cleared their driveways, some invited us into their kitchens to take off our gloves and drink coffee. It was good to look in the living rooms and see logs we'd cut stacked by the fireplace or stood up, drying against the wood stove, and it was satisfying driving up and down the frozen crushed stone driveways, watching the white-gray smoke ribbon out of chimneys. When it was Jon's turn to plow, when I was shoveling a walk or unburying a car, I liked to breathe it in.

Summer in the woods with the trees was the hardest season. We averaged three cords a day, cut and delivered. Even though we worked in the shade and it was cooler there than it must've been haying a field, filling pot holes, or shingling a roof, it was work that sent us home sore, and it seemed sometimes to be too much. Still, we liked it. The smells of sap and sawdust and gasoline and oil helped keep us awake and fresh, and we liked the system and order of our work.

After choosing a tree, we opened a triangle low in the trunk with a chain saw. If it needed help, if it looked like it might fall back into us or sideways, we stuck wedges in the gap and hit them with sledgehammers.

A falling tree shakes things up. It scatters birds. It can't be perfectly planned. It can take smaller trees with it on its way down, it can catch in a clump of birches, or it can get snagged in a bigger tree. Sometimes when this happens, all that's needed is your finger. You touch it and it's down. Sometimes it takes two men leaning on it. Other times, after you've already tried touching and leaning and you're standing back thinking of a plan, the wind blows hard enough for something to give, and it crashes, scaring the breath out of you.

When Jon and I had a tree on the ground, one of us took to its crown to zip off the thin, green, leafy branches, and the other marked the trunk with a four-foot measuring stick and red chalk. We then hooked the tree up to the tractor, pulled it to the clearing and cut logs. When we'd gone through enough trees for a cord, we stacked the four foot by eight foot box-frame four foot high, and cinched the load down with chains.

On the way to the woods in the mornings, I drove and Jon rode the empty wagon. In the afternoons we switched. Of course, then the wagon was stacked with wood—no room for passengers—so I rode on top of the pile. We had this arrangement because Jon was scared of heights. He lived in a one story house and couldn't get on a ladder to paint the trim or adjust his TV antenna, so I did those things for him, and at the end of a day in the woods I climbed the logs, sat in the middle of the wagonload for balance, and stretched my legs flat over the thick-linked chain in a wide V. I slipped my hand between the wood and the chain, a bull-rider's grip, and when I was settled, I raised my hand.

If I'd wanted, I probably could've squeezed onto the tractor in the space behind the driver's seat, but that's where we kept the saws, the other tools, and our water jugs, so it would've been tight. Plus I liked to kid Jon. Sometimes he'd look up at me on top of the pile and say, "It doesn't look that high from down here."

"About eight feet," I'd say, and I'd turn to one side and lean my neck and shoulders over the edge, and I'd put my hand over my heart. "But it's a high eight feet."

On the road we sometimes hit a bump or a pot hole and the logs under me would shift. I'd tighten my grip on the chain, find a new spot if I had to, and Jon would turn around and smile and shrug his shoulders. Sometimes while he was doing this, we hit another bump, but he never lost a log and I never fell off.

Once, working the first tree of the morning, I hit a knot and my saw kicked back. At first there were just ripped jeans and a white, empty gash above my knee, but then quickly there was blood, even some on my hands and arms. I fell back and yelled. Jon's saw shut off and then he was standing over me.

"My leg," I said. I was breathing fast and holding tightly onto fistfuls of leaves and sticks.

Without speaking, Jon ripped open the tear in my jeans. He looked and inhaled once quickly through his teeth before getting the water jug and flooding the cut. "Try to hold still," he said, and he took off his t-shirt, ripped it lengthwise, and tied it tightly around my leg above the knee. "How's that?"

"Tight," I said.

"Good." He put a hand on my arm. "I don't want to, but I think I'm going to have to leave you here and go get help. It looks like it could be bad and I don't think you're up for a wagon ride." He looked around the clearing and pointed. "Let's get you over to that tree so you can lean back." I nodded without turning to look where he meant. From behind, he grabbed me under the arms and pulled, and I pushed along the ground with my good leg.

When I was set up, back-straight, against an old oak at the edge of the clearing, he carefully raised my leg and rolled a thick log under my calf to keep my knee up. Once I was ok, he found my saw, started it, and let it scream for a few seconds before shutting it off and laying it beside me. My blood was still splattered across the blade.

"Just in case something smells you opened up and thinks about taking a look," he said. "It might not be a bad idea to let her rip once in a while. Keep them honest."

I nodded. "For a second there I thought you wanted me to finish up the rest of the order while you were gone."

"Only if you're feeling up to it." He kneeled and stuck out his hand, and we shook like we were making a deal. "Archie's house is closest. I'll call for help from there. You'll have to sit tight."

"I'm all right," I said. "Just don't stop by Piper's for a beer."

"Don't worry," he said, and he looked at his watch. "Not open yet."

When he showed up an hour later with ambulance volunteers and a stretcher, I was out cold. "Your face was white like cotton," he later told me. "I thought we'd lost you until one of the guys put his ear to your mouth, said you were breathing."

The doctor at the hospital in Bennington said I was lucky. He kept me overnight, but in two weeks I was back out in the woods, hardly limping, filling orders. "Another half-inch into your leg with that blade and there's serious damage," he said.

"That's why I give him the dull saw, Doc," Jon said. "Otherwise, he'd hurt himself."

In the winter, when we plowed, Jon and I always saved Henry Flint's driveway for last. After it was clear, we'd go inside and sit with Henry at his table, and at some point he'd get up, open the cabinet beside his stove, and take down a bottle of Jim Beam. "Well, look here," he'd say. We'd drink it straight or pour it into our coffee.

This past winter I plowed by myself. When I went in the houses to warm up, some customers spoke of Jon and asked me questions. They knew the basics of the story, but they wanted to get more from me, an eyewitness. I can't blame them. I can't blame people for wanting to know the facts about something like a bear killing a man.

I didn't tell them much. I didn't tell them how it latched onto Jon, pulling him off the tractor by his scalp, and I didn't tell them how it clawed one of his eyes out of its socket. I didn't tell them about coming down off the wagonload of wood and looking into Jon's chest, how I could see part of his heart, still as a stone.

After I plowed Henry's driveway for the first time last winter, he met me at the door with a mug and we drank to Jon. Later, at the kitchen table, Henry asked, "Why would a bear come within a quarter mile of you guys? All the racket you make with saws and falling trees? I don't understand it. The only thing I can think is rabies. Or maybe she was hurt, or her cubs were nearby and instinct kicked in. What do you think?"

I could've told him, "A deaf bear." But how I answered was true enough. I said, "Wrong place at the wrong time." He

moved his head in agreement and let a silent moment pass
before he changed the subject. He poured more coffee in my
mug, then more bourbon, and he invited me to take my boots
off and stand by the wood stove.

Jon didn't have any living family, so funeral arrangements
came down to me. I asked Archie Kenyon to sing at the service because I had faith in him. I knew he sang solos at
church–I didn't go much myself, but one Easter I made it to
hear him sing "Christ the Lord Is Risen Today," and I
remember thinking after he finished that we should all get up
and leave because we didn't need a sermon after that–and I'd
heard him sing along with the jukebox at Piper's lots of times,
nice enough so I sometimes thought about unplugging Way-
lon or Hank so Archie could take it home himself. He did a
good job at the funeral. Even made some people cry who I
didn't think had known Jon all that well.

The sun was hot that morning at the cemetery, but the
shin-high grass and goldenrod around the graves was still
damp from the thunderstorms the night before. People's
shoes and pant cuffs were wet through by the end of the service, and as Archie sang, I followed with my eyes the tracks
his wheelchair had made in the wet grass. That was just one
year ago, and the wet grass and Archie's "What a Friend We
Have in Jesus" are all I remember.

Thirty years before, carrying shingles on his shoulder,
Archie lost his balance and slipped off the roof of his father's
barn. He had Jon and me stack his wood out long and low
against the railing of his porch so he could reach the logs
from his wheelchair, sit them upright, measure them with his
ax, and split them.

He called me one day last November to help him carry
into his house a set of shelves that he'd built out back in his
work shop. Afterwards, I stayed and talked with him while he
split wood.

It was cold, down in the 20s, and the sky was gray and

heavy enough to suggest snow, although none had fallen yet. I stood behind Archie and blew into my hands until his ax came down, then I picked up what he'd split, threw it into a corner, and set up another log.

"You don't have to do that," he said.

"Keeps me warm," I said.

Archie wheeled his chair around to face me and leaned his ax against the outside of his knee. "I've been wondering something. It's something I hope is ok to ask."

"Only one way to find out," I said.

"All right. What happened to the bear that got Jon?"

"Sheriff didn't tell you?"

"He told me." Archie picked his ax back up and turned it so the business end was in his hands. He ran his thumbnail lightly along the blade. Out of his mouth he breathed heavy white frost into the air. "I didn't know you and Jon kept a gun with you when you cut."

"I'm telling you," I said.

"All right," he said and shook his head. "Forget it. That's it then. You got him." I wanted him to go back to swinging his ax but he didn't. He set it down, took off his wool hat, and scratched his head with both hands. "It's just a hard thing to move forward from. It won't settle with me."

I nodded and looked at Archie and then at the pile of wood he'd split.

"It's easier to look back," he said. "Hold onto what's left behind of him, like a joke he told or something else. It must be like this for you too."

"I saw him catch two trout on one cast," I said.

"I still don't know if I believe that one," Archie said. He smiled and started piling kindling in his lap. "When he forgot his gloves in my kitchen that time. I think of that. I reminded him whenever I saw him, but they sat on my table for two months."

"He used a pair of mine," I said. "I asked him where his were and he said he figured your house was a safe enough place to keep them."

Archie laughed out loud, and then was quiet for a moment before he spoke. "All right. We've got enough. Let's start a fire."

This is the truth. This is as close to the truth as I've come.

The bear wasn't there, then it was. With one swipe it knocked Jon from the tractor, then followed up quickly, not giving him a chance to get to his feet or roll over onto his stomach.

From the top of the loaded wagon I yelled, "Bear!," and I waved my arms to try to get its attention, to get it off Jon, but it didn't let up. Its back was to me so it couldn't see me, and no matter how loud I yelled it wouldn't turn away. By the time I was down off the wagon and had one of the chain saws started, I could see that half of Jon's face was gone.

Even with the saw buzzing, the bear kept its back to me, kept hunched over Jon with its head and both paws. It didn't know I was there until I was almost on top of it, but then suddenly it knew, and it whirled around, roared with bared teeth, and swung at me sidearm. I ducked, pushed the saw in front of me, blade up like a sword, and met the paw in mid-air. Only then did the bear reel and take off into the trees. I could still hear it, crashing and bawling, when I bent to Jon, his one eye and one empty socket both staring straight up through leaves into patches of gray.

I pulled the pin from the wagon hitch, picked up Jon, and climbed into the tractor seat. I held him across my lap. As we pulled away from the stacked wagon and out of the woods, the rain we'd been trying to beat started coming in slow, small, occasional drops, falling silently into tops of trees, thinning the blood on Jon's face and chest to pink.

When I went to bed that night, I expected to move violently in and out of dreams of Jon, perhaps of Jon and the bear together, wrestling ferociously. Maybe they'd take breaks to rest their backs against trees or fish the creek, each of them on all fours, stabbing at shadows in the water. Maybe

I'd be there with them, and maybe I'd have a gun. Or maybe I wouldn't have a gun, and Jon and I would just talk, or maybe we wouldn't talk, and the bear would be silent, too. There would only be the sound of rushing water, and if they wrestled, there would be that sound.

But there were no dreams that night, and there haven't been any since.

It was still raining the next morning. Sheriff Cropsey knocked on my door early to ask if I wanted to track the bear with him. He had on a camouflage slicker and there were beads of water on the clear plastic that covered his hat. "No need," I said.

The sheriff dropped his head and said, "Well."

"Took four slugs," I said, stepping out onto the porch. "Jon was already ripped up by the time I could get to the gun and start shooting."

The sheriff rubbed the back of his neck and squinted. "It's done then."

I nodded. "After I got Jon to Archie's and the ambulance came, after they told me for sure he was dead and I double-checked about where they were taking him, I drove the trac- tor back to the wood lot, to the bear. I buried it under dead wood and brush, emptied the gas can on the pile, and lit it."

"I'm sorry," the sheriff said. He stepped forward and clapped my shoulder. "This is a hard thing."

"It is hard," I said. "It took a long time. Every now and then it would burn out and I'd have to relight it. Smoldered until dark, under a tree with rain coming down around, lightly."

I'm not cutting wood this summer. I have a little extra money–the winter was a good one, lots of snow–and if I'm careful I should be able to stretch it enough to keep gas in my truck, buy groceries, and pay my bills.

Evenings I walk or sit on the porch and tie flies, eat fried fish, onions and potatoes, drink iced tea, and listen to the Red Sox on the radio.

In the mornings I fish. The weather's been good for it, hot and wet, so the creek is new and high and the trout aren't shy about coming up to eat. Casting sidearm from under a tree, I think about upstream, about a deaf bear running silently through the woods, dripping blood on rocks and rotten leaves, stopping at a deep pool to wade up to its neck and soothe its paw on a cool underwater stone, and I think about how Jon would fish this hole, more patiently and deliberately than me, and for a while I try to work it like he would, and I look up from the creek and scan the opposite bank, and then I look behind me, in the brush, up in the trees, and I try to concentrate on listening, but there are only birds and the creek and sometimes a jumping trout. Raindrops ripple the water, spread, are swallowed up. I dip a cupped hand and drink what I can get to my mouth.

Considering Work

According to the instructions on the box, according to Susan, if the dot turned blue, Derby was a dad, so it was he and I sweating it out behind Hardison's barn that day, leaning on shovels and hiding from work and trying to hurry up four o'clock so he could get over to Susan's to find out what was what.

The night before, after Susan had driven to the Rite-Aid in Tamarac to get the test–she figured buying the thing in Tamarac would cut down on the chances of running into someone she knew–she called Derby to say mission accomplished, and she told him she'd been thinking a lot about this. Derby stopped her to say he had been too, and he told her he'd wait on the line while she did what she had to. But she said, no, that the test called specifically for morning urine, and anyway, the more she thought about it, the more she realized how it was going to be a defining moment in their relationship either way it went, and she said she'd rather not discuss results and repercussions whispering into the kitchen phone, hoping that her mother wouldn't walk in. Besides, knowing that he was waiting on the other end of the line would make her nervous. She said, "I think I'd like it if you'd come over tomorrow after you're done working and you've taken a shower. We can go to dinner somewhere and discuss how things are and how they will be."

He tried to convince her he didn't think it was good for him to wait–he'd already thrown up twice and felt more coming–but she was set, and even though she felt bad that he was getting himself so worked up–didn't he know that when he hurt, she hurt?–she thought it would be better in the long run for both of them if they took this in stride and handled it maturely, like adults. Then she said, again in the long run, that the bottom line was she'd love him forever and she knew he'd love her forever, wouldn't he? "Of course," he said, and he said so truthfully.

After they said goodbye, he threw up again, and he spent the rest of the night with a bucket by his bed, staring at his ceiling, praying that what might be wasn't.

Derby started seeing Susan around the same time I met Julie Schmidt, early in our junior year of high school, eight or nine months before Derby and I were hired at Hardison's farm for the summer, and the four of us went around some.

After a while though, things got to be different between Susan and Derby than between Julie and me. They started calling each other "Hon" and they went places with each other's families some weekends, and when the four of us went bowling, the two of them held hands between turns so it was always either Julie or me keeping score and telling them when they were up. Eventually, the four of us didn't go out as four much anymore. But Julie and Susan still talked more to each other than to any of their other friends, and Derby and I trusted each other enough to share things we would've otherwise taken more care with.

Earlier that summer at Hardison's, Derby had told me what had happened with Susan on his parents' couch in front of a *M.A.S.H.* re-run. More than that, he told me he knew he loved her, that he thought he'd known for a while but now

was sure, and he was only letting me in on it with the understanding that I wouldn't think about Susan like that or wise-
crack, even just between the two of us. But no matter how he
would've said it, I couldn't have fought back the smile I
smiled–in my mind I was seeing it all in full color, hearing
B.J. and Hawkeye do the play-by-play–although it wasn't a
dirty smile.

"Come on. Seriously, Sam," he said.

"Sorry," I said, and I held my hand up like I was promis-
ing something.

We started baling later that day, so I couldn't have tor-
mented him much anyway. Mr. Hardison drove the tractor,
Derby and I stacked the wagon, and that kind of work is
silent work. The tractor is loud enough so it's hard to hear a
voice, and, even if you're in good shape, after a few minutes
of stacking bales you don't have enough breath to waste on
words, especially if it's hot, and you're into a rhythm with
the baler and each other that you don't want to break into
by speaking.

It wasn't too many days after the hay was up that Derby
and I began working together with ax and shovel against the
stubborn maple stump behind the barn, all that a bolt of lightning and then Hardison's McCulloch had left of the shade we
used to eat our lunch under. The tractor, unfortunately, had
given up the ghost right at the end of haying, so it was Derby
and me alone against the stump at least until Hardison got the
new transmission in. "There's nothing else pressing right
now," said Hardison with a smile, "so why don't you boys see
what you can do. You should be able to handle it on your
own." When Hardison smiled, the curve of his lips and the
puff of his cheeks half-closed his eyes. "Tools are in the barn."

Not a half-hour into swinging and digging, Derby told me
about the test and what Susan had said about waiting. We
agreed then, without saying anything, to stop, to take turns
peeking around the side of the barn for Hardison, to kick at
the dirt we'd turned up, upsetting night crawlers and gray
bugs, to look at the sky when we could stand it, when a cloud

would pass over and absorb some of the sun, and to wait for the time to pass.

At four on the dot, stump still in the ground, we found Hardison in his kitchen and promised that, first thing Monday, we'd finish it off. He nodded and rose from his chair and asked if we wanted to get paid even though we hadn't finished, and when we said yes, he said he'd go grab his checkbook. Derby said, "If you don't mind, Mr. Hardison, just give mine to Sam. I'm in kind of a hurry." He looked at me on his way out, and I nodded.

"Julie and I will be at the drive-in tonight," I shouted through the screen door at his back, and he raised his arm in full-sprint without turning around.

"Never seen him move that fast working," Hardison said, straight-lipped. While I waited for him to make out the checks, I drank the iced tea he gave me, cooling my forehead with the glass between sips, and I used his phone to call Julie to tell her I'd be there for her before dark.

A lot of my truck was Bond-O, but it ran all right and was good in the snow, and the bed was solid enough for drive-ins in the summer.

Some nights Julie and I stayed in the cab, but more often we set up folding chairs in the back and she filled a garbage bag with popcorn and I got beer from Ben, a friend of mine who worked down at the 7-11. Sometimes Susan and Derby would come with us, and we'd all four perch ourselves up in the back like it was the deck of our house, and we'd talk and laugh and ignore the movie and the cracklings that came, like ghosts' voices, out of the speakers.

When it was the four of us, deep into the night and the second feature, when conversation was tired and we smiled privately to ourselves at jokes made hours ago, Julie and I could sometimes hear Susan and Derby whisper about love. We'd pretend we didn't hear and find the screen so we wouldn't have to watch them, and I'd find Julie's hand or she'd hug my arm so we wouldn't have to look at each other, and we were quiet. Sometimes I thought about looking Julie full in the face to find out what we'd say, but I never did it for real.

On especially hot and humid nights, Julie and I played a game. We told each other winter stories. We tried to make each other shiver. I always told the same one, about Derby and I counting to three on the dock over thawing Burden Lake, me doing a fake jump, him doing a real one, his yelling when he hit the water, up the dock ladder, up the bank, back to the truck, and me, dry, staring into the icy black. Julie shivered every time.

Just as the sun reached its lowest and biggest and orangest point, I turned my pickup into Julie's driveway. She came out her front door on my third honk, hauling a puffed-out Hefty bag and wearing cut-offs and the shirt I'd bought for her birthday tied in a knot at her belly button. When we got out of sight of her house, she scooted over to me, kissed me on the cheek, and asked if I knew what had happened with Susan's test that afternoon. I said, "Not yet. How do you know about that?" and she sighed and moved her thigh so I could shift–she could feel a shift coming and that was one of my favorite things about her–and said, "Susan called this afternoon. She was supposed to call me back when she knew but she never did," and she moved her thigh again and I got it into fourth and she tapped the back of my neck like there was a radio and she was listening to a song.

Julie and I saw Derby that night. When he spoke he looked like he wanted to cry, and that was hard to take.

He found us by going up and down the rows of cars in his parents' station wagon. His headlights were on, so whenever he turned down a new row he broke people out of the trances they were in, either watching the screen or locked with one another in some variation of an embrace, and those who could reach their horns honked at him. When he hit our row and we recognized his car, we waved and moved the beer and the popcorn off the tailgate and situated our chairs so he'd have somewhere to sit.

"Have one," I said, and threw a can out into the dark.

Like that was her cue, Julie excused herself to use the restroom. When she got up from her chair, hopped down and gave Derby a hug, I noticed the white stripes the vinyl had imprinted on the back of her tan legs, and I thought of how beautiful she was, and I thought of how what might be beginning in Susan was weighing heavily in a different way on Derby himself, also even on Julie and me, and as Julie moved away from us into the darkness toward the far away light of the snack bar, things seemed to get more desperate.

Derby tilted back his head and emptied some of his beer before interrupting the static coming out of the speaker next to us. "She was in her bathroom and did what she was supposed to, followed the instructions and everything, and she was waiting however long the thing tells you to wait, and I guess she was nervous and forgot to lock the door," he took another swig, "because her mom barged in to put clean towels in the cupboard, and Susan panicked and flushed the damn test down the toilet."

"Man," I said. "So now what?"

"So now," he said, "so now we have to wait a couple days because her mom wants to take her to a gynecologist in Troy to get it done right. She saw the thing swirling around in the bowl, and she told Susan I was a son of a bitch, and she said, 'You better be ready to marry that son of a bitch if it turns out to be so,' and she cried and carried on and said she didn't want her daughter finding out if she was pregnant hiding in a locked bathroom."

He took another long swallow, and then he set down the can and burped and rubbed his eyes with both palms like it was morning instead of night and he was just waking up. "Susan's got an appointment for Monday morning. I have the whole weekend to wait this thing out, and Mrs. Hellmann won't even let me talk to Susan on the phone. I called there twice tonight and she said, 'I think you've done enough already, Derby' and 'Haven't you done enough already, Derby?' She said my name like she was cursing." Julie was back by then, and Derby asked if we wouldn't mind avoiding the subject for the rest of the night.

Because we were trying so hard to not talk about something, we ended up talking about nothing, and after a half an hour of this, Derby said goodbye. He told me he'd keep in touch but not to expect him at the farm on Monday, and he smiled at Julie and she did her best to smile back.

Although it was perhaps a kind of relief when Derby left, it took Julie and me a while to talk freely again. Before we said anything that meant anything, I remarked how terrible the movie was, and Julie commented how there were sure a lot of unpopped kernels at the bottom of the bag, and she apologized for that, and I for the movie, and then we told each other that things weren't that bad.

"What do you suppose they'll do?" I asked her. She was facing me, her back to the screen, and when I spoke, she leaned back as far as her chair would let her, getting as close to horizontal as possible, like there was sun, like she was tanning. She liked the recliner and I liked the straight–back, so it worked out all right.

"What if it was you and me?" she asked.

This, of course, had crossed my mind, and I guess I figured it had crossed Julie's, but I thought it was beyond either one of us to say, and when she did, it took me by surprise, maybe even struck me like she was breaking confidence or a promise or was being unfair, and I couldn't give an answer, not with words that would've helped either of us, not with words that were true. She sat up, her chair clicking behind her, and I got the feeling she was waiting for me.

"How could it be?" I said finally, and I smiled, trying to turn it into a joke, hoping that she'd smile back or punch my arm, and I thought then it would be dropped because we never argued or pushed each other.

"We don't have problems, do we?" she said. She made sure I looked at her—she wanted me to see she was smiling, I think, and I saw, although it wasn't a smile to put much confidence in—and then, before leaning back, she said again, "Do we?"

Monday morning I pulled into Hardison's. Derby's car wasn't in the driveway.

Hardison, though, was on the porch with a cup of coffee for me, and he said, "Derby called in sick today but said maybe he'd be in by noon." He offered me a cigarette—he always did and I never took one—then he put the pack back in his pocket. "I guess he's leaving room for a miraculous recovery."

"I guess so," I said.

Hardison smiled into his cup. "You might as well start on that stump. Listen, I have to get over to Albany today to see about some things." He said this and shook his head like he had the hard job and I had the easy one. "So you're the boss," he said, and he took his mug with him to his truck.

The ax and the shovel were in the barn where Derby and I had left them Friday, but it took me a while to get around to using them. I studied the stump for a while, trying to decide if Hardison had been at it over the weekend, but I couldn't remember exactly how Derby and I had left it. Eventually, I started picking at it a little with the shovel, but I knew my heart wasn't in it, wouldn't be in anything until I knew what the doctor in Troy would find or not find in Susan. And Julie was also in my mind, not so much Julie, I guess, as what I'd thought we'd begun to understand, maybe for closer to sure this time, about what wasn't and probably wouldn't ever be.

It hit me then how worrying can drain every ounce of energy from you, and I remembered hearing once that just sitting and worrying for a half an hour burns as many calories as running a mile. That thought dropped me down to one knee and I threw the shovel aside and picked a long and shiny green piece of onion grass and stuck it in my mouth and bit into it with my side teeth.

Through all this, part of me must've been considering work because the stump solution just came out of nowhere, just sprang up in the middle of all these other thoughts, and I first got the gasoline out of the barn, then headed to the house for matches.

When you splash gasoline on a gray bug, you can hear it sizzle. The first one I hit was by accident, but as they all came scurrying out of the wood, I couldn't help angling a splash here and there just to hear them. I soaked the wood and dug a narrow trench around the stump so there wouldn't be spreading. Then I threw the match on and the whole thing billowed up in one audible poof and I stepped away fast.

Derby came around the barn so quietly I didn't know he was there until I saw his boot through the wavy, hot air around the flames. We stood like that for a while, just the fire separating us, and although I wanted to ask and he probably wanted to tell me, we let the fire burn itself out before saying anything.

The flames didn't last long. After the fire licked up the gas, it died quickly on the moist wood, barely charring the edges. I picked up the shovel, Derby picked up the ax, and we chipped away at the black parts, but I couldn't help feeling let down, that it wasn't all that I'd planned, that we couldn't get rid of the whole thing that easily. "Nice idea," Derby said, taking a big swing, burying the ax-head a couple inches deep, creaking the wood, splitting its most center, oldest ring like a bull's-eye, "but it looks like there's no getting around it."

I nodded. "Well?" I asked.

"Well," he said, and he shook his head at the stump. "She's not pregnant." He turned to me full then, smiled, and wiped an imaginary sweat bead off his forehead with the back of his hand. "The doctor said sometimes things just get out of sync."

I didn't feel like I thought I would, and I think what I said came out that way. "So now what?"

"So now," he said, "her mom and the doctor put Susan on the pill. Mrs. Hellmann says I can go over there tonight and pick Susan up to take her out just as long as she doesn't have to look at me for a while. I think," he stopped there to consider what would come next, like he had to say it quietly to himself first to make sure it was true. "I think everything's back to all right."

"Good then," I said. "That's good. Happy ending."

He nodded like it was so, and I grabbed the gas can and started toward the barn and wondered why I felt like I did, knowing that all was well, that nothing was up in the air, that nothing was left to wait on.

Crowd Pleasing

I have to be ready to put on the suit. I have to be in the right frame of mind. There are two worlds: inside the suit, outside the suit. I can't forget this.

Like if my car's running badly or my checkbook won't balance or I've had another unresolved night with Justine or there's news of more layoffs at Boeing–how much more can we take?–I have to clear my head, let it go. This involves ten or fifteen minutes of lying on the dressing room bench with my eyes closed, a transition period during which I stop being Ed Osborne and start being the Wichita Wing-Nut. Like Clark Kent in his phone booth, Bruce Wayne in his Bat Cave. It's not just changing clothes, it's changing. You can't climb on top of a dugout in one-hundred degree heat dressed in a thirty-five pound fuzzy purple suit and expect to lead five-thousand Wichitans in the Hokie Pokie–they need it, they're desperate for happiness–if your mind is elsewhere.

I don't have to act like the Wichita Wing-Nut, I have to be the Wichita Wing-Nut.

What the Wing-Nut does before the game begins–for focus, for inspiration, by now he's in the suit and on the field– is scan the seats for a woman in a white tank-top. As he terrorizes the field during pre-game, knocking hats off opposing coaches, kicking dirt and bumping chests with umpires before they've even had a chance to blow a call, he's scoping her out through the eye holes in the suit's neck. When he locates her— a bottle blond with a bottle tan and a hint of a belly behind the backstop, a tiny brunette in cut-offs down the right field line, a statuesque redhead in heels and leopard stretch pants, turning heads as she sips the foam off her beer and climbs higher into the cheap seats—he dedicates the game to her.

When the National Anthem begins, the white tank-top releases the arm of the man next to her and rises. Her date salutes the flag in center field smartly. He's stationed at McConnell Air Force Base, and they met last night at a bar uptown. He walked up to the table where she sat with her girlfriends, looked in her soft brown or green or blue eyes and said, "fighter pilot," like it was a password, and it was. When the anthem's over, they cheer and watch their team, the Wichita Aeros, young men in short haircuts and tight white pants, take the field. Some players don't mind a good luck high five or pat on the ass from the Wing-Nut—those around during last year's championship series, though, avoid him like a curse—and then it's play ball for the defending run-ners-up of the Double-A Central League.

In Wichita's Lawrence-Dumont stadium, the outfield grass is real and all the seats are good and they're all comfortable. You have leg room. For $4 you're close enough to the field to carry on a conversation with an outfielder. Home runs fly over a wall covered pole to pole with advertisements for car dealerships, banks, fast food chains, and lawn care services, the longest ones clear a second fence and land in an empty lot, one or two a season reach the street, but only one has ever reached the Arkansas River. Billy Bingo back in '85. A couple walking along the water that night—perhaps they were kissing and startled by the splash; perhaps it interrupted a pointless but severe argument and saved them—was able to fish the ball out before it floated too far into the sluggish current, and after the game it was presented to Billy in the locker room, where he cried and cried because he was so happy, because he'd hit a ball so far, into a river, and because he'd just received a call from Kansas City telling him to get the hell out of Wichita, to come on up, that the right field job was his to lose.

The Royals, the Aeros' parent club, play in a different world, the major leagues, over 200 miles away. Everyone at a Wichita Aeros game wishes they were in Kansas City, even during seasons when the Aeros are good and the Royals are bad. The Aero players convince themselves they'll be Royals before too long, the Aeros' manager is heartened by rumors that have him slated to eventually take over as KC first base coach, and the Aeros' fans plan their once-a-year weekend trips north. They punch out at LearJet or PepsiCo early Friday afternoon and get on the Turnpike and set the cruise at eighty so they can check into the KC Holiday Inn by six and arrive at the ball park by game time.

At beautiful Kauffmann Stadium they watch instant replays in color on the mammoth scoreboard and stand in awe of long, majestic, center field home runs that splash wonderfully into a man-made, powder-blue waterfall. Their seats are stacked steeply on one another—from where they sit, it feels like they are closer to the sky than to the players—and when they get up, dizzy from heights and happiness, to go to the bathroom or the refreshment stand, they feel something pulling them down, like one misstep and they're done for, and they have to reach out for whomever's nearby, steady themselves, make sure they have their legs. After the game they go out to sports bars and drink bottles of red beer and Zima, take cabs back to the hotel, sleep in late, and return to the stadium just in time to catch the Saturday afternoon game. They hope it will never end—they pray for extra innings—but it always ends, and before they know it they're in their cars and on their way back to Wichita, to where they came from, and the land is so flat and the horizon no mystery and they can see where they're headed the whole way.

Through the early innings of an Aeros game, the Wichita Wing-Nut does what he can, but the seventh inning stretch is when he shines. He suggestively gyrates his pear-shaped torso, claps his mitten paws, and bops his crazed, smiling head to whatever comes over the sound system. First it's always, "Take Me Out to the Ball Game," a tough song to dance to, but then it's Van Halen, Michael Jackson, Garth Brooks, Billy Ray Cyrus. The Wing-Nut moshes, moonwalks, Texas two-steps, Achey-Breakys. A ballpark full of Wichitans goes berserk.

Through the first six and a half innings, the Wing-Nut keeps an eye on the white tank-top, and if he knows she's been watching, if he's kept her interest at all, he makes her a part of the seventh inning stretch show. He runs up to where she's sitting and kisses her, presses his long, furry snout tightly into her neck and wraps his arms around her. He pulls her to her feet and dips her. Her fighter pilot smiles at first and acts like it's OK, no need for alarm, good clean fun, part of the show. But the first hitter in the bottom of the seventh stands in—the Wing-Nut and the white tank-top still cling to each other, no sign of it breaking up any time soon, the white tank-top's eyes are closed, she's smiling, the Wing-Nut's hand softly cradles the side of her egg-shaped head, her soft and straight hair, some fans are beginning to whistle—and the pilot stands and touches the Wing-Nut's arm. The crowd boos. Over the white tank-top's shoulder the Wing-Nut tells the pilot to sit down. The pilot sits. The crowd cheers. To be challenged in public by the smiling and lovable Wichita Wing-Nut is a no-win situation.

I swear when the pilot sits, the white tank-top leans in closer and hugs tighter. She doesn't want to let the Wing-Nut go. She buries her head between the two yellow W's on his chest and squeezes.

Justine tells her friends and co-workers that I'm in advertising. She doesn't know I know this. Not long ago I answered Justine's phone when she was outside checking her mailbox, and the woman on the other end said, "Is this Ed?" and I said, "Yes, hello," and then she asked how the ad business was going. I said terrific.

Justine works as a customer service representative for two long-distance phone companies. Part-time for each. Of course, they don't know about each other. She's ready to quit one as soon as the other takes her on full-time, but so far that hasn't happened. So from 10 to 4 on Monday, Tuesday, and Thursday she tries to get people to switch, and on Wednesday afternoon and over the weekend she tries to get them to switch back. She sees nothing odd or wrong in this. To myself, I compare what she does to if I decided to be both the Wichita Wing-Nut and the Tulsa Red Demon, the Wing-Nut's arch enemy, a sleek, smooth-muscled man in a red leotard and goatee who, whenever the Wing-Nut wasn't looking during the championship series last season, consistently got cheap laughs by spearing the Wing-Nut's ripe grape of an ass with his pitchfork. Before the Wing-Nut could even turn around, the Demon had glided away, smiling slyly, his red, satin cape and evil, arrow-head tail whipping behind him in the wind.

Justine knows nothing about the Red Demon. She's never even been to an Aeros game or seen the Wing-Nut. She thinks he's too important to me—she's gone as far as to suggest counseling—and she believes that if she shows any kind of support or interest, it will only make things worse. She says the Wing-Nut is below me, that I'm selling myself short, that I'm settling for him when I could be so much more.

At first I believed Justine's concerns, however misdirected, were good-hearted and selfless, that her suspicion of the Wing-Nut grew out of her love for me. But I don't think this anymore. I still believe she loves me—she tells me so, quietly, at times she doesn't have to, like in the middle of a movie as she squeezes my hand—but her problem with the Wing-Nut is personal. I think that on the one hand she's jealous of the Wing-Nut, and on the other hand she's embarrassed that she's with a man who makes his living dressing up and clowning around. She's made a commitment to ignore the Wing-Nut. She thinks by doing this maybe he'll go away.

I've tried many times to explain to Justine how important the Wing-Nut is, not just to me or to the Aeros, but to Wichita. He's something we have that no one else has. When he Twists with a toddler or fills the umpire's hat with dirt or shares an embrace with a beautiful woman, he's doing it for the whole city. Pizza Hut and Coleman are gone—we imagined them rolling their eyes and letting out sighs of relief as they passed out their pink slips and packed their moving vans—but the Wing-Nut remains. Justine thinks the Wing-Nut is demeaning and silly, but he's not. He's crucial. He's hope.

During the pennant stretch last season, Justine wanted me to skip a game because her parents were up from Florida. She wanted the four of us to go to dinner. I told her I couldn't, that every game mattered this time of year, and I offered to go out the next night, but she told me it was now or never. We'd been dating for six months, and I hadn't met them yet, and Justine was using the situation as a test. We argued over the phone. She said, "Here's a newsflash. Most fans wouldn't even notice if the Wing-Nut retired. They're at the park to watch baseball, not some moron in a Muppet suit."

"Now I'm a moron," I said. "Thanks for that." Before I said anything else, I pressed the phone into my shoulder and took a deep breath because I didn't want to yell or make things worse. "Listen, Justine. I know you're angry, but you're wrong. People would notice. Maybe not right away, but after the first couple innings they would sense that something was missing, and then it would hit them, and they'd say to each other, 'Where is he?' It wouldn't settle with them." I was trying to make her see. "They would know they lost something. People know when they've lost something."

"I'm sorry for calling you a moron," she said, and then she hung up. We didn't talk again for two weeks.

We haven't discussed the Wing-Nut since, but that doesn't mean anything's been settled. Not talking about it has maybe even made it worse. Justine hasn't yet offered an ultimatum, but I know it won't be long before I have to choose between her and the Wing-Nut.

It's not just the Wing-Nut that stands between us, though. There are other things that together we are unsure of. When Justine leaves my apartment at the end of an evening or when I leave hers, the door closes and I feel something inside me release, like a balloon deflating, and I slump into my couch or behind the wheel of my car and breathe for what feels like the first time in hours. This isn't always how it is, but it happens.

Sometimes I think that being the Wing-Nut and running around a hot, heavy-aired ball park for four hours inside a cramped suit is easier than being me, is easier than sharing a night with Justine. I don't know why. I don't know if it's me or her.

This I sometimes think of doing to help get to the bottom of things: Send the Wing-Nut to Justine's for a night. Shed the head and neck assembly to eat and drink if she's prepared dinner or bought a bottle of wine, but put it back on right after and see how things progress. If things are slow, the Wing-Nut can go through a couple of his routines.

When she starts to clear the table, he puts her in a head-lock and gives her a noogie. When she's at the sink washing dishes, he sneaks up behind her, pulls her sweat pants down, and runs. When they're sitting in the living room, he gives her five, then when she tries to give five back—would she even try?—he takes his paw away at the last second, points at her, shakes his belly in silent laughter, and struts around the room like he's pulled off something big.

For the finale, he finds something to use as a bat, like an umbrella, and goes through his Babe Ruth impersonation: He steps out of the box, takes a long look to left field and slowly points in that direction, knocks the mud out of his cleats, digs in, and takes the first pitch downtown, right to where he pointed, watches it go, head tilted, hand shielding his eyes like he's watching a 747, rounds the bases with one hand in the air—the end table's first, the recliner's second, the closet's third, the couch is home—slides headfirst into home—she's sitting on home—lands on her, turns over on his back, his head now in her lap, and looks up to see how things are going.

How she reacts will mean a lot. If only she'd look deeply into his rolling bugged eyes and smile, spread her arms like wings and call him safe.

Rain is a mascot's most serious challenge. A cloudburst empties the stands like nothing else, but in a way it separates the sheep from the goats, those who love the game from those who just like to drink expensive beer in crowds. Still, even the most lion-hearted baseball fans come to be entertained, and when bad weather interrupts an Aeros game, it's up to the Wing-Nut.

If the tarp's on the field, the Wing-Nut gets a lot of mileage out of simply running across its slippery surface as fast as he can and then collapsing into a headfirst slide. From third base, he's been known to glide more than halfway home on one bellyflop. He's not the clean-up hitter in the bottom of the ninth standing in with the bases loaded, but what he does has its place. He gives it all he has. He gets Wichitans to cheer in the rain.

Mascots usually don't make road trips, but for the championship series last September, both the Wing-Nut and the Red Demon worked every game in both cities, enduring the four-hour bus rides with their respective teams.

It showered in the middle of the seventh and deciding game in Tulsa. The teams had played to a tie through five full innings and the sky was clear in every direction except straight up, so no one was going anywhere. Players waited out the rain on dugout steps, punched their gloves and pine-tarred their bats. Fans stoically raised their umbrellas, pulled on the hoods of their windbreakers.

The Wing-Nut was doing his Gene Kelly dancing in the rain number on the roof of the visitor's dugout when he was hit in the middle of the back by a baseball. He spun and looked down on the field, and the Red Demon looked back, wielding a bat, beckoning to the Wing-Nut with one hooked finger.

Fans smiled and leaned forward in their wet seats. The Wing-Nut tried to decline the invitation without losing face by aiming his rear end in the Demon's direction, shaking it derisively, and going back to his soft shoe number, but the crowd would have none of it. They booed him until he jumped onto the field, and then they cheered.

The Wing-Nut batted first. He knew he had no chance, but it was what the fans wanted, and even on the road it was all for them. The bat was slippery from the rain and hard to hold in his fingerless, furry hands, and it was impossible to get a good foothold on the wet tarp with his huge, nylon-bottomed feet, but he dug in best he could, waggled his bat and substantial hips menacingly.

The Demon kicked his red leg high and pumped in an assortment of ungodly fast balls and sliders, deceptive change-ups, treacherous fork balls. After each pitch he smiled, twisted both ends of his waxed moustache, raised his shiny black eyebrows, unabashedly adjusted himself in his leotard.

A Tulsa bat boy served as catcher and laughed maniacally along with the crowd as the Wing-Nut missed pitch after pitch. He swung too late, too early, too low, too high. The Wing-Nut's ninth and final swing, at a tempting, too-good-to-be-true, underhand, backspinning, high-arcing floater, was so hard that he stumbled and fell into a puddle. Behind him the ball landed perfectly, softly, in the hysterical bat boy's mitt. The crowd stood in the rain and cheered. The Demon raised his arms. He threw kisses to every corner of the ball park.

They switched. The Wing-Nut toed the rubber and glared past the Demon for the sign. Fast ball. He reared back and let fly.

The Demon cocked his bat, lifted his front leg smartly, and with an effortless-looking swing drove the ball high and long over the left field wall into the bullpen. The stadium erupted. The Demon twirled the bat like a baton all the way to first base, from first to second he rode it like a horse, from second to third he did cartwheels, from third to home he was carried on the shoulders of two drunk, shirtless Tulsa fans

who'd spilled from the stands in a frenzy while stadium security staff laughed and applauded. "We Are the Champions"
came over the sound system. The clouds parted. The sun
broke through.

In the bottom of the ninth, score still tied with the bases
empty and two out, Tulsa's nineteen year-old, first round pick
center fielder, with a swing as sweet as heaven, lost a hanging
curve ball in the darkness over the right field fence.

The Red Demon stood on top of the Tulsa dugout and
looked down with satisfaction on the celebration. He spotted
the Wing-Nut across the field and to the delight of the crowd
took his pointed tail in his hands, hoisted it onto his shoulder
like a bazooka, and fired.

This season the Aeros won't be playing in the championship. Most of the best players from last year are now in
Omaha, Triple-A ball. A couple are in Kansas City. This
year's Aeros aren't bad, but they're not good.

So the Wing-Nut's season will be over by Labor Day
weekend, and Justine wants to take time off from her jobs and
go to Vegas. She wants me to go with her. She knows I can
because I usually take a week or two before starting my off-
season job at the mall. Every August a college kid heads back
to school, and I take his or her place ripping movie tickets at
Cinema 6, folding jeans at The Gap, or running the blender
behind the Orange Julius counter.

I know how I answer Justine will matter longer than the
time we're in Vegas together or longer than the time she's
there alone because it's not a question of whether or not I feel
like taking a trip, it's a question of us being together. She's
right in asking.

We're on her couch when Vegas comes up, and I say I'll
get back to her. I run my finger all the way down her arm
when I say this, from her shoulder to her wrist, and she shivers, and she doesn't look at me. Then I ask her a question.
This way the whole weight of the thing isn't on me. Would

she go to the last home game of the season next week? See what the Wing-Nut's all about? Give him a chance? The first hundred fans get a Taco Bell watch band, so what does she have to lose?

She says she'll get back to me. Maybe, maybe not. Things are left up in the air. So I have to go home because we're both getting back to each other. You can't stay with someone after that's been established. You have to leave so you can get back.

The Aeros' last game is against Tulsa, who have already locked up a spot in the playoffs. Rumor is, the Red Demon is making the trip even though there's nothing at stake.

It's hot, but the fans are all right. They press cool beers against their necks and remind each other they're at the last game of the season, and this, in a way, is sadly satisfying, like the end of summer. There will be no playoffs this year, but the boys played hard and enough good happened to hold most Wichitans over until next spring. It's Saturday evening and they're where they want to be, watching baseball under a clear sky, and things could be a lot worse. In KC there are thunderstorms–the tarp is on the field, there's no mascot–and in the paper there's talk of the Royals sending their best pitcher to New York for nothing but money.

Season finales are tough for the Wing-Nut. He wants to finish strong, give the fans and himself something to hold onto during the long, windy, brown-grassed winter, but at the same time he's tired. Sixty-five games. Over five-hundred innings. He wants it over. He wants it never to end. To do the Funky Chicken in this state of mind is emotionally draining.

It doesn't help that the Tulsa Red Demon is here, that he has a new suit, brighter than last year's, complete with red, high-top cross-trainers. He's faster and looks like he's been working out. His chest and arms are broader, his neck thicker, his moustache shinier.

Before the game the Wing-Nut surveys the seats for the white tank-top–he knows he needs her today–and spots her behind first base. She stands and waves. He can't believe it. She came. It's her.

Suddenly the Red Demon appears in the aisle next to the white tank top's seat. He watches her wave and follows her eyes down to the field, and when he sees the Wing-Nut looking back, he raises his eyebrows and smiles. He gestures to the white tank-top and nods, licks his top lip, gives the Wing-Nut a thumbs-up—the thumb is long and thin, the nail is painted glossy red and glints like glass in the stadium lights—and then turns back to the white tank-top and says something.

When the white tank-top turns and sees the Demon for the first time, she eases into her seat—the Wing-Nut thinks he sees her catch her breath—and the Demon moves in closer. Looking only at her, he slides his hand onto the back of her seat, and out of nowhere—was it up his sleeve?—he produces a red carnation and slips it gracefully behind her ear. Nearby, a little girl in pig-tails and a sunflower t-shirt—she's lived in Wichita all her life and has never seen magic so up close—opens her mouth and claps.

When the white tank-top blushes and reaches for the flower, the Demon takes her hand, brings it briefly to his lips, and then spins away back into the aisle and down the steps to the field. The white tank-top is left to shift in her seat, cross her legs and smell her flower, and then, as if remembering her purpose, she smiles down at the Wing-Nut, runs her fingers through her hair, and shrugs.

The Wing-Nut stands in the middle of the field by second base attempting to formulate a plan—it's come clear that today he must be better than he's ever been, there's no tomorrow—when he gets his head knocked off. A perfectly executed flying body block from behind. From the ground—he's writhing in the dirt, sucking dust—the Wing-Nut sees the Red Demon scoop up his head without breaking stride, hold it in outstretched arms, look into its ludicrous eyes, bite the end of its bouncing snout, and laugh. The Demon then raises the head high like a trophy and takes laps around the stadium.

The fans who notice—most of the crowd is still filing in—

boo at first, at the dirty play, at the cheap shot, at all that is vicious and unfair, but the Red Demon keeps running—it seems as if he'll never stop—and the crowd's boos begin to turn to smiles, then chuckles, then reserved and reluctant cheers, like the circling Demon is slowly sucking applause out of them, like they can't help it, like they're caught in a whirlpool. They realize cheering for the Demon is the same as forgetting and forsaking the Wing-Nut—this hurts a little, especially as they watch him, beheaded and wincing, struggle slowly to his feet—but they also know themselves well enough to admit they love laughter more than loyalty—they get so few opportunities—and deep down in their souls they know happiness is more cherished than a true heart.

The cheers become deafening and the Wing-Nut doesn't know where to turn. The white tank-top—the Wing-Nut still can't believe it's her—is standing with the rest of the crowd. Her flower is tucked under her arm and her hands are cupped around her mouth and she's screaming. The Wing-Nut wishes he could hear what she's saying.

Out of the corner of his eye, the Wing-Nut sees a flash of red, and with a sudden burst of anger he surges across the field to cut off the Demon. The crowd sees what's coming and cheers even louder. They're happy and hopeful; maybe tonight something will be settled once and for all, something they need to know, and maybe after the game they'll be able to drive past the bars and go straight home and sleep well. But the Demon sees the Wing-Nut in time and escapes up over the third base railing and into the seats.

The Wing-Nut follows. His face is as purple as his body. His teeth are clenched. He has trouble pulling himself up and over the railing—he's almost made it when his foot gets stuck—but two fans help him, two capped, tan-armed wheat farmers who've come to the city to see some good country hardball and to cheer for the underdog, to pull him up by his purple padded elbows if need be, to pound him on his back and get him turned in the right direction, toward the smiling Red Demon who hasn't taken advantage of the delay, who's stopped running like a good sport and waits just a few yards ahead until the Wing-Nut is ready to continue.

The chase starts up again and the fans love it. Their cheering is rhythmic and unified and they're using their whole bodies. They can't wait to see how it ends.

The Wing-Nut follows the Demon through the seats behind home plate and then around toward first base. It is there where the Demon stops and turns, right in front of the white tank-top. He gently places the Wing-Nut's head in her hands, and she smiles shyly and mouths thank you, like she's accepting a gift. The crowd has never been louder.

The Wing-Nut's almost there, he's closing in, when he trips over something, a fan's outstretched leg, his own wide, purple feet, he doesn't know for sure. He lands flat out on his padded belly, hands stretched above his head like he's diving back to first to beat a pick-off. He gasps for air and tastes blood–he's bitten his tongue–and above him, all around him, are laughing umpires calling him safe, pounding his back.

With some help the Wing-Nut rolls over onto his back–his torso is sticky with spilled soda and beer, covered with popcorn, peanut shells, warm gum–and he slowly sits up. He stares achingly into bright stadium lights, head pounding–no crowd anywhere has ever been louder, no crowd has ever cried out as desperately for something they were not sure of–and sees the white tank-top stretched across the red leotard lap, her neck curving gracefully to meet the Red Demon mouth, her fingers stroking tenderly the Red Demon heart.

Stumps

rs. Kaiser, our next door neighbor, butchered chickens on her clothesline. She hung them by their necks until their flapping and flailing stopped, and then snipped off their heads with garden shears and strung them by their feet to bleed dry in the grass. Later she heaped them into an old laundry basket and took them into her house, and I imagined her folding them neatly and placing them into drawers.

She did a dozen birds at a time and sold them, along with green beans, squash, and rhubarb, at our town's weekend farmer's market. The chickens she slaughtered in winter, when the market was closed, she piled in her freezer. Although my father disapproved of her butchering method, he was impressed with a widow going on seventy-five spry and determined enough to pull it off. She would've butchered the chickens properly, she told him, but her sight was failing, and she was afraid she'd hurt herself. "At my age, I have no business swinging anything any more," she said, "let alone a hatchet."

When my father offered to do the butchering for her, she refused at first, saying he had enough to take care of putting food on the table for his family, but she seemed grateful despite her protests, and when he insisted, she agreed. He said he'd do it for nothing, of course, but she wore him down until he agreed to take a bird for payment. They shook on it. Then she smiled and offered her hand to me which I took tentatively, frightened that I'd squeeze her bony fingers to dust.

I was young when my father began killing Mrs. Kaiser's chickens–too young, he said, to wield anything with an edge on it. I watched him, though. He'd butchered while growing up on his grandfather's farm, and he was quick and accurate. With the compact arc of his arm, he brought the hatchet down on the neck while the bird was still alive. "A strangled chicken," he told me, "isn't fit for soup."

Most of the chickens my father killed died meekly–after cleaving the bird, he'd brush the head away with the hatchet, and with his free hand hold the thrashing body on the block for a few seconds until it stilled–but occasionally a bird showed extra grit and endurance in fighting death to the end, to even beyond the end, by wriggling free from my father's grip and making one last frantic, horribly blind run around the yard, blood spraying from its stump like water from a garden hose. Before each round of butchering, I'd study the inhabitants of the coop to try to pick a runner even though I mostly believed what my father told me, that it wasn't anything special about the bird, but simply the luck of the hatchet, the right nerves spared by chance.

My job was to clean up afterwards. I manned the shovel, scooped the heads, carried them to the edge of woods, and flung them as far as I could into the trees for the raccoons and possums, but my aspiration was to swing the hatchet.

I was convinced it was a matter of maturity, or at least physical strength, and I schemed of ways to show my father I was up to the job. For days before a butchering, I'd do chores at what I considered superhuman speed, and when I thought he was within earshot, I whistled to show him what work meant to me. Whenever I asked him about butchering, though, regardless of how dedicated or cheerful I'd been, the

answer was always, "Not yet." Once he added sharply,
"You'll be the first to know. Don't ask any more."

Soon after that, I snatched the hatchet down off its nail in
the barn, took a couple practice swings through the air to get
a feel, and chopped the handle off my Louisville Slugger. I
held it on the floor like it was a chicken and hammered until
it splintered. This didn't make me feel better—I couldn't
believe how many swings it took me; each one disheartened
me more—and I had to lie to my father later by saying I'd forgotten the bat at the field where my friends and I played. "I
went back for it an hour later, but it was gone," I said.

"That's too bad," he said. "It was a nice one."

It was nearly two years later that I finally stood squinting
over a chicken, hatchet in my twelve-year old hand, on a
bright, harsh January morning. My father had gone through
all the chickens but one after he'd told me to watch him carefully, and I'd watched him, with concentration and anticipa-
tion. Now the sun bounced its rays off the snow so there was
nowhere to look to avoid it, and I had to keep wiping my
eyes with my coat sleeve so the tears wouldn't freeze on my
eyelashes.

My father stood next to me, calmly barking reminders
between even, frosty breaths. "It's a new, sharp edge, so just
swing nice and clean. You don't have to put it through the
block. Hold the body down firmly on the wood, look at the
neck, and swing where you're looking."

I nodded and grabbed my victim with confidence. I felt
useful in a way I hadn't before, and I sensed my father saw
me newly as he watched me focus and situate my hand on the
bird. "Good," he said, and pulled the brim of his hunter's cap
down to shield his eyes. "Now hit him."

My next action was a blur of light and feathers and
blood. On the downswing, white spots danced in front of my
eyes, and the bird squirmed under my hand. The hatchet
came down with good weight, smoothly and powerfully, and
stuck in the block like when my father swung it. The bird, a
runner, took off clumsily toward Mrs. Kaiser's house, and I

swept away the head. Only after hearing my father's yell did
I realize I'd also brushed away more than half of my index
finger. Only then did I feel it gone.

Moments later, in her kitchen, a white-faced Mrs. Kaiser
kept asking, "What happened? What happened?" as she dish-
towel wrapped my hand and thrust it, pulsing numb, into a
Wonder Bread bag filled with snow, but I couldn't answer her.
All I could do was watch out the window as my father went
through the pile of heads and found my finger, pointing like a
compass needle, in the direction of the slumped, headless bird
that stained the snow purple in the middle of the yard.

During the half-hour ride to the hospital in Erie, my finger
set between my father and me on the bench seat, chilling in a
snow filled bread bag identical to the one I held in my lap.
Neither of us said much. Once I looked at him, and he shook
his head at the windshield and said, "I knew it," and pounded
the steering wheel. After that I looked out my window and
concentrated on not crying.

The doctor couldn't do much with the finger. He told us
he could try to sew it back on if that's what we wanted, but
it would cost us, and even then it would never move or
bend like before. "It would probably turn out to be more of
a hindrance than anything else," he said to my father. "It's
off his left hand, so it's not going to ruin his curve ball."
Then he chuckled and punched my shoulder lightly, and I
felt like asking if that was his best shot, but I just nodded
and smiled weakly.

My dad said, "So be it."

None of us considered Felice Stevens–in all fairness, how
could we have?–who, under a lemon wedge of a moon,
would reach nervously for my left hand after the Sophomore
Dance four years later, only to find that we couldn't interlock
fingers, not all of our fingers, in a man and woman way. I
tried to get her to switch sides, but by then the mood was broken, and the moon was under a cloud, and she knew I wasn't
whole, and when you get to that point, it's too late. The next
year she went to the Junior Prom with Tony Debella, and

after the last slow dance, I watched them walk hand in hand out past the football field to the equipment shed, and I imagined the negotiations of their bodies among the mesh ball bags, yellow pinnies, and tackling dummies.

It wasn't until we were almost home from the hospital that I wondered what had happened to my finger. I didn't think the doctor had slipped it to my father, and I knew I didn't have it.

"Dad, you don't have my finger, do you?"

"I'm sure I don't," he said.

I looked at his hands wrapped around the steering wheel, and then I looked at my own. I held them away from me as I'd seen women do checking to see if their polish was dry. "Where is it?"

"What?"

"My finger."

"I don't know. Back at the hospital." He looked away from the road for a moment and saw me inspecting my outstretched hand. "Why?"

"Just wondering what they're going to do with it." And then I wanted to tell him we should go back for it–that it was my finger, and I had a right to it–and I felt a surge of disappointment, even anger, that he'd let them keep it. He'd given me a job–a job I'd wanted and begged for, sure, but it was a job–and despite the accident I'd done it. My bird was as dead as the ones he'd finished off. Even with the sun in my eyes, half-blind, I'd gone ahead and swung and brought the hatchet down. I wanted my finger even if all I could do was keep it in a box on top of my dresser.

I didn't suggest we turn around. A few days later my father told me the pills the doctor gave me weren't aspirin and that he was supposed to keep an eye on me to make sure I didn't have a reaction. He also said the doctor told him that his son was one tough son-of-a-bitch, not even crying in a situation where a lot of grown men would've passed out or whimpered like babies. He patted my back. I asked then if I could try again, and I told him about the sun, but he just breathed out through pinched lips and said to give it a while.

I never got another chance. I still watched him—he did it for a few more years before Mrs. Kaiser died and her nephew razed the coop—but I didn't ask to help. I watched from farther back, too—over the years I'd crept up until I was practically on top of the block—but I was still there every time sitting on the snow drift, watching the steam rise from the severed heads when they hit the snow, waiting for the fighters who held on a little longer than the others.

I'd sit and watch and wait for him to miss, for the sun to pulse a blaze into his eye so he'd swing down through his own bone and scream. I'd then come down off the drift and throw his finger far into the trees and say, "It's all right. A man doesn't have to fill a glove to be a man," and then I'd stop his blood, taking his hand tightly in mine, and we would know each other.

Parables

Joe

There's a steep four-foot drop at the edge of my backyard where I stop mowing. Down the bank and
stretching two-hundred yards to Black Rock Creek is a
hayfield that used to belong to my neighbor, Russell Cropsey.
Until he died two weeks ago, Russell lived across the street
from me, surrounded by rusty guts of old cars, in a gray, two-
story home that creaks in the wind like it's pulling apart from
itself. Now that it's empty it's even louder. It wakes me.

Russell was a mechanic who spent his spare time drinking
and meditating on how he'd been wronged. He did not need
or use his field for any practical purpose–I never even saw
him walking it–but a year ago, just after I'd moved to
Chatham after doing twenty years at Coxsackie State Prison,
Russell made a point of knocking on my door to ask if I
fished. When I said that I used to, he told me I should feel
free to drop a line in the creek whenever I wanted. He said I
could do this even if what he'd heard was true, that I was a
friend of Rev. Wade's, because he wasn't looking to drag others into what was between Wade and himself. Besides knowing of my connection with Wade, he also knew my name was

Joe without me saying, but he didn't let on whether or not he knew I was fresh from prison. I only shook his hand and thanked him for his offer, told him I'd probably take him up on it.

I rent my house from Union Gospel Church. Wade's parsonage flanks the church on the east side, and I live on the west side. My house originally belonged to Russell's aunt, who left it to her church instead of her nephew because she disapproved of his drinking. She didn't leave Russell empty-handed—she willed him his house and the field—but in the mornings when he looked out his bedroom window, and in the evenings when he sat on his porch with a drink in his hand, it was my house he saw standing between him and his field, and I imagine he felt interrupted and incomplete. These feelings sometimes turned into anger. I might've felt the same in his place. I know what it is to be divided and what that can lead to. Because of this I sympathized with Russell, at least in my heart, even though I knew liquor sometimes made him mean. Even though he had a sincere hate for Wade.

It's been hot and dry lately, getting on towards August. It won't be long before Russell's nephew spends a Saturday afternoon in the field his uncle left him, circling with tractor and mower, slowly closing in on the middle until all that's left is a final strip he can get with one straight swipe. But now the field is tall enough so that it's even with my close-cropped lawn at the top of the bank. At dusk, from my kitchen window, it looks like level ground stretches from my back door all the way to the creek, like the grass would reach no higher than the tops of my boots, like it wouldn't take any faith at all to walk the whole way without missing a step.

When I've done my dinner dishes, I ring the washrag out and drape it over the faucet. I flip off the light and pray at the window, in the same breaths offering thanks and repentance because I'm not sure which it should be. When I open my eyes, dark gray outlines of rabbits move from the lettuce row in my garden to the bank where they take long, fading leaps into darkness, disappearing, as if swallowed by earth.

Wade

I was still in seminary when I first met Joe. I didn't yet have a church, but I wanted to minister, put to practice in the real world what I was learning in school, so I volunteered my time to serve as chaplain at Coxsackie State Prison.

I was young then, just beginning to work out my faith–twenty-one years later and I'm still not finished–and I wished to test it and to test God, to see Him move in clear and unmistakable ways through me. I thought a prison would be a good place for this to happen.

I led prayer meetings there twice a week, and on one of those nights Joe walked in and sat in the back. He told me later that he was there for one reason: he was considering the worthlessness of his life and trying to summon up the courage to end it. He wanted to ask someone who'd know what happens to the soul of a suicide. He'd heard hell, but was close to deciding that hell didn't scare him any more than living did.

That night, and every night in those meetings, I talked about how God wanted to restore to Himself the men sitting in that room. I tried to look each of them in the face, one at a time. "No matter what you've done to get in here, even if you've done worse things that you haven't been convicted of, God's power to forgive is sufficient. He'll take your sin away so that nothing separates you from Him. He'll make you new."

The inmates weren't allowed to talk to me individually right after meetings, but the guards always passed around a list to get names of men who wanted visits later in the week. Joe got his name on the list, and for three days, while I sat in lecture halls taking notes on the minor prophets and trying to learn Hebrew and Greek, he thought about what he'd heard.

When we finally met in the prison's visitors' room, surrounded by tables of blank-faced women, a few restless children, and silent men, he told me he'd never before thought of his sins–running around on his wife, Lydia, hitting her sometimes, killing her lover, George Regan–as separate from himself. He rarely looked up from the table and kept his hands still and folded in front of him. When I told him that God wanted to help him bury his sins and move on, he shook his head slowly and looked me in the face for the first time. "I believe that, Pastor. But when they're gone—with somebody like me, I wonder—what's left? Maybe sin is all I am."

"A new man takes the old man's place," I said. "You'll die, but then you'll be reborn."

Joe ran his hands roughly through his hair and smiled faintly. "Like suicide then," he said. "That's what I've been thinking lately, Pastor. Better if I was dead."

"Not like suicide at all," I said. "This death results in life."

I stayed with Joe as long as I was allowed. When the guard told us we had five more minutes, I asked Joe if he wanted to pray. At first he was hesitant, embarrassed, but then he looked around the room and realized no one was paying any attention. When we were finished, he raised his head, breathed deeply, and leaned back in his chair. He nodded to me and told the guard he was ready to go.

I'd prayed with many men like Joe in that same room, and after the first few, I'd become skeptical. Prison is a desperate place, and men are willing to try anything to ease the pain they feel, even a relationship with a God they might not wholly trust or even believe in. Salvation is an ongoing process, a life-long commitment, and many of the men who wept into their hands across the table from me I never saw again. The emotion and drama wears off in a matter of days, and they realize that although they've had a spiritual experience, physically they're still in jail, and those who thought getting in good with God might mean a miracle, like an angel coming in the night to spring them or the walls falling down like Jericho, begin asking themselves what's in it for them. They're back to themselves within weeks. Lost.

Joe was different. He requested a few follow-up visits, and eventually we set up a regular weekly meeting. I completed seminary in another couple years and started pastoring the church in Chatham, but I continued to see Joe when I could over the twenty years he was in Coxsackie, and when I was unable to visit, we wrote letters.

Joe stayed strong over the years. He devoured the devotional books I gave him and with my help read through the Bible ten times. His twentieth year in prison he was scheduled for a parole hearing, his second, and like I'd done before the other one, I volunteered to speak to the board on his behalf. Minutes before I addressed them, Joe and I prayed together in the hall outside the hearing room, in front of a silent guard and Joe's state-appointed lawyer, a tall, thin man with a huge wristwatch and patchy beard.

Just before we entered the hearing room, Joe's lawyer reminded Joe that the board would want to hear him say he was sorry for killing George Regan, and when the time came, Joe said it and meant it, but he wasn't emotional or dramatic. The lawyer said a cracking voice or tears might help, that if the board could see some physical evidence of something like regret, it might move them. Joe looked at me and then told his lawyer in an even voice that if tears came, fine, but he wasn't going to force them out, he wasn't going to stage weeping about something he'd wept about genuinely for twenty years, in his bunk at night, silently, even after he knew he was forgiven.

On the drive to Coxsackie that morning, I'd been wrestling with my conscience, thinking about the man Joe had murdered and asking myself if I was sure of Joe's faith. The answer he gave his lawyer eased my mind, convinced me that I was doing the right thing.

I delivered a sermon to the board. *The Joe Cooper who sits before you today is not the same man who came to this prison twenty years ago. He's a new creature, a repentant child of God who resists evil and embraces good. I've known Joe for twenty years, he's my friend, and I've never seen more change in a man than I've seen in him. God's forgiven Joe and has mercifully released him from the shackles of guilt and sin, and I pray you'll do the same in a physical sense. Not because he's innocent, but because he's new, so he can live out the rest of his life as an example to the world of God's redeeming and transforming power, of His unfathomable grace and mercy.*

As Joe and his lawyer and I waited in the hall for word of the board's recommendation, I thought about how doubting Joe at that point, after God had brought him so far, wouldn't be much different than doubting God Himself, and I was reminded of the Pharisees in the New Testament, who for generations prayed fervently for a miracle, a savior, but then doubted blindly when their prayers were answered. I remembered this again recently when I learned of Russell Cropsey's death, when for a brief period I again struggled with doubting Joe. Ashamed, I prayed for forgiveness and then called Joe to go fishing.

Joe doesn't speak well in front of people–his head dips; his voice is quiet–and his lawyer talked for less than a minute, said that Joe was fully rehabilitated, a success of the system. I believe what God said through me had a lot to do with Joe's release, and when Joe and I learned of the board's decision and smiled at each other, not sure what to say, I remembered myself twenty years before, just beginning to work at the prison, charging God in my youthful brashness and zeal to work through me in changing men's lives in miraculous ways.

I met Joe on the free side of the gates the morning he was released from Coxsackie. I'd set up a job for him and a place to live in Chatham, next door to my church, and I'd arranged it so I could serve as his parole sponsor. I told him all this within the first five minutes of his freedom, on our walk to the parking lot. "God's been doing great things for you, Joe. He's been moving in wonderful and mysterious ways."

Joe

It seems like long ago, and it was, me standing on my own front porch, shooting George Regan out of spite and jealousy for loving my wife, Lydia.

Lydia and I weren't living together at the time. We'd been separated for a month. She and George might've been seeing each other even before that. I don't know. If they were, it wasn't because Lydia didn't love me any more. It was because she was angry with me like I was angry with her, because marriage wasn't what we'd thought. We weren't living up to each other's expectations, and our days were too much about groceries and late bills and laundry. After a year we began to question if we'd made a mistake. I admit I drank too much and had women during our separation and lied about them, but Lydia and George set up living together like husband and wife in the house I was paying on. When I found out it burned in my chest so that I couldn't hold down food.

I was sober when I called the house one night from the motel room where I'd been staying. I called my own home to ask my wife if what I'd heard was true, that she'd taken up with a lazy, unskilled carpenter, a bald man with a big stomach who had a reputation in bars for borrowing cigarettes and dollar bills. George answered the phone like it was his right, like he was claiming all that was mine by picking up the receiver. I could hear Lydia clanging pots in the background, making him dinner.

I hung up without saying anything. I drove to the house and rang the doorbell. It was snowing, large, wet flakes, and I was shaking, warm and cool at the same time, and when George opened the door and saw the .38 in my hand, he fell back and his arms went out and his eyes and mouth melted into a look of pleading. He said, "Joe."

I shot him in the face. I heard Lydia scream, but I didn't see her. I drove back to my motel room and waited. Sitting by the window, I imagined her pulling up in a cab, coming to the door and crying for us to go somewhere far away together, maybe Mexico or Alaska. Somewhere we could change our names and begin again now that we knew the things not to do.

It began to snow harder as the police cars slid into the parking lot. I moved to the door and opened it. In the flashing lights I watched flakes stick to tree branches and parked cars. I never saw Lydia.

Twenty-one years later, on the morning Russell Cropsey died in my hands–twenty of those years I'd spent in prison–I recognized the hate that was in Russell as the same that had stirred in me when I killed George Regan. I recognized what was growing in Russell like you do an old enemy. You know it's them even if they're grayer or heavier. Even if you're someone else now.

I know that only the Lord can look on the heart, see it truly and clearly for what it is, but for a brief moment that morning Russell died, God allowed me to see Russell like He saw Russell. The scales fell from my eyes like they fell from the Apostle Paul's, and I saw the darkness and felt the lead-heavy weight of an unredeemed human soul. I was moved through God to act as God, Who beyond our understanding offers mercy to some, justice to others.

I realize that if God hadn't reached down and strengthened me that morning, Russell might still be alive and Wade might be dead.

Looking back, not only to two weeks ago when it was Russell and me in his kitchen with the morning sunlight slanting through the window like a sign, but also to George Regan and me on my porch, to Wade and me praying at a table in Coxsackie's visitors' room, I realize that my life has been a constant testimony to how God can work through all things for His good, to how His plans reach far beyond one man's understanding in that they're always complete enough to protect His own. God chooses His vehicles according to His own good and divine purposes. He called me like He called Moses and Abraham, but also like He called Cain and the Pharaoh of Egypt and Judas and Barabbas, who even through their sin were used to fulfill His will and make it real. Even though they themselves were sacrificed.

I have to remember these things. Over the last fourteen days I've prayed for peace of mind. For a while I was comforted by remembering my first day out of prison, the car ride to Chatham with Wade. We talked a lot about Lydia. Even after twenty years the first thing I wanted to do when I was free was find her, if for no other reason than to ask her to forgive me, to tell her how I'd changed. Wade calmed me down.

He helped me realize I had to let go of her. He said that through no fault of her own she was part of my old life. There was no looking back. He talked about the man in Matthew who tells Jesus that he wants to follow, but then asks if he first can go back to his home and say goodbye to his family. Jesus answers by saying that no one who puts his hand to the plow and looks back is fit for service in His kingdom. I don't think about Lydia as much anymore. When I do, I just see her not doing anything. I just picture her. Then I go back to this passage for strength.

Since the board's decision a few days before I was released, I'd thought constantly about being in the world again and tried to imagine how it would hit me. I wondered if I'd be able to take in as much as I wanted. But as Wade and I drove toward Chatham with the windows down, passing trees and birds and cows and other cars—models of cars I'd never seen except in magazines, and some had women in them—I could only think of what Wade had done for me, what God had made possible. Twenty minutes into the trip I asked if we could pull over.

After Wade steered us onto the shoulder and turned the car off, I walked twenty or thirty feet down the highway embankment, into a patch of thick, shiny-leafed bushes and healthy trees. They were mostly maple, a couple birch. I was out of Wade's sight but he trusted me. I sat at the base of the biggest tree and spoke out loud. Mostly it was thanks, but I also brought up killing George Regan twenty years before and how I'd wronged Lydia. Even though I knew it all was in the past and had taken to heart what Wade had said about not looking back, I repented one more time because I felt the need to take stock of where I'd been and where I was. I wanted to have a time, a specific instance, that I could look back on later and recognize as a new beginning. With a stick I loosened three large flat rocks from the dirt and balanced them on top of one another. I stood over them for a few minutes before going back to the car. I stepped away from them, then moved close, then closer, watched them move down my shadow, from my head to my heart to my feet.

Wade

While Joe was still in prison, I would sometimes mention to him the problems I was having with Russell Cropsey, my neighbor and the son of a woman in my church. On several occasions, Joe and I even prayed for Russell.

I met Russell through his aunt, Ginny Cropsey, who'd raised him after both his parents died young. Soon after I started pastoring at Union Gospel, Ginny asked me to visit Russell, and I did one August afternoon. He was pleasant and hospitable enough at first, asking me into his kitchen—it was up in the nineties outside, not much cooler in the house, no fan anywhere, no air conditioning; the glass of ice water he handed me was sweaty and almost slipped out of my hand—but when talk about the weather stopped and I suggested he visit church on Sunday, that it would mean a lot to Ginny and others who were concerned about him, Russell's face fell, like he thought he'd been deceived. He ducked into the pantry and came out holding a hunting rifle. He didn't point it at me, the barrel just hung at his side.

"Visit's over, Pastor," he said. "Got some things to take care of. Thanks for stopping by."

"You don't need a gun to tell me that, Russell."

"I know it. The gun's for if you don't want to leave." He smiled and waved me to the door. "Before you go though, Pastor, I'd like to make a request as a member of the community. Sunday morning I'd like you to ask the organist and the choir to pipe down some for the benefit of us drunks who like Sundays to be true days of rest."

After that, I didn't talk to Russell for almost a year, but then Ginny died the next summer, and Russell became angry because, just before passing away, she told him she was leaving her house to the church. He would get the land on which he already lived and the field, which she advised him to sell so he could make a little money to put into his repair shop, but these things weren't everything, so to him they were nothing.

After Ginny died, Russell accused me of swindling him out of her house. During that phone conversation on the afternoon of Ginny's death, I tried to explain to him how the deacons and I had been surprised by such a large gift to the church, and how she'd said she was sure she wanted to do it when we asked, and how we now felt we must stand by her wishes. Russell hung up with a promise of legal action but none ever came.

On the morning of the funeral, Russell walked into the church late with uncombed hair and muddy boots. He opened and closed the outside doors loudly, fell into an empty pew in the back, coughed thickly during my eulogy, and left in the middle of the closing prayer without a word to me or anyone else. When I got outside, I noticed his truck was gone from across the street. He didn't make it to the burial.

Late that night, Russell, drunk, ran over my mailbox in his pickup. I wouldn't have known who it was except that he called the next morning and apologized for doing it and for acting the way he had at the funeral and for not going to the cemetery. He promised he'd be in church that coming Sunday and that he'd be by soon to fix the mailbox.

A week went by, though, and then a second Sunday, and I didn't see Russell in church or fixing the mailbox, so I went out one day to fix it myself. Russell saw me working and stumbled across the street, drunk again. "Trying to show me up? You going to tell people I'm not a man of my word because I have to work for a living?"

I shook my head. "I just want to get my mail again, Russell. Mailman said it had to be fixed."

At this, Russell lunged for the hammer in my hand. I pulled it away and pushed him with my other hand, and he fell backwards and hit his head on the road.

He needed eight stitches at the hospital. I drove him to the emergency room, thirty minutes away, and by the time we got back, he'd sobered. He rolled his window down and rubbed his face with his hands, and then he sat back and fingered the stitches at the back of his head. When I pulled into his driveway, he thanked me for driving him, apologized in a whisper, and got out.

A week later, three tires on my car were slashed. The one unslashed tire bothered me almost as much as the other three because I thought there should be a meaning in it that I couldn't find and because it suggested to me a dangerous and unbalanced mind. Either that or Russell had been so out of it that perhaps he'd thought he'd gotten all four as he weaved and tripped back to his house in the dark, mumbling to himself about last laughs.

After that, for years at a time things would be quiet, but then something would happen. A pile of empty bottles would show up on my lawn, or my porch light would be shot out when I wasn't home and I'd have to dig a slug out of the siding. There were a few instances of more serious consequence. I returned from a fishing trip one spring to find the fruit trees I'd just planted uprooted and ripped apart, and a few years later, during a sweltering August heat wave—at the time I was attending a pastors' conference in Vermont—my enclosed porch was broken into and a whole deer carcass left. I smelled it even before I turned in the driveway.

Eventually, though, the pranks stopped altogether. Russell was getting older and drink was breaking down his body, but I'm sure, too, that he was discouraged by my lack of reaction. I never called the police, never even told anyone in the church, and through it all I waved to him when I saw him sitting on his porch or driving by in his truck. More than once I feared him swerving into me, but I continued because I believed God was testing me to see if I could really love my enemies.

And then both of us got dogs. A week after I brought home Harper, a six-week-old beagle puppy—Joe had just started living in Chatham and had gone with me to the kennel to pick out Harper—Russell got Simon, a broad, deep-chested, shepherd-hound mix who quickly earned a bad reputation around town, but was actually usually fine with people if they took time with him, if they let him sniff the backs of their hands then moved carefully to scratch the top of his thick head or the scruff of his neck.

Although Simon was all right with people, he fought with other dogs and was a problem for neighbors, even for those without pets, because he liked to chase cars, get into garbage, dig up flowerbeds, and eat bread crusts people intended for birds. Even after a complaint, though, Russell wouldn't chain or fence Simon. He was insistent in his belief that to restrain an animal was cruel, and he wouldn't be a party to it. When Alice Buck, the owner of the horse farm up the road, called Russell to complain that Simon was spooking her horses and that one man had even been thrown, Russell responded by swearing that if riders ever strayed onto his property, he wouldn't think twice about grabbing his rifle and blowing them off the backs of the poor animals. When Alice threatened to complain to the sheriff, Russell told her he'd long considered reporting her for cruelty to animals because a woman her size had no right getting on a horse. When Mrs. Fredericks from a few miles away called Russell to complain that Simon had killed one of her ducks, Russell politely said he wouldn't be held responsible for millions of years of evolution, a natural hunter's instincts, and before hanging up, he told her that if Mr. Fredericks wasn't a giving man, she was welcome to drop by any time.

The two fights between Simon and Harper took place on my property, and both times Harper had the disadvantage of being chained. It wouldn't have mattered, though. Harper was too young to be much of a fighter, and Simon outweighed him by forty pounds and was capable of collapsing him to the ground and opening up his belly or neck. Twice I took Harper to the vet because of Simon. The second time Harper lost half his left ear.

After the first fight, I tried reasoning with Russell. A month before he died, I took a meat loaf over to his house—at my suggestion, Joe went too—but nothing got settled. Russell was obviously suspicious, but he asked us in and invited us to sit. Most of what he said he directed toward Joe. He told a few jokes and asked Joe some questions about prison. Not insulting questions. He didn't even ask what Joe had done to get in there, and I thought this showed respect and restraint. After a while he also made an effort to include me in the conversation by looking in my direction on occasion and nodding toward me when he spoke. He seemed to be getting comfortable, and at one point he got up and took three plates down from the cupboard and put the meat loaf in his oven to warm. When I got around to mentioning the dogs, though, Russell picked up two of the plates, put them back in the cupboard, said thanks for dinner, and on his way out of the kitchen he said we could show ourselves out.

Joe

I don't make much at the job Wade got for me. I'm cutting trails through the woods not far from my house for a group of men who bought the land with intentions of opening some cross-country ski trails. I've been at it for a year now and have made good progress. After nine or ten hours in the trees I come home tired–in the summer, mosquito bit, in the winter, cold–but knowing that I'm working well is satisfying, and knowing that there's a future is a good thing to know. The owners plan to open this coming winter, and they've asked me to run the place full time: maintain the trails, rent skis, sell coffee and hot chocolate, and keep a fire going in the lodge, so it's turned into a good situation. I'm praying for snow.

From my bedroom window I can see across the road to Russell's. When Russell was alive, there was always a light on in the upstairs window, even all through the night. I'd get out of bed to go to the bathroom or get a drink and his window would be glowing like an eye. That's what it reminded me of. A never-blinking eye that watched over me even while I slept.

I don't always understand the meanings behind the illustrations Wade uses in his Sunday sermons. I see more clearly when he explains them to me later in the afternoon while we watch football or sit at his kitchen table and drink iced tea. In the pew, though, I'm often lost. It's like this sometimes when I'm reading the Bible by myself. I'll hit a passage and it's like I'm reading it for the first time, or it means something different to me because it's sunny or raining outside or I've just finished watching my team win or lose on television.

There are simple parables with obvious messages. Some seeds fall in the rocks and blow away, some fall in the thorns and get choked, and some fall in the soft, deep soil, take root and grow strong. But the kingdom of heaven is like yeast? And new wine bursting old wineskins is like what? Still, those first nights out of prison when I'd wake up in my new house at three a.m. not knowing where I was, in a strange way scared because I couldn't hear other men sneezing or coughing or talking in their sleep, I'd stumble to the window and think of how Russell's glowing light was like God's eye, never leaving me through the whole, long, dark night that was my life.

Now that it's not there anymore, some nights I wake up and have to explain to myself how it's not Him I lost. It's just something that was there temporarily to remind me of Him.

Two weeks ago I was in my front yard, drinking a Coke and barbecuing a steak. I haven't had an ounce of alcohol for twenty-one years, truly haven't even been tempted much, but when I grill steaks I admit I think about beer. I saw Wade walk into Russell's yard and onto his porch. He didn't turn up the driveway. Instead he cut across the overgrown lawn, moving quickly with big steps and swinging arms. When Simon rose to his feet and wagged his tail in greeting, Wade circled him.

I saw Russell answer the door. I could hear Wade from my yard. "My chained dog's sleeping in the sun on its own porch and it gets mauled. There's no sense in that, Russell. I'm sorry, but I see Simon on my property again, anywhere but on your property, I'm calling the county to take him away."

Russell stepped out onto the porch with Wade, letting the screen door close. It was hinged tightly and slammed loudly. I could hear it slap shut even from my bedroom on weekend nights when Russell got home late from Busby's or wherever else he'd been drinking. It was always the screen door that woke me, not his truck rumbling into his gravel driveway.

As soon as I heard Russell, I knew he was drunk. His voice was breathy and didn't correspond to his slowly waving arms. My steak spit loudly and I turned it. "And you call yourself a pastor? Here's a prophecy for you: My dog dies, you'll have trouble. Come onto my property again, I'll put a slug in you." Wade turned to go. "I'm telling you, Russell. I'm telling you." He walked across the yard and back down the road to his house. When he saw me, he shook his head and threw up his arms but didn't stop walking. His face was red and his voice was loud. "Enough is enough, Joe. Enough is enough." Russell saw me then. "What's your problem?"

"Don't have one," I said. Simon heard me and trotted into my yard, his nose getting higher and working harder the closer he got to the grill, and he sat down beside me on the grass. Russell made a sound, as if to call him back, but he cut himself off and went back into the house, snapping the door shut behind him.

When the steak was done I ate it on my front steps. I cut off a small piece, let it cool on the tip of my knife, and flicked it to Simon. We'd gotten to know each other during the last year. I passed him every evening on my after-dinner walk. Sometimes he accompanied me for a while until something else caught his attention, an interesting scent, a low-flying bird. He swallowed the meat I'd given him whole, like an aspirin, and looked for more. I cut the whole thing down the middle and gave him half. He licked my plate after.

When Wade was young, before he entered seminary, he worked with his father as a chimney sweep. There are scars on all his fingers from banging and scraping brick and stucco. He has huge hands, naturally big, but made even larger from hard work. When we fish, I have to tie his knots for him because his swollen knuckles get in the way, and when he holds his Bible and reads from it Sunday mornings, his hands swallow it up so it looks like he's reading his palms.

When I saw Wade the morning after he and Russell had argued on Russell's porch, he was holding his face in his hands. He'd just killed Simon.

Wade

I saw Joe walking over fast from his yard, and before he even got to me—so quietly, he might not even have heard—I said, "He's dead, Joe."

"I heard your tires screech," Joe said. "I was at the stove frying eggs and I heard it and knew." He was on one knee looking at Simon. The body was on its side, its head resting on the driveway at a horribly impossible angle, and blood was coming out the ear.

"I could've swerved," I said, "but I thought he'd move. He's always moved."

Joe put his hand on my arm and told me to go inside.

I went in and sat at the kitchen table for an hour or so by myself, and then Joe came in and made some coffee and eventually my hands stopped shaking. Joe told me that, as for dealing with Russell, he thought the best thing would be a mediator. Before I could argue he was out the door. I could've followed him and stopped him, or I could've said, "Let's go together," but I didn't.

Joe

I finally got Wade to go inside. His hands were shaking so badly he couldn't even fold them together or stick them in the pockets of his jeans.

When he was gone, I picked up Simon and carried him to my backyard. His weight and open eyes surprised me, his head swiveled freely, resting against my forearm. I put him down in the wet grass, grabbed the shovel off my porch, and dug a shallow hole in the corner of my garden, close to my tomato plants.

When I filled the hole back up, I tried not to look into it. I tried to concentrate on moving dirt, shovelfuls of moist, sweet-smelling soil.

It was around nine o'clock when Russell, bare-chested and heavy-lidded, greeted me at his door. His sour breath hit me through the screen. He gestured me inside.

I'd been around a lot of men who drank like Russell, and at that hour on a Saturday morning, I thought I'd be breaking bad news to someone rendered mellow and quiet, just reaching the end of a long-night, hard-earned drunk. What I wasn't expecting was a freshly opened beer on the kitchen table. He sat down in front of it and pushed out the chair next to him with his foot. "There's one for you if you want, Joe."

"Thanks anyway, Russell."

"Suit yourself." He pointed his can in my direction like a toast, but he started to say something before it got to his lips so he had to put it back down on the table. "I'm glad you're here, Joe, because I believe I owe you an apology. I did some drinking last night, enough to forget some things, but I think I remember being rude to you at some point. I apologize."

"No need."

"I was upset about Wade bitching about my dog acting like a dog, and I believe I looked up and saw you after he left. I'm sure I probably said something regretful to you even though you had nothing to do with anything I was angry about."

"Forget it." I pulled myself in closer to the table. "I know about regrets. You can't let them hold you."

He nodded and looked down at the table. "I never wanted to be any man's enemy." He sipped his beer and smiled. "Wade was mad, wasn't he? Never seen him like that. A man of God getting that worked up. Makes me think about him a little differently. Easier for a sinner like me to identify with."

"There's something you need to know, Russell," I said. "About Simon."

He looked at me. "What's that?"

"He's dead."

He pushed his can away and shifted in his chair. "How? Wade called the county?"

I shook my head. "No. Backing out of his driveway. It was an accident."

"Accident. And he sent you over here to tell me because he's too much of a coward." Russell said this more quietly.

He looked all around the walls and the ceiling but he didn't look at me.

"No, that's not it, Russell."

"You want to see accident?" He rose and moved a few steps into the pantry and grabbed his rifle from the corner. "I'll show you accident."

When I moved to him with an outstretched hand, he swung the butt of the rifle and opened a gash above my right eye. I was stunned for an instant. We both were, not just by the blood but by where we were and what was happening. When he tried to move past me again, I punched him in the jaw and he dropped the rifle. We scuffled to the floor and I got behind him, locked his neck in the crook of my arm.

He tried everything to get out of it. At first he was intent on standing up and then on prying my right hand from my left wrist, but I was stronger. He tried to lunge for the rifle, but it was out of his reach and I yanked him even farther from it. I looked at his face, noticed the way the sun lit up only part of it, one eye, half a nose, half a mouth. I watched him sputter and curl his lips over his teeth, and I knew things were out of my hands. Blood seeped into my eye from where he'd butted me, but I couldn't spare a hand and had to let it burn. His eyes darted around the room, at the rifle, up at the ceiling. I said, "Sorry, Russell." He tried to flip his legs back and kick me. Then he tried giving up, going limp, so I would think he passed out. At the very end he tried to bite me. When he did that I snapped his neck.

When I let him go I felt my head throbbing and it hurt to straighten my arm. I put two fingers on his throat, my ear to his mouth. I washed my face at the kitchen sink and found a clean towel in one of his drawers. I cleaned the floor and wiped my blood off Russell's shoulder and back. I put the rifle back in the pantry, wiped it down with the clean side of the towel, then pressed the towel tightly against my head.

I'd never been upstairs in Russell's house before. That morning I climbed the stairs twice. The first time I was alone. I found Russell's bedroom and went to the window. On the table next to it, the lamp was on even though the curtains were open, and sunlight shone through the glass so brightly it hurt my eyes. It was like the whole sun was aimed at the window. Through it I saw my house. Three birds on my porch railing. Two robins and a grackle.

The second time I climbed the stairs I dragged Russell up with me. At the top I held him upright and pushed.

When I left Russell's, I kept my hand on the screen door and made sure it closed quietly. I walked slowly across the road to my house. No cars came by. Wade wasn't in his yard.

I closed the gash on my head with a butterfly band-aid. I worried at first that it wouldn't be enough to hold me together, but the Lord reached down and healed me. The first time Wade saw me after Russell's death, I was calm and ready for questions. I said I'd tripped on my throw-rug and crashed into the edge of my kitchen table.

As soon as I took care of my head, I buried the bloody towel in a box of papers and went outside and lit a fire in my burn barrel. When I got back inside, the phone rang. I took a deep breath before picking up because I knew it was Wade and I knew I had to lie.

Wade

Joe said he knocked and knocked but Russell never answered. He said he thought it was strange because Russell's truck was in the driveway. He said the only thing he could think of was that maybe Russell was still sleeping off last night. He said he'd try again later.

It was the next day that Russell was found by his nephew at the bottom of the stairs, his neck broken. When the nephew called to ask me to do the funeral, I told him bluntly that I didn't think I could, that his uncle wouldn't have wanted me to, but the young man said he wasn't so sure, convinced me that it would be like accepting a peace offering extended by Russell through him, a blood relation, the best a dead man could do.

Joe has taken Russell's death hard. They weren't friends,

but they weren't enemies either, and I think perhaps Joe saw some of what he used to be in Russell, and I think because of that, Joe has been remembering and reliving people and things that were part of his old life. I'm worried about him.

I admit when I found out Russell was dead and thought back to Joe heading over there to break the news about Simon, I worried that something had happened between the two of them. The first few times I talked to Joe after Russell's death—he hasn't been to church since the funeral, two Sundays, but he tells me he's been working, and I've gotten him to fish with me one or two evenings—I found myself studying him—his voice, his face—for confirmation of innocence or guilt, but I discovered that I don't know what either looks like, or that they look very much the same. Finally I decided that I was trying to do God's job, and I stopped trying.

I've come to have a peace about Joe.

Joe

Those hours during which only God and I knew Russell was dead, I spent in my house, praying and reading my Bible. I opened first to Psalm 11. ***For the Lord is righteous, he loves justice; upright men will see his face.*** I read it over a few times and thought of the man who wrote it, David. I turned to First Samuel and read about how David had to hide in the hills from Saul, the man who wanted to kill him, in a place called the Crags of the Wild Goats. He could do nothing himself but wait for the Lord to deliver him, just pray and wait. I read the stories of the times David had had an opportunity to take care of Saul himself. Once in a cave, Saul, his back exposed, pissing against a wall, unaware of David behind him. Another time at night, Saul sleeping, his spear stuck in the ground by his head, David standing over him. I was amazed by how David spared Saul both times—in the cave just cutting off a piece of the king's robe, the other time just stealing a spear and a water jug—and by the faith this showed. David believed fully that God would spare him, that God didn't need his help. I thought of how long Wade had put up with Russell, wondered how many times he'd asked God to take care of things.

But I also read through Judges, about Samson who killed a thousand Philistines with a donkey's jawbone and how God rewarded him by quenching his thirst, by splitting a rock out of which cool water came. And I read about Ehud, who with his left hand stuck a double-edged sword into the belly of Eglon, the fat Moabite king, and with God's help delivered Moab into Israel's hands.

Even after two weeks of prayer, it's hard for me to understand that the God of David, the God of Wade, is also the God of Samson and Ehud, is also my God. I think about Russell every day, and every day there are questions. When Russell grabbed his gun, was he thinking of Harper and not Wade? Would he really have taken a man's life for a dog's life? Couldn't I have claimed that it was me who accidentally killed Simon? Wouldn't Russell have been more likely to forgive me?

The world is never quiet now. I'll be working in the woods and a voice will come with the wind, out of the leaves. I'll be in my house cutting up vegetables for a meal I won't be able to force myself to eat, and one will echo in the ceiling, whisper in the walls. Even fishing the creek—like Russell, his nephew made a point of assuring me that I can go down to fish whenever I want; unlike Russell, he also told this to Wade—I think maybe it's Wade speaking to me, loudly, above the rush of the water, but I turn to look and his mouth is closed, his eyes intent on the end of his pole or up in the sky or in the trees, following a bird.

I ask the Lord daily to deliver me from doubt, but I know it's something I'll always struggle with. Sometimes I feel sorry for myself, compare my faith to Wade's. I think of myself as Moses, beating a rock and losing his future, or as Abraham in tears, raising a knife above his son. I think of Wade as Joshua, leading people into the Promised Land, or as Isaac, resting comfortably on the altar, listening closely and faithfully for an angel, a rustling in the bushes.

Sleeping Through Mountains

Brad falls asleep just after midnight, and then I might as well be alone, and that suddenly makes it real, what I'm going through with. We'll reach the cabin in another hour or hour and a half. Two o'clock at the latest. We're almost done with Vermont, and once we hit New Hampshire, we'll be only forty or fifty miles away. A while back I set the cruise at 75, and all by itself it's inched up to 78, so we're making good time, but what's that worth?

Brad's head rests on the window, vibrating with the road, and his hair, thin and blond like his mother's, clings to the glass in wisps. He's asleep in my pickup instead of his bedroom—still in his jeans and jacket, face unwashed, teeth unbrushed, an empty McDonald's bag and crushed Coke can at his feet—because a few hours ago, pulling out of the drive-thru back in Albany, I knew all at once that I couldn't take him back to Rachel, at least not right away, and I first headed east to think this over, and then I headed north. My eyes should be on the road, scanning shoulder-to-shoulder for deer and troopers, but I can't help watching him. He's so still. Every few miles I have to reach over and rest my hand on his chest to make sure he's breathing in and out.

When his mother and I shared a bed, she slept this deeply–probably still does, though not tonight, I'm sure– through cat fights outside the bedroom window, neighbors' parties, storms. During the time when we were just getting started–Rachel and I married three weeks after Brad was born–I worked second shift at Troybilt. This was before I got on at the car dealership in East Greenbush, began working daylight hours like normal people. Sometimes while working nights I wouldn't get in until two in the morning, even later if I went for a beer and a game of pool, but Rachel and Brad always slept through my getting home. I could clang keys on the dresser, switch on lights. Nothing but hunger would wake Brad, and only his crying would wake Rachel.

One night, only a few months after Brad was born, lightning splits an oak in our apartment complex. The window above our bed lights up, and the glass rattles. I mean, the tree is twenty yards away. Had the physics been a bit different, it could have ended up in our bedroom. I wake up on my feet with my heart in my ears. I'm thinking gun shot, but then, no, because the sound wasn't crisp enough–there was crackling and it lasted too long. Not a peep out of Brad from his crib at the foot of our bed, and Rachel doesn't even twitch. I mean, the rhythm of their breathing doesn't change.

That kind of sleep has to be good for you, like eating a bowl of spinach every day, which Rachel does for lunch. If not spinach, then Swiss chard, drizzled with olive oil and red wine vinegar. Sometimes tuna mixed in, solid white only, for protein, but never a hard-boiled egg, and never cheese or creamy dressing. It adds up, right? As far as dessert goes, even at restaurants, it's fresh fruit or nothing. More than likely she'll stick with coffee, watch you eat your cake or pie or torte or whatever, and then she'll go home and knock out ten hours of hibernation-quality sleep while you're up watching Letterman, chewing Rolaids. On top of this, five times a week she'll pull her hair back, put on headphones, and walk for an hour, briskly, swinging her arms, pumping blood through her whistle-clean arteries. All kinds of weather. She

and I were born the same year, but I guarantee that on the
twentieth anniversary of my funeral, her name will still be in
the phone book, and if you call, she'll answer, and you won't
have to yell to make yourself heard. Vampires live forever.
Not that Rachel's a vampire. But we're on different timetables
to be sure, and that could be behind this urgency I'm feeling.
Like I'm pressed for time.

Although hurting Rachel is not what I'm out to do, I realize it's part of what I'm doing. She's not a vampire. I don't
think of her like that. If there's one thing I wish she could
know, it's that this wasn't planned. This isn't about strategy or
the hatching of some long-in-the-works scheme. She and her
boyfriend are moving to Miami on Monday, and they're taking my son with them—who's scheming who?—and I'm sure
she thinks I've launched this plot to throw a wrench into that,
to get back at her. But that's not what's going on. People out
for revenge map things out. I have no idea what comes next.
If I had to give her reasons right now, I don't know what I'd
say. Time and space, Rachel. For Christ's sake. Perspective.

We split a year ago, and I still find myself preparing expla-
nations for her as if there were reasons and it mattered to her
whether or not I knew them. I'll be driving to work or lying in
bed, and I'll remember an argument we had, and I'll say out
loud to the windshield or the empty space next to me what I'd
meant to say, what I should've said. If I'd had the chance to
rehearse before Rachel and I got together—if I could've nailed
my lines ahead of time, studied my cues—we might've worked
out. I'm not talking about lies I wish I hadn't told, or even lies
I wish I had told. I'm saying I missed opportunities to tell her
some true things, and if I had to do it over again, these things
would get said. Maybe if I had a whole other life before this
one just for practice. Like spring training, a whole schedule of
games that don't count. You can misjudge flies, let routine
grounders through your legs like you're a croquet wicket, miss
signs, pull your head and step in the bucket as you swing at
first-pitch breaking balls in the dirt. No sweat. You're just getting it out of your system, working out the kinks.

I've tried to think of Brad apart from Rachel, like he's present and future and she's past, but how's that supposed to work? I'm supposed to see him living and breathing and not think of her and me? Not that Brad exists only as a sum of Rachel plus Quinn. I shouldn't boil him down to that, but on some level, isn't it true? I'm saying this matters because when I'm with him, a part of why I love it is because Rachel's there, too, in a way, and this is also a part of why I don't love it.

Brad was quiet, concentrating on his dinner until we hit Route 7. When he asked where we were going, I told him I was giving him his last tour of the North. "Look out your window," I said. "I don't want you forgetting what woods are when you're bumming around those beaches. I want you to remember what a mountain is. Coming up on your left is a pine tree."

"They have nature in Florida," Brad said. "The ocean teems with life." He says things sometimes. School for him is a breeze. He spends half his time there waiting for the other kids to catch up. Rachel's got him set up for tests in Florida to see if he should be in advanced classes. This without consulting me. For the most part, I learn things after the fact.

Brad took off his cap and spun it on his finger. "Besides, I'll be back here three weeks this summer." He turned to look at me when he said this. His voice steady, like assurance. Rachel would do this sometimes. After a guy I didn't know would smile and nod at her across a bar, Rachel would squeeze my arm and whisper in my ear, and after her mother would call and make doomsday predictions about us, she'd get off the phone and kiss me with her eyes open.

"I know one thing," Brad said. "I'm wearing my Jets cap to school no matter how many kids like the Dolphins."

"It's April," I said, "and you're thinking football."

Brad rolled his eyes, twisted in his seat belt to face his window. "Baseball sucks. I even like hockey better than baseball. Football, basketball, hockey, baseball. That's my order. Wait, even soccer's ahead of baseball."

"What's this?" I said.

"All they do is visit the mound to talk it over and spit, and then they throw over to first to keep the runner close." He turned to face me. "Baseball's for old people. Keeps them company." He closed his eyes, let his head fall back and started to snore. He's got a strain of smart-ass in him.

When we hit Brattleboro, I thought about turning around, but I didn't. Instead I got on 91, headed north. At Rockingham I pulled into a 7-11, sidled up to a gas pump. "I'll fill the tank, you get the windshield," I said.

"What are we doing?" Brad said.

"How about fishing?" I said. "Let's fish. My buddy keeps a cabin in New Hampshire. You know Jim. From the dealership. He says I can use it whenever I want. Fishing. Up for it?"

"What about Mom?"

"I'll put a call in," I said.

On the way into the store to pay for the gas and get drinks, Brad told me he didn't think Rachel was going to go for it. "I can hear her now," he said, and his voice turned high and squeaky. "'He's moving on Monday. His room isn't even packed yet. He doesn't have warm clothes with him. He'll catch cold.'" He turned his head and spit. "She never lets me do stuff. Always bitching."

I caught his elbow and wheeled him around. I did this more roughly than I'd intended. His neck jerked. Sometimes your hand will slip when you're holding a baby, and that weak neck will flop, and the baby's eyes will open wide and roll back, and it scares you. You feel like dirt.

"Is that how you talk about your mother?" I said.

"No." He shook his arm loose and stepped back. The look he had? Half of him wanted to fight me, half of him wanted to cry into my chest. I shouldn't have grabbed him like that. Now his jaw was tight, and he was doing that thing where he'll look anywhere but at me. You can't react with kids. You have to think before you move your muscles. You know who pays for it most when you mess up? You do.

"She's your mother," I said. I opened the door to the store, and Brad walked in ahead, under my arm. The girl behind the counter looked up from a magazine and smiled.

Maybe she saw me put hands on him, maybe not. "Besides," I said, "she didn't say no yet. Give her a chance." I pressed two dollars into his hand. "Large coffee, two creams. Careful pouring. Get yourself a Coke."

He watched me walk to the phone. I actually took the calling card out of my wallet and pretended to read it as I punched numbers. I dialed 555 like they do on TV. The digits that get you nowhere. I put the receiver to my ear, held it in place with my shoulder, and talked to the recording telling me that my call couldn't be completed as dialed. "Rachel, Quinn. . . . No, Brad's fine." After I said this, I looked at Brad and rolled my eyes. "Actually, I was wondering if I could keep him the weekend. . . . Fishing. . . . I'll get him what he needs. . . . I know. . . . All right. . . . OK. . . . Bye."

I hung up and walked over to Brad. He hadn't budged. His arms were folded high on his chest.

"My coffee?" I said.

"What'd she say?"

"We're going fishing."

"No way!" he said. "She went for it?"

"What's not to go for?" I said. "A father–son fishing trip? You have to have the touch. You have to know how to work it."

"Yeah, that's you," he said. "Smooth." He thrust at me the money I'd given him. "Here. I need to drain my main vein."

"Nice mouth," I said.

The cashier, grinning, pushed the key to the restroom across the counter. "Around back," she said.

After fixing my coffee and getting a Coke from the cooler, I paid at the counter. "This and gas," I said. The cashier nodded, tucked her long, dark hair behind her ear and rang me up. She wore large wooden earrings, like miniature totem poles, and when she reached for my money, they swung back and forth, brushing her neck. She looked sixteen or seventeen, the same age as Rachel when we'd first met, and I imagined the girl's boyfriend, around here probably the son of a logger or farmer, wiry and tan from working in the weather, daydreaming about her black hair and her neck as he cut trees and drove his tractor. I wanted to tell the girl something that would help the both of them. Something subtle that would fit into normal conversation, but then later, when she remembered it, would take on significance, and she could share it with him. I get like this sometimes. Who doesn't? Like I think for a moment that I have something to say. It's a feeling that passes.

"How old's your boy?" she asked.

"Ten," I said. "Just turned."

"My nephew's eight," she said as she handed me my change. "They remember everything they hear, then they wait until they're in public with you to let loose."

"Right. You've got them figured out."

"I'm glad his mom is letting him go fishing," she said as I turned to leave.

"Yeah," I said. "We weren't sure which way that would go."

I waited for Brad in the truck. I rolled the window down, faced the cooling air and hung my arm out. I drummed my fingers against the door and watched another truck pull in, cruise slowly past the gas pumps, then turn out onto the highway again without coming to a complete stop. I thought, You either need gas or you don't, buddy.

When Brad climbed in, I clapped him on the knee, handed him his Coke and told him I'd forgotten something, that I'd be right back. I told him to stay put.

I went back into the store, to the phone. The cashier raised her head from her magazine again, and those earrings swung under her lobes in tight circles, orbits, like she was the center of something. "Don't I know you from somewhere?" she said.

"Not me," I said. "I'm a stranger."

I put my hand on the receiver and stood there a few seconds without picking it up. A chance to rehearse. The cashier looked at her watch, closed her magazine and walked out from behind the counter to look out the glass doors.

Rachel picked up on the first ring. She sounded anxious and tired, nasal, like she'd been crying. I got all this from her hello. I said, "Hey. Brad's fine. Sorry about this. I'm working it out," and I hung up. As I walked out of the store, the cashier held the door open and said, "Have a good one," and I waved with my left hand without looking up or speaking.

Over the next few miles, Brad went on and on about how he was going to catch more fish than me. He was wound up. "You want to see something funny?" he said.

"Sure," I said.

"You can't get mad, though," he said. "Promise."

"What?" I said. He was already cracking himself up. Watch your kid giggle himself red in the face and try to keep it together. He reached into the pocket of his jacket and pulled out the gas station bathroom key.

"What's the matter with you?" I said.

"Accident, I swear," he said. He was hugging himself and kicking his feet. A smuggled restroom key? Hysterical. "Totally an accident," he said. "Seriously."

Just then we hit a bump in the road—a pothole, maybe road-kill—and coffee splashed onto my jeans. "Way to go, Grace!" Brad said. We were talking to each other like this, laughing, but the whole time I'm thinking, Back there, that was the first. One lie, told to your son.

When we cross into New Hampshire and pick up Route 10, Brad's still asleep. The signs tell me that in daylight we'd be catching glimpses of Smart Mountain, but even in the dark I can sense it somehow, rising up from the evergreens like a ghost.

Brad sleeps through more mountains. Piermont, Carr, Cushman. He sleeps through the radio tuning in and out, the rain changing to wet snow. Even when we downshift to climb the steep stretches of road. We keep turning left, twisting our way up. Even when the pavement ends and we're driving on gravel, then dirt. Even when we stop. I have to shake his shoulder, say his name twice.

I hadn't thought about it on the road, but now, standing in the dark, in the snow, my hands on the rock and about to lift, I worry about the key. What if it isn't here? How much depends on a key staying put during a New Hampshire winter? What if Jim moved it or took it home with him the last time he was here? Would I break a window to get in? Will this come down to something like me breaking a window? But it's here, stuck a half-inch deep in the stiff April mud. I wipe it off on my pant leg, unlock the door, and let Brad in ahead of me.

I switch on all the lights as we walk through the cabin. The bedroom is east off the living room. Brad sees the cots and heads for one. The sleeping bags are in the closet like I remember. By the time I get one unrolled, Brad's already asleep again, flat on his stomach. I pull his shoes off and then his jacket—I'm rolling the kid over, yanking on his limbs, and his eyelids don't even twitch—and I fold the jacket twice and slide it under his head for a pillow. I lay the bag over him.

I turn the bedroom light off and go back into the living room. I sit in the recliner by the wood stove and decide against a fire. It's chilly, but I'm not up to crawling around in the dark under the cabin, hooking up pipes and switching on the pump. The one rule Jim has is no water, no fire.

Jim sells cars with me. He went through a divorce about a year before Rachel's and mine, and he talked me into staying in his cabin for a week last October. I had nine empty days of vacation facing me. I'd put in for the time almost a year before because Rachel wanted to go away for our anniversary. We'd sat at the kitchen table one evening and flipped calendar pages. She marked the days with a pen. We didn't know where we'd go, but that night I think we both were comforted by the promise of those days. We planned to do something with Brad the first weekend, maybe even keep him out of school for a day, and then we'd drop him at a friend's and have four or five days of just the two of us being quiet together. We thought it might be enough to save us. We never said this to each other, but I know that's what we thought. We knew we needed saving.

But we didn't make it that far. We had several serious arguments in the next few months—one that ended with me kicking a hole in our screen door, threatening our next-door neighbor, and spending the night at a motel—but worse than the arguments themselves, worse than the actual time we spent in the same room being cruel to each other–both of us knowing that Brad was up in his bedroom or in the living room watching TV, at the same time listening and trying not to listen–were the long, lonely spaces in between. It took us too long to forgive each other.

With some couples, splitting isn't an option. They might even end up hating each other, but for some reason they stick it out. Is this strength or weakness? With Rachel and me, it was never like this. Even when things were good, it seemed like we were always only one or two mistakes or conversations away from losing it. I don't know why, but we were always fragile like this, desperate for each other, but never a sure thing.

Rachel and I never discussed the specifics of when she started with Tim, but looking back–this I've done–I think I know. It was a Sunday, and I was home watching a game. She was grocery shopping, gone for three hours and then back with only half of what had been on her list. She went straight into the bedroom without putting anything away, and was unusually talkative when she came out, asking me who was winning and, before I could answer, apologizing for having taken so long. She'd run into Pam Franklin and Debbie Russell both, and traffic.

A month later she asked me to leave. It was early July and Brad was at camp for the week. I was hanging my wet jacket in the hall closet–the rain that had been expected all day had finally come full force as I was leaving work, but already it was letting up, tapping softly on our living room windows– and I remember thinking later that she couldn't even wait until I had my jacket hung up. I was angry–at the very moment she said the words, I felt sick–but I wasn't surprised. She said she'd been trying to decide which was the lesser evil, staying with me or being without me. Have someone say that to you and then go live your life. I put my jacket back on and left, and she watched without trying to stop me, like relief.

The first time we split we were just kids, back in Cleveland. She said we needed space to grow up. I was doing stuff that convinced her that loving me was not a good move for her future. She left town, moved to New York. The next time I saw her? Six years later. She was home visiting her parents. We ran into each other at the grocery store, both still single, went for coffee. That's how Brad happened. That afternoon in my apartment. A few days later she returned to Albany. When I found out she was pregnant, I followed. Would I have eventually went to her anyway, even without a baby? That's what Rachel's mother asked me on the phone once. Right after I say, Hello, she asks this, like she's been waiting for the opportunity. It's a bad question because it doesn't matter. Hypothetical equals irrelevant. Things don't happen any way, they happen one way.

I should've told Rachel's mother this: Those six years I spent in Cleveland without Rachel are forgotten, as in one big, black blind spot. Like memories of a coma. How did I fill them up?

I saw Tim for the first time on the day Rachel and I finalized the divorce. He was leaning against his car in the parking lot of the law office building, smoking. This surprised me, Rachel going for a smoker. We looked at each other and knew. He was probably more sure than me. I imagine he'd seen my picture at some point. Maybe he'd even been by the house when I still lived there, before I knew, maybe even when I was in the shower or mowing the back yard he and Rachel had been on the couch, or in the kitchen, or in the bedroom. When I started toward him, his cigarette fell from his fingers. He tried to make it look like he'd dropped it on purpose, proceeded to ground it into blacktop with his shoe, but it was only half-smoked.

"Tim?"

He nodded once.

"You have no right."

"I'm not looking for any sort of trouble."

"Then why come here?" I said. "You thought this was the place to come today to stay out of trouble?" Rachel came out of the building, saw the two of us and froze. "Nice touch," I called to her, motioning to Tim. "Bringing a date."

"I didn't know, Quinn. I didn't ask him to come." She started to cry. "I wouldn't do that."

As I pulled out of the parking lot, I looked in my rearview and watched Tim move to hold her. She pushed him away. This gave me some satisfaction until I played it out in my mind on the drive home. He would tell her he was there only to support her. He was sorry if it showed bad judgment, but he wanted to be there for her, he didn't want her to be alone through this. Eventually she would let him slide an arm around her, rub her shoulder, there in the parking lot, and then he would follow her home. They had two hours before the bus dropped off Brad. They'd go to the bedroom, the afternoon sun streaming in the windows.

Eventually Rachel moved in with Tim, so Brad did, too—no custody battle, the question never even came up; I never even considered separating Brad and Rachel—but when I'd stop by to pick up Brad on weekends, I rarely saw Tim. He was always out back or at the store or upstairs. One time early on, Rachel answered the door and said Brad would be out in a minute. Without saying anything, I stepped inside and kissed her and moved a hand onto her waist. I opened her mouth with mine. She didn't pull away or cry out, but she caught my wrist and pushed my arm back. When I turned and walked back out onto the porch, the door closed behind me. When Brad came out a few minutes later, I could hear her running the vacuum.

One of the few times Tim was around—he answered the door—was a month ago, the day Rachel told me he was being transferred to Florida. They asked me inside, offered me coffee. Tim got the mug down from the cabinet. I nodded to cream, and he poured a little into the mug before he poured the coffee. This way, no stirring, no clinking. No coffee puddles on the tablecloth when you put down your spoon. No spoon at all. Little trick he picked up somewhere.

Rachel told me she'd given it a lot of thought and decided that she and Brad were going to Florida with Tim. While she spoke, Tim stood behind her, silently, propping himself against the counter with one arm, looking at the floor and then at Rachel's back and then at me, and I'm sure at least part of him was wondering—as a part of Rachel was, as a part of me was—how we'd gotten to this moment.

Months before, just days after the divorce was finalized, I sat in the break room at work. It was a Friday afternoon, hours before my vacation. Jim drew a map for me on one side of a napkin, and on the other side he sketched out the cabin's floor-plan and yard. He was enjoying himself. "My father built it in the early seventies after he and my mom split. He took weekends and vacations there, and when he retired, he moved in for good. Lived there until he passed two years ago. I took my two weeks there this past summer, right after Carla and I made it official. I signed the last batch of papers, stuck them in the mailbox, and got in the car." His pencil moved as he talked. "So it has history. A place for losers at love like you, me, and my dad."

"That hurts," I said.

He grinned and angled the napkin so I could see. "Plenty of split wood right here by the front porch, but even if you run out, there are logs out back under canvas that should burn. Sledge hammer, wedge, and ax by the door. Walk in, turn left, they're leaning in the corner. You should keep plenty warm. The stove is serious. You can swelter in the middle of January if you want. One thing. The water's not on—I don't want pipes freezing—so when you get there you'll have to go under the front porch to hook up the pipes and turn on the pump. Hook up the water before building a fire, OK? Safe side. Bathroom's here. Flush toilet. In the kitchen, there's an electric stove and a small fridge. Just plug them in." He stuck his pencil back behind his ear, picked up the napkin, leaned over, and tucked it in my shirt pocket. "It's a good place, Quinn. What the doctor ordered. This time of year no one else will be around. You can disappear."

And that's what I did for two weeks. I fished and read and cooked and ate and kept a fire and slept. I didn't talk to anyone or even see anyone except once in a while a car passing me on the road near one of the spots where I fished. One driver caught a glimpse of me through the trees and waved out his open window, but I didn't wave back. Instead I looked down through the water at the mud and smooth stones, wondered why someone would have their car window rolled down in late October, in New Hampshire, with freezing drizzle coming down, and I realized that I felt a little better about things, that I was settling down, that I might be able to go back to Albany and sell a car and sit through a movie or a ball game.

Jim doesn't know I'm here now, but I wonder if the possibility will cross his mind tomorrow when I don't show up for work. I'd planned on going in this whole weekend. I knew Rachel and Brad would be packing boxes, and I thought that the dealership would be a good place for me to be, better than alone in my apartment or sitting at a bar. I wonder if Rachel and Tim and maybe a cop will show up at work looking for me tomorrow, asking if anyone can think of where I might be. Rachel will head right for Jim. She and I sometimes went to dinner and movies with him and Carla, and she'll suspect that I might've confided in him. "Do you know?" she'll ask. "Can you think of anywhere? This is about Brad, Jim. This is about my son."

There are no curtains on the two windows in the bedroom, and Brad is up with the sun. I never made it to the cot the night before, instead falling asleep in the living room chair by the cold stove.

"Dad."

I come out of my sleep slowly, conscious of one thing at a time: I'm cold, I have a kink in my neck, I have to piss, I'm hungry, I'm in New Hampshire with Brad, Rachel's with Tim in Albany, frightened and hating me. I imagine the two of them drinking coffee at their kitchen table, red-eyed, exhausted. No spoons, no words. "He called once," Tim's saying. "Maybe he'll call again."

Brad's piling up questions. I answer one. "Yes, we're fishing this morning. But first we have to take care of business."

I head out the front door and Brad follows. We trudge through the crunchy mud and frosted grass to the edge of the woods and unzip. "Fire one," Brad says. He's speaking puffs of frost into the air, and when our piss hits the ground, steam rises. We stand ten or fifteen feet apart and look up into the trees. I close my eyes and roll my neck back slowly against my shoulders. I could've used a pillow. Squirrels skip from branch to branch, charge each other, and occasionally drop to the cold ground, just for the sake of moving, it seems.

Before we head back inside, I have to crawl under the porch, connect the pipes and turn on the pump. Righty-tighty, lefty-loosey. I have to keep reminding myself, pipe after pipe. I'm not the brightest bulb first thing in the morning. When I think I've got it all hooked up, I yell for Brad to go in and try the kitchen faucet. In a minute I hear him yell, "Good!" and then run back onto the porch, directly over my head. When I slide out into the open, Brad laughs. "You have dirt and spider webs in your hair. You look like a zombie." I get up and start toward him slowly, my arms outstretched and my knees locked. You can die and then come back to life if you want, but it's not going to be like it was before. You can count on stiff joints.

I turn on the water in the bathroom and let the water run for a few minutes. It's cloudy at first, rusty orange like the clay around the cabin, but eventually it clears. I find a few towels in the hall closet and clean up at the sink, and I tell Brad to get in the tub. "I'm going for supplies. It might be an hour or so. Will you be all right, or do you want me to wait so we can go in together?"

"Give me a break."

"Right. Sorry, sir."

I drive ten miles to Lincoln and pull into a shopping plaza. At K-Mart I buy two hats, two coats, two flannel shirts, two pairs each of gloves, heavy socks, long underwear, pants—I don't know Brad's sizes, I have to guess—two rods, two reels and tackle. In the grocery store next door I buy bread, eggs, bacon, orange juice, ice, toothpaste, toothbrushes and soap. On the way out, I notice the pay phone by the door, and I think about it, but I don't.

When I have everything loaded in the truck, the groceries next to me in the cab, and the clothes and fishing gear in the back, I climb in, and when I settle back in the seat, it hits me all at once how tired I am. My body, but my brain, too. Spent. Like I'm in an old private eye movie and someone's slipped me a mickey because I'm getting too close to the truth. Should've bought coffee. Rachel and I used to polish off a full pot each morning. I don't make it for myself. Weekends I do diners, and weekdays I drink the slop at work. It tastes like metal, but we gulp it down. Each morning Jim and I stir in heaping spoonfuls of Cremora and bump our Styrofoam cups together in a toast. It coats your throat. The cup I drank with Rachel and Tim in Tim's kitchen was the flavored stuff. Either the coffee itself or the cream. Something nutty, like almond or hazelnut. Barely coffee at all. It smelled like dessert.

I dig through the grocery bags until I find the orange juice. I open the carton and take a few swallows. Across the parking lot, a bread truck pulls up to the curb in front of the grocery store. The driver opens his door, hops down, and hurries around to the back of his truck. He's moving quickly. He likes his work and being out in the morning. In seconds he's striding toward the grocery store with two trays of bread balanced on his shoulder and a clipboard in the opposite hand. He's looking at the clipboard when he almost collides with a woman on her way out of the store. The woman's wearing jeans and boots, an untucked western-style shirt under an open denim jacket that looks too big for her—probably her boyfriend's or husband's—and she has a folded newspaper in her right hand that she's reading as she walks and a cup in her left hand that she swings away from her and above her head at the last possible second, when she looks up from her paper and thinks that the delivery guy is going to run into her.

They don't collide, though. The delivery guy looks up

from his clipboard just in time, and the two dance around one another–her shoulder might brush his clipboard as he spins away in a tight circle; that's as close as they get–and once they are out of danger, each out of the other's space, they both slow and turn just long enough to smile at one another before continuing on. I'm waiting for the bow and the curtsey. I look at my watch for the first time since last night. Not even nine o'clock. I take one last sip of juice and put the carton back in the bag, drop the truck into drive and pull out onto the road. I'm gurgling, acid from the juice sloshing around in an empty stomach, but also my nerves because I know that the thing to do next is the hardest thing. In the last hour, not having Brad with me, I've gained some perspective. I know that I don't want my time with him to be empty like a lie. I want it to come down to something. I'll come clean, tell him about the phone call at the gas station, and when I'm finished, I'll ask him what he's thinking. We'll go from there.

I'm feeling more settled, even feeling relief, but at the turn-off for the cabin, just as I steer off the pavement and into the mud, my mind shifts again to Rachel, and I see her sitting alone in Brad's room, crying on the edge of his bed, and Tim's standing behind her, darkening the doorway, a mug in each hand, and my fist surprises me as it comes down on the dashboard and swings back against the passenger seat, and it surprises me when it swings back against the passenger seat a second time, and when my anger is spent, I can see the world again, and I can see smoke pouring out the open door of the cabin, and Brad running toward the truck.

I stop and get out, and he's screaming, "Sorry! Sorry!" I run past him into the cabin, to the stove, and I open the flue and rush to the kitchen sink and fill a pot with water. I take it over to the stove and open the top–I almost reach for the handle with my bare hand, but I stop myself in time and pull my fingers up into the sleeve of my jacket–and I pour the water, and there's more smoke, and I'm coughing, and my eyes are burning, and I run outside. Brad's leaning over the hood of the truck, crying into his folded arms. When he feels my hand on his back, he faces me and says quietly, "I'm sorry. I was cold. I thought I knew how." I tell him all right. I tell him he just needed to open the flue. I tell him I'm sorry. In a while the smoke clears, and I go back inside the cabin and dump more water into the stove to make sure. After that I crawl under the porch and turn off the pump and disconnect the pipes, and then I go back inside and turn on all the faucets to let them run dry.

The whole inside of the cabin is gray with soot. The walls, the furniture and appliances, the windows. I'll come back next weekend to clean up the place. Scrub it. Monday morning at work I'll explain to Jim what happened, and I'll tell him I'm going back to clean it up. I'll tell him I'll pay for any damage, but, really, everything looks OK. Just a scare.

I lock the door, put the key back under the rock, and Brad and I climb into the truck and head into town to find a diner. Along the way, to show Brad we're all right, I ask if he wants to steer. I pull over and he takes the wheel. At first, he wants to watch his hands and not the road, but I explain to him how that's not going to work. When he gets the hang of it, I tell him he's a natural.

After breakfast we spend the day fishing a lake with rubber worms. Between us we catch four fish, Brad three and me one, two sunnies and two perch. We throw back the sunnies, and in the middle of the afternoon, we sit together on the damp bank and clean the two perch on a rock. Brad wants to bring the knife toward him as he cuts until I explain how it should work the other way. We build a small fire with half a box of matches and wet pine needles and wood, and we cook the fish on sticks. The fish takes forever, and there's not much of it, and it's still cool in the center when we eat it. Brad says, "Sushi."

We get back to Albany just after dark. From the truck, I watch Brad try to let himself in the house, but the door's locked. He has to knock. I keep the headlights on him until he disappears inside, and then I back out of the driveway and pull away slowly. I imagine the embrace. Rachel, I'm sure, tells him he smells like smoke, wants to know why he smells like smoke.